Fct: '94 Suppl.

D1480670

F
DIC   Dickinson, Peter,
        The yellow room
        conspiracy

$18.95 Baker & Taylor 6/94

3 2790 00059 0321

THE YELLOW ROOM CONSPIRACY

Also by Peter Dickinson

The Glass-Sided Ants' Nest
The Old English Peep Show
The Sinful Stones
Sleep and His Brother
The Lizard in the Cup
The Green Gene
The Poison Oracle
The Lively Dead
King and Joker
Walking Dead
One Foot in the Grave
A Summer in the Twenties
The Last House-Party
Hindsight
Death of a Unicorn
Tefuga
Perfect Gallows
Skeleton-in-Waiting
Play Dead

THE YELLOW ROOM CONSPIRACY

PETER DICKINSON

THE MYSTERIOUS PRESS

Published by Warner Books

A Time Warner Company

SOMERVILLE PUBLIC LIBRARY
35 West End Avenue
Somerville, N.J. 08876-1899
(908) 725-1336

Copyright © 1994 by Peter Dickinson
All rights reserved.

 Mysterious Press books are published by Warner Books, Inc.,
1271 Avenue of the Americas, New York, NY 10020.

W A Time Warner Company

The Mysterious Press name and logo are registered trademarks of Warner Books, Inc.

Printed in the United States of America
First printing: May 1994

10 9 8 7 6 5 4 3 2 1

Library of Congress Cataloging-in-Publication Data

Dickinson, Peter, 1927–
    The yellow room conspiracy / Peter Dickinson.
        p.   cm.
    ISBN 0-89296-556-8
    1. Man-woman relationships—Great Britain—Fiction.   2. Scandals—
Great Britain—Fiction.   3. Murder—Great Britain—Fiction.
    I. Title.
PR6054.I35Y4   1994
823'.914—dc20
                                        94-1980
                                         CIP

THE YELLOW ROOM CONSPIRACY

Editor's Note

The late Lady Seddon's instructions were that I should leave the material by Paul Ackerley as it stood, but that I should "tidy up" her transcribed tapes. To this end the present Lady Seddon lent me a number of letters from her mother-in-law, with which I found the voice on the tapes to be remarkably consistent in style, making allowances for hesitations, repetitions, etc. I have to the best of my ability based my version of the transcription on the letters, including such details of orthography as the spelling of *alright* as a single word. Otherwise I have made no material alterations at all.

—PD

Paul

ONE

Summer 1992

Normally I'd have switched the radio off the moment I heard the name, but I was trapped in the middle of the Yellow Border, poisoning bindweed, a tense and delicate process demanding far greater physical control than most other activities that come my way. I've tried various methods, including the one with the rubber glove and the old sock, but nowadays I do it with a plastic bag and a cheap little hand sprayer. So I was poised in the midst of all the late July uprush (I keep my borders pretty crammed) with my feet twisted into two small clear patches, and my hands, having disentwined the growing tips of the bindweed and eased them into the bag and sprayed them there, now trying to withdraw them and at the same time shake any excess poison from them back into the bag so that it didn't drip elsewhere. Disentangled bindweed is intransigently floppy. My left calf was on the verge of cramp. I had left the radio on the gravel path twelve feet away.

It was that jokey political quiz, with Critchley and Mitchell, and a couple of columnists as their guests, attempting to give politics a good name by answering questions about politicians as bitchily as the facts allow. If they are on form they can make it work.

Part of the format is that there comes a point when the

contestants are given two minutes to answer, competitively, using buzzers to get in first, as many questions as they can about some past event. Only a week or two before, I had heard them doing the Profumo affair, and it had then crossed my mind that they'd probably get round to Seddon. Still, I wasn't ready for it when it came. I suppose I am still emotionally unable to believe that anyone could regard it as a fit subject for mirth (though most people now do), because for me the central fact about it has always been the appalling and tragic week-end at Blatchards, whereas, in the public view, that was marginal to the revelations that made it newsworthy: hypocrisy and corruption and sexual shenanigans linked with hitherto respectable household names.

Anyway, there I was, teetering in the middle of my sunlit border, when the voice said, ". . . two minutes to answer as many questions as possible about the Seddon Affair. Which year?"

Buzz. Bizz. (The rival teams use slightly different notes.)

"Julian?"

"Too easy. Suez. 1956."

"One point. Which sport—"

Bzuizz.

"Julian again?"

"Cricket."

"That was the *outdoor* sport."

(Studio laughter.)

"One point to Julian, and one to Austin for a relevant intervention. What was the name of the East End pub—"

I had started to lurch towards the radio, trodden into an eryngium that I had already spent several minutes teasing into natural-looking elegance and propping in place with twigs, and stopped. The momentary and trivial discomfort was not worth the damage I'd cause by trampling around. I had the garden open next day. I could bear two minutes, surely.

". . . Dirty Dick?"

(Wild studio laughter.)

"Come on. This isn't Blackpool Pier. No one know? It was The Wooden Leg."

(I had forgotten that.)

"How many Vereker sisters—"

Bizz.

"Austin?"

"Five."

"One point. Nancy, Harriet, Lucy, Janet, and Belinda. How many husbands?"

Buzz.

"Julian?"

"Nine. Or was it ten?"

"Neither. Austin?"

"I'll plump for a round dozen."

" 'The Dirty Dozen'?"

(Animal cackles and brays from human throats.)

"May I remind you you have only two minutes. And you're all wrong. It was eight. I'll give half a point for each name. Forget your buzzers."

"Lord Seddon, Edward Voss-Thompson, that crook who killed himself . . ."

"Gerry Grantworth."

"That Italian playboy. Gino Arrezzio?"

"Arrizzio, but it will do."

"Paul Ackerley."

"No. Not married. Three to go."

"Wasn't there a Smith?"

"Bobo Smith. Married to Harriet. Any more? David Fish, Richard H. Felder III, and—I don't know how you managed to leave him out—Michael Allwegg."

"Aren't you going to ask us how many of them Lucy had slept with?"

The studio brayed. I'd been trying to prop the eryngium back onto its twigs with the hand that wasn't holding the plastic bag and sprayer. I straightened, snatched the secateurs out of my hip pocket, and slung them at the radio. I was never any use at ball games, but I have often been amused to notice how accurately I can toss weeds into a bucket several feet away, missiles whose differing weights and air resistances my hand and eye seem to estimate without the intervention of a calculating mind—that is, until the moment of noticing, when I can do it no longer. Had I been told that I must fling the secateurs at the radio in order to save my life, or the human race or something, I should certainly have missed, but I flung them without thought in the pang of shame and anger, and they hit, point first, bang in the centre of the loudspeaker grille, and speared in. The cackles snapped off as the radio crashed over, and in the sunlit stillness I heard a collared dove calling. Shuddering with swallowed fury, both at the insensitivity of my species and at my own lack of control in ruining a perfectly adequate little radio, I crouched to finish dealing with the eryngium.

It refused to lean as I'd had it, with its blue heads and stems casually haloing the mahogany and orange daisies of a rudbeckia, so I stayed crouched for a couple of minutes getting it right, with the result that when I rose the blood drained from my brain and I had to stand helpless in the drumming dark, swaying, until my head cleared. As light came back, I heard footsteps on gravel and opened my eyes to see Lucy coming slowly up the path with a full glass of sherry in each hand. It was only Saturday, so without thinking about it, I registered that she had been listening to the same programme while she was getting lunch ready and had brought me a drink because she'd known I'd need it. A decent-size glass of sherry was typically thoughtful. Left to myself, I'd probably have made a violent martini, and then felt stupid all afternoon.

She stepped round the radio, which lay in the path with the secateurs speared dramatically into the grille.

"Are you all right?" she said.

"I stood up too fast. I'm OK now."

Her hands had begun to tremble. Sherry dribbled down her wrists. I picked my way out and took the glasses from her.

"Bother," she said. "I thought I was going to make it all the way."

I grunted. Shock, emergency, a quick little surprise sometimes, can do that. The shakes go away for a few minutes. It's a commonplace of the disease. If she needs to, Lucy can make use of it—deliberately, as it were, shocking herself into momentary full control—but of course there is a law of diminishing returns. She put a quivering hand on my elbow and let me lead her up to the bench at the top of the border. It's only there for looks, and the occasional visitor—as far as I'm concerned, there are always more interesting things to do in a garden than sit down. But now the sun-sodden stone was delectable against my spine, as necessary to me as the drink. Two doves answered each other, from the orchard and from beyond the stables. The patch of common hemp agrimony at the top of the Maroon Border murmured with insects, which is one of the things it is there for. Something honey-scented drifted on the imperceptible breeze. Lucy leant against my side, her shakes dwindling from their aftershock extravagance to their usual steady tremor. Only the radio was wrong. It was like the focal point in a Magritte, deliberately placed in the perspective between the borders in order to deconstruct the idyll. The black casing contradicted the sunlight. The shape, mean proportioned, square edged, embodied the unnaturalness of artifact among all the growth and green. The object itself snapped at me about what I'd done.

I put the glasses on the bench, strode down the path, slid the secateurs into my pocket, took the radio into the scullery yard and dropped it in the bin. When I came back, Lucy appeared to have fallen asleep, bolt upright, a knack she'd always had. She was wearing a sleeveless linen shift with nothing, I guessed, underneath. (She could still dress herself, but simplified the process as much as she could.) Though I'd done her hair well that morning, by now it had half-loosened itself from its bun, but that had always been her style. I remember a diplomatic reception, presumably while she was still married to Tommy Seddon, as she was hostess. Royalty of some kind had just arrived and she was greeting them. I was admiring the way she made her formal curtsey look like a friendly and natural gesture when her sister Harriet, standing beside me, whispered, "Trust Lucy to look as if she'd already started going to bed when she suddenly remembered she was supposed to be here."

Now straggles of fine grey hair hung down by the pale slant of her cheek. The "masked" look, symptomatic of the disease, was only slightly present, subsumed for the moment into the mask of beauty she had always worn. Her thin white arms seemed frail as paper. Her whole attitude cried to me of her vulnerability (though both frailty and vulnerability had, until her illness, been almost pure illusions). Once again, for the thousandth time, the pang of love stabbed through me. I stood letting it fade away, much as I had done with the blood loss a few minutes before, and then walked on. My footsteps woke her, or she had not been asleep, but she didn't open her eyes till I settled beside her.

"I switched it off as soon as they said the name," she said.

"I was stuck."

"Yes, I saw. That was a terrific shot, Paul. I'll buy you a new one for your birthday."

"See if you can find a waterproof one. They have them for camping."

"May I have my sherry?"

I held it to her lips so that she could empty it enough for her to hold without spilling, then picked up my own and sipped.

"What a perfect day," I said.

"It's all looking too beautiful," she said.

"I only see what's still wrong with it. Oh well, I suppose it's not bad. Let's hope the weather holds."

"You always say you prefer to look at gardens in the rain."

I must have sighed. Despite the banalities of contentment, the aftertaste of the radio programme kept regurgitating itself in my mind. Lucy read my feelings.

"I'm sorry," she said.

"Don't let's talk about it."

"I think we've got to. As a matter of fact, I've been thinking about it a lot. I'm going to start getting worse soon."

"Nonsense. There's no reason why you shouldn't stay pretty well as you are for years still. You're on a plateau. I had a long talk with Liz Sterling, when was it . . . ?"

"She doesn't know. I'm the only one who knows. It's been quite a nice plateau, and I'm glad it's lasted as long as it has, but I can feel the edge coming. It doesn't matter what Liz Sterling says."

I opened my mouth to snap at her, and closed it again. What was the point? I'd lied to her about what Dr. Sterling had told me.

"What's for lunch?" I said.

"It's cold. Let's stay here. It's lovely here. Please, Paul. I want to talk to you. I'll make it as easy as I can for you."

"You don't have to make it easy for me."

"It's really just two things. . . ."

I was aware of some inner effort taking place. This itself was a rare event—not the effort, but my awareness. I suppose I know her better than anyone else in the world, but I am nowhere near understanding her, why she is what she is, says what she says, does what she does.

"I'll have the good news first. If any," I said.

"I don't know if it counts," she said. "Will you marry me, Paul?"

I was startled into laughter and spilt some sherry. Years and years ago, lying sleepless in a dirty little hotel in Samos, I'd heard faint rhythmic murmurs from her and realised she was counting.

"Greek sheep?" I'd murmured.

"Men who've proposed," she'd said. "It's your fault—you set me off, teasing me about Waldemar."

(He was some kind of international financial brigand who'd had a plush cruiser moored in the harbour. Lucy had spotted him and let on she'd met him. I'd suggested making ourselves known in the hope of an invitation on board. Lucy had refused, saying that he was one of her rejectees and hadn't taken it well. I rather crassly—I was in a bitchy mood—had asked how long the list was and where he came.)

"I've got to thirty-seven," she said. "Not counting the ones where I didn't speak the language so I didn't know whether actual marriage was part of the proposal."

I'd already known, even then, what she'd been telling me, that part of our unspoken contract was that I should not figure in that list.

"I want it soon," she said now. "While . . . while I can still understand what's happening. It's all right, Paul. I'm not trying to tie you up. I've got everything worked out. While you were in Scotland, I got Timmy to come, and we went round and looked at some homes and found one which will do. He's going to sell enough of my shares to buy an annuity, which will cover the fees. And we'll have a marriage contract which will say you've got to let me go there as soon as it's no fun living with me."

Timmy is her son, now Lord Seddon. I like him. He and his wife, Janice, come and stay two or three times a year. Lucy's daughter, Rowena, is beautiful in her mother's style but has opted for a life of near-fanatical uprightness, and so is uneasy with Lucy and me.

"As your husband," I said, "I shall surely—"

"No, you won't. I'm going to tie it up like a miser in a novel. Timmy says . . . Does that mean yes?"

"A provisional yes, subject to contract, as the estate agents say. Do I get a kiss, or must I listen to the bad news first?"

She sat still. Again I could sense the inner process. It wasn't the proposal of marriage that had caused it earlier, either. It must have been whatever was coming now. I waited, steeling myself.

"This is while I can still understand, too," she said. "Will you tell me how you killed Gerry? I think I know why, but how? How did you get into the room? And out again?"

The drumming dark that I had experienced in the flowerbed returned. This time it can have lasted only a few seconds. Lucy seemed not to have noticed.

Silence. The doves. Bees. The far drub of a helicopter. Sunlight. The flood of memory. In my mind's eye a large lawn, also sunlit, but the air dense and still. Four women in sports gear gazing towards the facade of a large house, their postures tense with amused alarm. The tinkle of breaking glass. All different, all long ago, but in my own throat and chest the selfsame sickness and oppression that I was feeling now.

"I had always imagined it was you," I whispered.

Lucy

ONE

Summer 1992

This was my idea. We tried talking about it, but I couldn't keep my end up. We tried to tell each other why we'd done what we did and thought what we did, but it was too tiring. I couldn't keep my thoughts in order. I started to stammer, which is a very bad sign. There seemed to be so much the other one didn't know. So in the end I said, "You'll have to write it all down and then I can put bits in. Don't do it for me—do it for someone else. Otherwise you'll leave things out because you think I know them."

So that's what we're doing. I watch the telly in the evenings and Paul puts his earplugs in and sits beside me writing in a notebook. He still has the most beautiful, neat writing, just like him. Everything in order. Mine was always all over the place with letters on top of each other. And of course Paul can't help wanting to get it right. The words, I mean—the way people talk, the pictures, the feel of things. If he takes anything seriously, he has to do it as well as a professional. That's why his garden is so beautiful.

I'm not like that, and anyway I hardly write at all these days. My hand shakes worse because I'm trying. Even pressing the buttons on this machine brings the shakes on worse. If there are gaps, it doesn't mean I've gone to sleep. I'm thinking.

I never used to think much about things, once they were over, but I do now, back and back and back. I'm pretty sure my mind's still alright—they say it oughtn't to go till last of all.

The first thing I've got to say is, Whoever you are, don't pity me. People think it must be awful being like this, but it isn't. It's a nuisance, of course, stops me doing things I'd like to, means I have to be looked after—for instance we have to get a nurse in if Paul goes away. I want him to get one all the time so he doesn't have to do so much for me, but he says not yet, and I don't feel even slightly guilty. There's lots I enjoy, things I took for granted before. Sitting at the top of the borders, letting the sun drill through me, drinking my sherry, waiting to see what Paul was going to say, I felt life was so good I wanted to cry. Not so-good-in-spite-of-everything. So good. Like that.

Especially don't pity me about not being beautiful anymore. Actually I'm not too dusty. Being ill has given me a sort of holy, marble-saint look. A saint who's been kissed by so many pilgrims that she's worn away a bit, which makes her look a lot more interesting than when she came all polished out of the sculptor's studio. I suppose I'd better get this business about being beautiful over. Last winter there was a *Life of Churchill* on the telly. When he was old but before he went gaga, he got Vivien Leigh and Laurence Olivier to come to lunch with him at Chartwell. He sat her next to him and didn't say anything, just kept looking at her. Once or twice he told her how beautiful she was. That's all. For God's sake, I thought, that's not what you go and have lunch with Churchill for! I don't think being beautiful was the only reason she was a nut case, but it can't have helped.

Don't worry—I'm not going to start a special brand of feminist hoo-ha. "Beautyist" it'd have to be, I suppose. Aesthetic harassment. Of course when I was very young and didn't know how to handle it, I sometimes wished it would go away, and it doesn't help when you're in a real teapot-throwing temper to be told how terrific you look when you're cross. And of course you want to eat your cake and have it. You want the pluses and not the minuses. You want the fun and the attention and the parties and you don't want the slobs barging up and expecting to get off with you. I know I wouldn't have preferred to be out-and-out plain, but suppose I'd been about as good-looking as Harriet—not a head-turner, but not bad . . . I don't know. . . .

People who know me well, Paul for instance, say they can tell if I'm upset because then I look specially calm. I suppose it's true. I've heard singers being interviewed and they have this funny way of talking about what they do. They don't say "my voice," they say "the voice," as if it was right outside them, not part of them at all, like a cello or something. It's a bit like that with me, not that I've ever talked about "the face," but that's how I felt. It was something I wore. "Me" was the person who wore it, quite different, much brighter than I looked for a start, but not specially brave or calm, erratic, impulsive, silly about some of the risks I took, like everyone else, really, only I had this face to hide behind. Just a few people—Father, of course—Gerry was another—they didn't seem to pay any attention to the face, so the person they saw was me.

No, Paul wasn't one of them. He still isn't.

I think that's probably important. If you don't understand it, you won't understand a lot. But it certainly doesn't explain everything. Nothing ever does, about people, does it?

Now I'm afraid I'm tired. I hope I get better at this. I'm going to have a snooze, because Paul's at his Historic Dorset committee and he'll ask me if I have when he gets back.

Paul

TWO

1934–39

Though we were almost exact contemporaries, I knew Gerry Grantworth only slightly at Eton. For one thing he was in College, at a phase when there were marked social barriers between Collegers and Oppidans, Collegers being there on scholarships, and so assumed to come from families who were unable to afford the Eton fees. Then I belonged to a different group of unacceptables, having been brought up as a practising Jew. To judge by old photographs, I was not very obviously Jewish; in fact as my connections with my ancestral faith and nation have withered over the decades, my appearance seems to have gone in the other direction, so that now I am almost a caricature—apart from the damaged side of my face—of a certain kind of elderly Semite: slight, quick eyed, smooth voiced, saurian, cultured, mysteriously wealthy.

(To get it over—though it has no connection with what follows, apart from the fact that I have always been able to afford what I wanted and to arrange my time as I chose—there is no mystery about my wealth. I inherited from my father, who died shortly before the end of the war, a business dealing in office equipment. From my Intelligence work in the war, I was able to grasp, sooner than most people, the enormous changes that would come with the so-called information revolution. I am good at analysing documents and reports. I have a natural understanding of how bureaucracies and other organisations function. I was lucky in one or two people I met. I acquired the right agencies, backed new enterprises which fulfilled their promise—I won't go into detail. My father's modest fortune, enough to send his only son to Eton, but at some sacrifice on his part, became considerable in my hands. That's all that need be said.)

To return to Eton: it is difficult for anyone much younger than me to appreciate the nature of the anti-Semitism that pervaded our culture in those days. I am talking not only of the class of people who sent their sons to the major public schools, but the considerably larger class of those who would have done so if they could have afforded to. It was not the virulent, Hitlerian strain of the disease (though I believe it could, under different circumstances, have mutated to that), but it was the air we breathed, so familiar as to have no odour in our nostrils for most of the time. Jews were outsiders, not "one of us." You blackballed a Jew from your club as automatically as you blackballed a candidate who had been seen wearing brown suede shoes with a blue suit. I can remember myself looking at another boy—my second cousin, as it happens—who conformed much more closely than I did to the stereotype—oily black curled hair, loose, sensual features, and so on—and wondering with a kind of distaste why he needed to seem so blatantly Jewish. His parents, more ambitious for acceptance than my father, had Christianised, but that made no difference. People nowadays make a fuss about the hints of anti-Semitism in writers such as Kipling and John Buchan, and the more-than-hints in the egregious Sapper, and seem amazed that we didn't reject them out of hand. It crossed very few people's minds to do so. A Jew myself, I read such writers with pleasure and accepted the passing slurs as the way things were. As I say, that was the air we breathed.

I've always found it easy to make friends, so after the first few weeks I got on well enough with boys in my house of my own age. I had trouble with some of the older boys, particularly with Bobo Smith, who later married Harriet Vereker. He became Captain of Games in my house and used the position to pick on me unjustly, more than once. Though I was no use at games, I had the wits to conform to the petty rules about compulsory exercise and so on. Still, he found excuses. Being thrashed on your arse with a cane by an athletic eighteen-year-old hurts almost as much as any pain I have so far known. Any physical pain, that is. Bobo was a bully, and if I had not been available, he would have picked on someone else. My Jewishness made him choose me. Even then, it seemed to me part of the natural order of things, and I don't believe I resented it much.

I've strayed. What I was attempting to explain was that both Gerry Grantworth and I were members of despised minorities, he as a Colleger and I as a Jew, but that that did not put us on the same side of any fence. We might have spent five years at Eton and still never have spoken to each other, but in my last year I got to know him a bit, through cricket.

From my second year on, I had messed with Tommy Havers and Dick Hall-Fisher. Both died in the war, Tommy from a mine at Alamein, and Dick run down by an American truck in Salerno, during the Italian campaign. Dick was a quiet, dull, self-sufficient boy, pleasant enough but never important to me. Tommy and I became close companions throughout our time at Eton, met when we could afterwards, and wrote to each other till he died. He was not a natural games player but possessed the most extraordinary willpower, so that if he decided he was going to achieve something, he nearly always succeeded. Early on he had told me that before he left, he intended to be in the First Eleven—cricket—and School Field—a weird form of ur-soccer that the school in those days took with great seriousness. (I believe it is still played, but it must be more as a sort of folk ritual than as a living game.) It was as Tommy's hanger-on that I came to know Gerry.

Gerry was a natural athlete. Indeed, he seemed to me then to be a natural everything. This is not to say he was the traditional young Apollo, golden haired, dreaming on the edge of strife. For a start he was not obviously handsome. Striking, yes, with his slightly too-large head stiff-necked above wide muscular shoulders. I have seen him stripped, in changing rooms. His torso appeared gnarled with strength, his legs like those of a billiard table, but he was by no means muscle-bound. His large hands hung loose and low; he walked lightly and could move with unbelievable speed and precision. Boys think much of sport and are impressed by abilities such as Gerry's, even when allied to a dull mind and brutish temperament, but Gerry seemed gifted at anything to which he turned his attention. He had won his scholarship in a perhaps unprecedented manner, on his mathematics, coming from a prep school where they taught Latin to a moderate standard at best and no Greek at all. Having won it, he crammed Latin and Greek through the summer holidays and arrived pretty well level with boys who'd had their noses rubbed in the languages for five years. He read voraciously. His conversation at seventeen, when I first knew him, was electric with unpredictable thoughts and phrases, quite as good, even then, as anyone's I have met since. My sole physical talent is that I am a tolerably good dancer. Women I have spoken to on the subject have told me that Gerry was the best—most proficient, most exciting—partner they had ever taken the floor with.

I know of two blemishes on the image of the easy, all-achieving demigod. First, he had no head for alcohol. I learnt this in the summer holidays before my final year. (Drink was forbidden at Eton. If you were seen in a pub, you would very likely be expelled—certainly if alcohol were found in your room. Senior boys could drink a very mild beer bought from a source controlled by the school. My father regarded a cocktail before supper as a necessity of life, and since I was sixteen I had joined him, but home practice among the boys varied considerably.) There was a short cricket tour that holidays, playing village teams around Tommy's area, and I went along as scorer. (I have to explain that despite being a duffer at cricket, I enjoy watching the game. I have the compulsory games system to thank for this. Being forced to play two or three times a week all summer, though with other incompetents and at a level of farcical dullness, at least gave me an imaginative grasp of the skills involved in the performance of serious players.)

On our first evening at Tommy's, there was wine for supper. Gerry had never tasted wine before (nor was he the only one). After one glass his talk became excited, but not quite to the point of incoherence. After his second he passed out and we had to put him to bed. We all thought this a great joke and made further experiments, to which he submitted a couple of times, and then went on the wagon.

Gerry's other blemish, if I can call it that, was vaguer. My first intimation of it also came to me by way of cricket. One afternoon I was watching a match against some other school— Charterhouse, I seem to remember. They had a notoriously big hitter at number five. Soon after I arrived, Dirty Dan settled into the chair beside me. He was, I suppose, the most notable figure of fun on the Eton staff in those days. He earned his nickname by shaving irregularly, reeking of male odours only partly concealed by his dreadful pipe tobacco, and wearing clothes a tramp would have refused. The boys in his house held sweepstakes on how long he would sport the same pair of trousers, identical pinstripes that could be told apart by the food stains on them. He was spectacularly shy of women. Mothers were said to have interviewed him without discovering what he looked like, so thorough a smoke screen rose from his pipe under the stress of such a meeting. He was a savage dispenser of punishments but a better teacher of French than most in that dismally taught subject. His passion, his genius, his life blood was the boys in his own house. They dreaded him for their first two years, but left adoring him—I am told that a cabinet minister was seen weeping at his memorial service.

Tommy had opened the bowling and had a good spell with his fast-medium inswing, taking a couple of wickets. There was a minor stand, another wicket fell, and the big hitter—I have forgotten his name—came in. Such players depend to a great extent on a self-confidence that amounts to a kind of psychic dominance over their opponents, and this chap had it, and to spare, that afternoon. He hit two fours and a six in his first over, cleanly, not slogging, but with stylish violence. Dirty Dan took out his binoculars, normally used only to study the performance of boys in his house. Anyone watching must have been aware that we were in the presence of something unusual, a player who might be captaining England in years to come, though of course that kind of startling early talent can disappear as quickly as it came. We were never to know. The boy was drowned at Dunkirk.

The score rattled up, Tommy was brought back on, but the ball had lost its shine and barely swung. He was no threat, and suffered. In apparent desperation the captain, a boy called Thayer, put himself on to bowl at the other end. He was mainly an opening bat but could at need bowl slow leg tweakers, spinning them a mile but without much control of length and line. Dirty Dan hummed with excitement—Thayer was in his house. The first two balls spun all right but were such long-hops that I felt I could have hooked them for six myself. The batsman did so with disdain.

"Ground bait," muttered Dirty Dan.

Another master, I forget who, chuckled derisively from the chair beyond.

The third ball was no improvement but spun far enough

across the wicket for the batsman to decide to pull rather than hook it. His stroke was beautifully timed, and made by a powerful young man from the meat of the bat.

Gerry Grantworth was fielding at short leg. This was in the days before helmets, and it was lunacy to have left him there against such a hitter with such erratic bowling. I have no idea how fast the ball was travelling. I saw Gerry leap, his hands full-stretch above his head. His upper body whipped back so that for an instant I—and others, to judge by the gasp— thought the ball must have caught him in the face. Then he had landed and was tossing the ball back to Thayer as unconcernedly as if he'd picked it up in a net. I was on my feet and yelling, and so was the master beyond Dirty Dan and most of the other spectators.

"That's the most extraordinary catch I've ever seen," said the other master as he settled into his chair. "You know, I believe that boy is capable of anything."

Dirty Dan was relighting his pipe (he expended far more matches than tobacco), so his answer came late enough to seem isolated from what had prompted it, and thus vaguely oracular.

"Including, ultimately, his own destruction," he said.

The other master grunted questioningly. Further pipe-suckings repeated the pause.

"He believes himself invulnerable," said Dirty Dan.

"All adolescents do," said the other master. "What's more, he broke his thumb in last year's Winchester match."

(We all remembered this event, because Gerry had retired hurt, but returned at eighth wicket down to bat one-handed, scoring thirty-odd and achieving a draw.)

"Morally invulnerable," said Dirty Dan. "Automaton in armour, eh?"

I heard another grumble of incomprehension from the master. Dirty Dan sighed.

"Adolescent invulnerability I grant you," he said. "This one's different. Cap-à-pie on the outside, no moral innards.

What's he for, eh? Merely to be Master Grantworth. His own purpose, that's all. All bets are certs, because he's risking nothing, his side. Only they ain't. As he'll find out. But a sly bit of bowling from young Thayer, eh?"

As I say, we considered Dirty Dan a figure of fun, and I didn't take his comments seriously. I don't believe I've thought about them again until I came to write these words, and even now I am not sure what weight to give them.

I think that's all about Eton, except that I remember having the Vereker girls pointed out to me at Lord's in my last year. They were all five there. Nancy was already in the gossip columns, and Harriet occasionally mentioned. The story as told at Eton—as reliable as any other gossip among adolescents—was that old Vereker had explained, when he proposed, that the object was to produce a male heir to Blatchards, and that the future Lady Vereker, a lawyer's daughter, had replied that she would bear five children and no more, and that done, he should keep her in hunters for as long as she was able to ride. If all five were girls, it was either his fault, biologically, or his bad luck, actuarially. If true, my guess is that it was no more than a joking bargain between a couple who were marrying for love. When I knew them later, they gave no hint of discontent with each other, or with the knowledge that the inheritance must now pass through the female line.

I regarded Lord's as a bore. Whatever interest the cricket might have had was obscured by the social event. I can no more than have glanced at at the Vereker party. They belonged to a world in which I had no prospect of moving nor, then, any wish to.

The war swept that world into abeyance. Unlike most of my Eton contemporaries, who were concerned to get themselves into congenial regiments, I took no special steps and let myself be hoovered up in the general melee of conscription. Then there was a bureaucratic hitch, which resulted in my presenting myself at a camp at Bury St. Edmunds as instructed in my call-up notice, only to be told that as far as the camp was concerned, I didn't exist, and I must go home and wait for my position to be clarified. This took some weeks, with the result that I did my basic training not with the main flood of public-school leavers but with a far more heterogeneous bunch. An odd thing happened here. Having been picked on in my early days at Eton for being a Jew, I was now picked on for being an Etonian. The corporal in charge of my platoon, a lively sly Welshman, seemed fascinated by my education. He was always bringing it up.

"And where were you at school, lad?"

"Eton, sir."

"And they didn't teach you to wash your neck of a morning, then? You're a dirty soldier, aren't you, lad?"

"Yes, sir."

I didn't mind. I made friends, including the corporal before long. Having been in the Eton OTC, I could drill. I kept myself neat and obeyed orders, though it was clear that I was never going to be much of a fighting soldier, being physically inept and a hopeless shot. On the other hand, I turned out to have a natural grasp of the needs and habits of military bureaucracy, and was soon able to work it to my advantage and to advise my friends on how to do so.

Basic camp lasted only six weeks. Its function, apart from simple training in drill and weapons, was to assess us for posting on to whatever unit we were thought suitable for. The system could be crazily haphazard but worked for me. My mother was Viennese, and I had been brought up bilingual, adding fair French by staying with families during two summer holidays. I was not bothered about getting a commission. My object was to get into Intelligence, where I thought I might be most useful. Many weird and incompatible Intelligence setups proliferated as the military machine expanded, and in the nature of things, suitable officer-quality staff was more available than other ranks. The officer who assessed me at the camp had a memo on his desk asking him to look out for men with almost exactly my qualifications.

"Good God!" he cried. "We have a round peg here, and a hole to match! I think we're going to win this bloody war after all!"

So I was booked for a week's Christmas leave, then to join the Signals for a wireless course near Salisbury, where I would be interviewed by someone from the organisation that had sent the memo, and if that went well, move on to a secret location. Eight days before I was due to finish at Bury, I spotted Gerry in the canteen, alone in a corner, reading. Delighted I went over to say hello, and when he looked up, he seemed as pleased as I felt. I could see from the stiffness of his khaki that it had been issued only in the last few days. The book was Demosthenes' *Philippics* in Greek. No crib.

"What on earth are you doing here?" I said. "I'd have thought you'd be in France by now."

"I may very well be. What you see, Paul, is, as far as I can make out, a phantasm, the wrong half of a doppelgänger. If I vanish of a sudden, it will mean that my true self has stood in the way of a bullet somewhere in no-man's-land. Or possibly been shot for a deserter, in the attempt to unite himself with me. Has the War Office a Surrealist Department? When I leave this place, will I be sent to smother the German defences with giant melted watches with ants inside them?"

"I didn't exist for a few weeks," I said. "Then they conjured me back into being. I know I'm real. I have pay books to prove it."

"Ah, but I have two sets of pay books, two numbers, two existences. There is actually pay accumulating for me some-where so that it can formally be taken away from me after my court-martial. When I collect my pay on my other pay book, they tell me that I shall have to sign a document admitting that if I turn out to be my other self, I shall not have been entitled to it."

"Seriously?"

"Seriously. There are documents to prove that I was called up, trained, posted and shipped to France. Only at that point does someone seem to have noticed that I wasn't there. The first I knew of it was when two military policemen showed up at home and wanted to arrest me as a deserter. I was in my bath. My aunt charmed them with Marmite sandwiches, but that didn't stop them from taking me off to the glass-house. In the end I was able to persuade someone that I had never left home and had simply been hanging around waiting to be told what to do. Now I am here. But my other self refuses to go out of existence. What are your plans for this Sunday?"

"Nothing special."

"Care to walk over to Blatchards with me?"

"Blatchards?"

"The Vereker girls. You haven't run across any of them? How refreshing. Nancy told me to bring anyone I liked. No? I promise you, their reputation belies them. Or they it."

I wasn't, I believe, even curious to meet the Vereker girls. On the other hand I was confident of my ability to look after myself socially. Sunday afternoons were a desert. We were let out of camp for a few hours, but looking back, it is astounding how little a town the size of Bury had to offer by way of entertainment when it chose to shut down.

"It's about three miles," said Gerry.

"All right. Thanks."

I don't wish to give the impression that Blatchards was any kind of Brideshead or—a mistake occasionally made in the memoirs of writers who should have known better—that the Verekers were at all similar in attitude and style to the Mitfords. To take the house first. We walked out on a dull December afternoon, just short of rain, and so still that the last few leaves seemed likely to hang forever in the listless air. Suffolk is a closed, rolling county, without wide views inland, and with neither heights nor levels. We came to a small village, beyond whose church a weedy drive began between nondescript Georgian lodges. As we trudged through parkland, the house began to emerge, but as a rectangular dark shape part-screened by clumps of trees, so that it was never fully in view until we were almost on the turning circle of gravel before the East Front, with its out-of-scale porte-cochère. It was a large house, of course, by my standards, though moderate by those of its time, around the end of the eighteenth century. I saw at once that it was nothing special. It was not only the porte-cochère that made it look as though the first Lord Vereker had simply instructed a local builder to build him a house of a certain size and left the rest to him: "Rooms? Oh, around fifty should do the trick. Look like? How the devil can I know what it should look like until I see the demmed thing? Modern, mind you, but none of these gothick frills. Oh, get it out of a book. Lady Vereker? What the devil . . . oh, she'd better have a boudoir or a parlour or something, if you can get her to make up her mind. Now, about the Stables . . ."

"Not much to look at," said Gerry. "And it's worse inside. There isn't a picture you couldn't buy in a junk shop for twenty quid. The curse of the Verekers, passed from generation to generation, has been a uniquely boring taste. Not even positively bad, no quaint excesses of vulgarity, just the most absolutely mediocre of which their period was capable."

"Are they like that themselves?"

"Far from it. Not the girls, as least. There is marked sexual dimorphism, as in birds, only the other way round, the males drab and retiring, the females decidedly striking."

We were still a few paces from the door when it opened and a girl backed out, wearing Wellingtons and riding breeches. Glossy dark-brown hair, rippling at the ends into crinkles, flowed down her shoulders over a dark green jersey with leather patches on the shoulders and a hole in one elbow. She turned, stared at Gerry for a moment with her mouth half-open, took me in, and laughed.

"A whole army!" she said.

She was about sixteen, lightly freckled, not merely pretty but already beautiful in an earthy-elfin style, unlike that of anyone else I've ever known, though I've caught glimpses of it sometimes in her sisters.

"The elite corps only," said Gerry. "This is Paul Ackerley. He was at school with me. Lucy Vereker."

"Hello," she said. "Nan's in the library."

"What is Nan doing in a library?" said Gerry.

"Practising ping-pong with an eyepatch."

"Paul is a bit overcivilised, so I thought it would do him good to spend an afternoon among the Visigoths."

"Aren't you going to ask me about the eyepatch?"

"I assume she's bet someone—your father?—that she can beat him like that."

"Was he always as irritating as this?" she said.

"I find it restful to know there's no point in competing," I said.

"That makes two of them," she said. "Him and Nan, I mean. Rule one of all games is that Nan wins. Come and give me the low-down on Gerry while I get the eggs."

At what point did I first fall in love with Lucy? There were second, third, and fourth times, at least, with longish intervals between, when we met only by accident and corresponded through Christmas cards, but in that sense "falling in love" means something different from what happened that afternoon. Still, that was when everything began, as I watched her scatter corn among the chuckling mottled birds, helped to search for clandestine nests among the bramble stems, was shown how to ease the blood-warm eggs out from under a mutteringly indignant broody. That is my AUC, my manger cradle, my hegira. I have wondered whether, supposing I had gone in with Gerry and met Lucy along with the rest of the family, I would have had quite the same feelings about her. I was an urban child. We lived in Wimbledon, but our whole bent was towards the centre of London and away from the increasing rurality south and west of us. I had not touched a live hen before that afternoon, or held in my palm an egg with the mother warmth still glowingly in it. One is very easily deceived by such things. They seem to possess "reality," a touchstone quality that must for me have contrasted strongly with the dreamlike, irrational procedures of conscription. But as I say, that was when it began, though as I walked back to camp with Gerry, I cannot have thought of myself as being in any way in love with Lucy. Any of the five girls (the school holidays had just begun, so they were all there) might have been an equally good, and equally unattainable, target for my affections.

I had better describe the Verekers at this point. As a group, a family, that is. Individual traits will no doubt emerge later. I was an only child of only children, and though I had stayed with families of friends, the culture, the instinctive sociology, of a family network was almost as alien to me as the business of egg collecting. The Verekers were a genial group. They liked each other, most of the time. They also, all the time, loved each other, perhaps more than they were ever to be capable of loving anyone else. They liked other people, too, and made no apparent effort to exclude them, but however apparently welcome (even, perhaps especially, when married to one of the girls), we others remained outside that inner circle. We could feel their love for each other, like a centre of warmth, but we could not sit with them as they sat, seeing each other's faces golden in the glow from the stove. Moreover this warmth existed, and could only exist, at Blatchards. (I speak symbolically. The house could be hyperborean in winter.) Blatchards was the context of their mutual delight, necessary to it, part of it. Things might have been different if there had been a male heir, but though it was openly accepted that when Lord Vereker died, Nancy would inherit, all five girls spoke and behaved as if they had equal rights, and so did their parents.

The girls were Nancy, about two years older than me (it seemed typical of Gerry that he should have attracted the attention of a girl who might be expected to prefer men several years his senior); Harriet, my age; Lucy, eighteen months younger; Janet, fourteen; and Belinda, invariably known as Ben, twelve. Lady Vereker, handsome in a hoydenish fashion and as boisterous as any of the girls, must have been in her early forties. Lord Vereker was some fifteen years older. Slight and scholarly-looking, he was never seen to read anything except the *Times*, perfunctorily, and the local paper, assiduously. He seemed a good listener, bright eyed and eager, but though I never caught him out in an unintelligent response, his comments other than grunts of encouragement were so few that I came to wonder whether he understood all that was being said. I have met dogs with a look like that—or children watching a conjuror, unable to form any notion of how the trick might be done, simply delighted that it should be done at all.

I have fallen into the trap of introducing later impressions. I can't have had more than a few words with Lord Vereker that afternoon. We had tea in a room mysteriously named Gloucester. "Because it had to have a name" was all the explanation I was given. In any other large house it would have been the Nursery, or the Schoolroom, or something like that. The table was rectangular, and I was near one end with the younger girls, who chatted pleasantly about their own doings and interests. I was aware of Gerry and Nancy at the other end of the table, Nancy very lively and aggressive, and Gerry coping easily with her assault and obviously enjoying himself, as if facing a good quick bowler, while Lord Vereker, seated between them at the head of the table, twitched his head back and forth like a tennis umpire.

After tea the girls were eager to play something called "The

Game," which was best done four-a-side, but Gerry and I were due back at camp by six, so to my relief we had to disappoint them.

We walked back in the dark to blacked-out Bury. Gerry was at first unusually silent until, as we reached the main road, he laughed and said, "The question is, how does one acquire wealth? Not a mere competence, Paul. Riches."

"Luck, intelligence, nerve, knowing the right people, hard work," I said.

"I doubt intelligence has much to do with it, if one judges by some of the boneheads who could send several sons to Eton."

"They inherited their money."

"I believe that if I had something to start with, I could find ways to increase it, but how does one begin? Don't tell me. I am talking to myself."

"Is it that urgent? We've got a war to get through first."

"It has to be thought of, Paul. It has to be thought of."

Lucy

TWO

1938–39

It's funny what people remember, and how they remember it. I know I must have collected the eggs with Paul, because he says so—he's often talked about it—and anyway it was my job in the holidays. I do remember Gerry bringing this other chap out from Bury, and me turning round and seeing them on the drive, and my heart stopping. And I remember tea, and feeling absolutely sick with jealousy because Gerry was sitting at the other end of the table with Nan and making her laugh, and Mother was making such a noise in between that I couldn't hear what they were saying, and me flouncing round and saying something thoroughly aggressive to the funny little chap Gerry had dredged up, so obviously different from anyone I knew, like a foreigner almost, and him not minding and not letting me feel ashamed about being so rude, but smiling and coping and giving me a chance to talk—I don't know what about, the family I expect—and then telling me about Gerry and Eton because of course I asked.

And I do remember when I first met Gerry. It was the August before, when Nan got him down for a House *v.* World cricket match. I'd better explain. When Father realised he was only going to get girls he'd said in that case we'd all got to learn to play cricket well enough to play for the House. They

started having House *v.* Worlds before the First War, and
there'd been women in the teams sometimes, even then, but
because of us it became a regular thing. It was a bit of a cheat
having Gerry to play for House as he wasn't really, but old
Lord Seddon, who was bringing the World team over, had a
couple of ex-Blues, so we thought it was fair. That year was
special, as we all knew there was going to be a war and we
thought it might be the last match.

Anyway, I always went in last, and we were still forty behind
and Gerry was at the other end, and of course we tried to make
it so that he got most of the bowling, but I couldn't help
having some. They started off bowling me dollies because I
was a girl and the youngest playing (Janet had been furious
about that), so I'd got a few runs before they realised I wasn't
a duffer and started taking me seriously. By then we'd got
about twenty to go, and it was getting really needle. Gerry
was wonderful, treating me like a real player, letting me see
he trusted me, keeping me going, and I got into a sort of
excited trance. I *knew* we were going to do it. Then we were
one behind and I had the last ball of the over to face and I
glanced it for two—Janet said afterwards it was a snick, but
it wasn't, I'd done it on purpose—glanced it down to where
fine leg wasn't and Gerry and I walked in together waving our
bats while everybody cheered. Everybody was just the teams
and about twenty spectators, but it didn't matter. It was the
best day of my life, till then. I'm not sure it still isn't.

So that's how I got my crush on Gerry. I kept it to myself,
best I could. I thought I knew about crushes. I'd read about
them. I'd seen it happening to school friends. I thought they
were like measles. You have them around that age and you
recover and then you don't have to worry anymore because now
you're immune. But with me it wasn't measles, it was chicken
pox. Two summers ago Paul had shingles, and Dr. Sterling
explained it was because he'd had chicken pox when he was
small, and the chicken pox virus had been hiding in his body

all those years and now for no known reason it had decided to come back in that different, horrible, painful way. That's what my crush on Gerry was like. I thought I'd got over it. It was so long ago and such a lot had happened that I thought I'd forgotten about it, and then, out of nowhere, back it came— not just once, either—and it really hurt like blazes. It made me behave like a complete bitch, too. Looking back now, I simply don't understand myself, then. I sometimes think I can't even have been quite sane, those times.

Of course I've asked myself why, often. My only idea is that it might have had something to do with Father. You read bits about the Vereker girls and Blatchards in memoirs and books like that, because we were supposed to be rather glamorous and eccentric—and then there was the Affair, of course—but nobody ever says much about Father. Just a line saying he was a bit odd but mainly boring. That's pretty much what Paul says, too, isn't it? Well, I thought he was the most wonderful person in the world. When I was small, I thought he could do anything and knew everything, and even when I got older and found out it wasn't really like that, I still adored him. I can remember sitting in our pew in church (second row back on the left) under the window of St. George killing a very sheepish-looking dragon. I was right against the wall and Father was on the aisle as usual because he read the first lesson, so all the others were in between us, and suddenly I had this thought, strong and clear as if somebody had spoken it in my mind, that I wished they were all dead, so that I could go to bed with him and sleep in his arms all night, like Mother did. I couldn't push the idea away all through the rest of the service, though I was trembling all over with the wickedness of it, and as soon as church was over, I rushed up to Mother and hugged her till she told me not to be a nuisance.

I dare say that sounds terribly ordinary. Probably a lot of little girls have the same sort of feelings about their fathers. Not that Father did anything to encourage me, as far as I

know—in fact I remember feeling pretty frustrated sometimes
because he didn't always remember which one I was. All I can
say is it was extremely strong—in fact it was a lot more like
being "in love" than sometimes since, when I've persuaded
myself I was in love with some man or other. And it went on
for years. I've never talked to any of the others about it, of
course—I was too ashamed.

But what's it got to do with Gerry? I think I can see a sort
of pattern, though I don't know if it will make sense to anyone
else. I suppose it depends on whether they can understand how
much that cricket match meant. We all knew it was the last
one, the end of everything, because there was a war coming.
Father said we were all going to die of poison gas. Not that
he did anything about it, apart from moving some camp beds
into the cellars and laying in an immense stock of dog-biscuit,
because he said it didn't go mouldy as fast as human food.
Everyone talked about the war as if it was certain, so we knew
that even without the gas it was all over, and nothing would
ever be the same again. Good-bye, Blatchards. Good-bye,
happiness. Good-bye, being fenced off from horrible things.
(Mind you, we'd never been rich. There were servants, of
course, but they didn't get paid much, and there weren't nearly
as many as Blatchards had been built for, thank heavens. Father
was always thinking of ways to save money, which usually cost
more in the end. I remember how delighted Ben was when she
shot up and couldn't wear Janet's castoffs anymore. There was
a particular green dressing gown which had gone through all
five of us, and Mother was furious when we ceremonially burnt
it, because she'd noticed that the rector's collie was going bald
and she'd been going to offer it to him as a dog coat.)

Sorry. The cricket match. One of the boys staying to play
for the World had tried to make me let him come to my room
the night before. I was used to boys wanting to kiss me, but
this was different. He wasn't a lot older than I was, but I could
tell he knew what he was up to. He'd done it before. I was

frightened. I had to get Nan to tell him to lay off. (No use asking Mother or Father, of course.)

And then there was the match, and me going in last, all wound up, and Gerry at the other end, who really could do anything and did know everything (everybody said so) and being *my* partner, just us two—not even anyone else to come in if one of us got out—and paying proper attention to me, the me inside, not this face, this shape, but the person who was his partner and was helping him win the match—so totally different from the boy who'd tried to come to my room, so much what I wanted. . . .

I suppose it explains the crush, but I don't know that it helps about the way the crush came back, like shingles . . . and I suppose there was knowing I couldn't have him because he belonged to Nan, the way Father belonged to Mother. . . . So I'd be doing something, some job, or living with some man—both maybe—and gradually, without me noticing, there'd be this feeling building up that this wasn't what I really wanted, because what I really wanted was . . . was . . . and still I wouldn't understand, only this sort of vague hunger, until something triggered it off. That time Gerry showed Nan how to tango was the worst—and that was after a House *v.* World match too, come to think of it—and it would burst out, or rather it wouldn't burst out because there was nowhere for it to go, this furious, hurt, crazy jealousy for something I knew I couldn't have and certainly didn't want with any of me that was left still sane . . . I suppose. . . . That's what I tell myself now, anyway.

Does that make sense? Remembering that we aren't clockwork? No wheels going round, cogs fitting into other cogs, only this mess of currents and swirls, pushes and pulls, soft as water, strong as an opened sluice, making us what we are?

I'm not sure.

I meant to say something about Paul, but I'm too tired.

Paul

THREE

1943

I spent what time I could with Gerry during my remaining few days at Bury. A definite empathy seemed to develop between us, and a rebalancing of our relationship. Hitherto I had felt myself to be almost totally overshadowed by him in everything he did, and no wonder, but now to my surprise I found an area in which I was very much more competent than he was. Gerry turned out to be hopeless at grasping how the military machine functioned. As a result I was able to help and advise him in useful ways.

We exchanged home addresses, I went on leave and then reported to Salisbury, only to find that the Intelligence setup that had wished to recruit me had lost out in the cannibal competition with similar rivals, and that particular future was closed to me. I was now in the Royal Signals, so was posted on to Catterick for more orthodox training, but after a few weeks in those bleak northern barracks, I was sent for to London, my file having seeped through the cannibal digestion to reach a desk whose occupant had decided that his own organisation might have a use for me. Thus my time in Intelligence began. I was always a bureaucrat, never an agent. I found the work interesting and was good at it. My name appears in the indexes of several official and unofficial histories of British clandestine activities, but never with more than a couple of minor entries.

During this time I corresponded erratically with Gerry. We made one attempt to arrange a meeting, but without sufficient determination on either side to overcome minor obstacles of timing. In one of his letters, however, he mentioned his boredom and frustration with regimental life—this would have been after Dunkirk but before Rommel's campaigns in Africa. My organisation had a touchy relationship with the Special Operations Executive, but I got on well enough with some of their people and suggested Gerry as someone they might have a use for, intelligent, hardy, good at languages, and conforming to a stereotype of the British gentleman, then thought likely to impress simpleminded peasant partisans. Again, this is a step that Gerry would not have known how to take for himself.

I had consulted him, of course, and he wrote to say he had been taken on. Our correspondence ceased, and I heard no more from or of him until late in 1943, when I was in Cairo. Greece and Crete had fallen, and the desert campaigns were largely over. We knew by then that the war was won, and my organisation had transmogrified itself yet again and was now chiefly concerned with building a base of contacts and information which might allow Britain to influence, if not control, events in southeastern Europe in the aftermath of war. We existed, we believed, as a result of one of Churchill's momentary whims, expressed in a memo: "We must now be looking forward. Trouble has always brewed from the Balkans. Storms that engulfed Europe began as thunderclouds in those remote passes. We must know what is going on there. Let me see your proposals." Well, something like that.

There were already half-a-dozen feuding agencies, all more or less deluded by their own preoccupations, supporting various partisan groups and running agents and intelligence out of different countries. Our task was to assess and collate what they came up with, and since we were not in immediate conflict with any of them, and since my boss had a genius for dealing with the several types of maniac who ran them, they were for the most part more cooperative than might have been expected. My work was largely files and committees, but from time to time agents would come into Cairo for what is now called a debriefing and a rest, and at some point we would talk to them, and I would take them out for an evening on the town, or whatever they regarded as a good time, presenting myself as the junior dogsbody who got landed with that sort of task. Their own organisations let us do this largely because we had funds, and this allowed them to use their own entertainment budgets for other purposes. Some agents wanted drink and a woman, or a boy; some the pyramids by moonlight; some an evening's bridge. My most exotic achievement was to muster four performers of adequate standard for my then charge to play Schubert and Handel quintets with. The idea was that they should relax with me. I wasn't there primarily to pump information out of them, but to try to form a judgement of the depth and bias of the information they were bringing in.

Most agencies concealed the true names of their people, for obvious reasons, so there was no way that I could have known, when summoned by my boss to meet a Maj. George Gissing, that I was going to be confronted with Gerry Grantworth. We both laughed. My boss watched us unsmiling, the piggy little eyes in his big blank face glancing back and forth.

"Lieutenant Ackerley, Major Gissing," he said. "You have, I gather, met."

"In the far show of unbelievable years and shapes that flit, in our own likeness, on the edge of it," said Gerry.

The quotation was presumably a fluke, my boss being a Kipling fanatic, but at the same time it seemed an affirmation that Gerry hadn't changed in his capacity for getting things effortlessly right. My boss nodded.

"In that case I won't keep you," he said. "Thank you for

your help, Major Gissing. Have a good time. Let Paul know if there's anything we can do for you, in any way."

We left.

"Just two pips, Paul?" said Gerry. "I'd have thought you'd be running your own show by now."

"My rank's a bit variable," I said. "How would you like to spend an evening?"

"Talking," he said at once. "How are you set up here?"

"I've got a flat. Is that what you mean?"

"Perfect. If it suits you, that is. Or is there someone else there?"

"She's gone north for a family wedding. Lamb chops and a bottle of burgundy. Oh, no, of course—"

"A glass of decent wine would be agreeable. Possibly two. My head has grown a little stronger with the years. But if I venture on a third, you'll need to hire a barrow and wheel me back to the hotel."

"I hope not. Your people will assume that I've been trying to get you to tell me things they'd rather you didn't."

"Isn't that your job?"

"Not really. I've seen a rather uninformative file. You're in liaison with a group of pretty intransigent Reds on the Albanian frontier. That's all. This way. There's supposed to be a car for us."

I was living in the Armenian quarter, on an upper floor of one of those yellow, apparently unplanned, vast, shambling houses above an alley too narrow for vehicles. The driver dropped us at the corner. I could sense Gerry's wariness as I led him between two bead-workers' stalls and into the courtyard, where I shouted for Farzi. Farzi's eldest daughter, a demure fourteen-year-old, appeared and explained that her father had not expected me back and so was smoking and already sleepy. I gave her the chops I'd bought on the way home and told her what I wanted. She nodded and stalked off to see to it herself. Gerry didn't relax till I had settled him into a chair, facing eastward out over rooftops and a minareted skyline.

"You're looking a bit worn," I said.

It was true. The changes of puberty are the ones that get the literary attention, but there is another set between adolescence and manhood that I find more interesting. Though the muscles harden and the mouth firms up, more takes place in the character and mind. Between one page of a notebook and the next, a poet stops writing his juvenilia and finds his own voice. Or whatever. For those of my exact generation, the war became a rite of passage, marking and reinforcing this change. The effect in the case of Gerry was to my eye very marked. He was obviously fit and well. He walked with a spring, and his body, when I had lurched against him as the driver took a corner Cairo-style, had felt as hard as a wooden idol; but the lines of his large face were deeper etched than a normal three years would have worn them, and even when he smiled, I sensed that he had every face muscle under control.

"With cause," he said. "You described my cohorts as intransigent Reds. The epithet at least is correct. They are elemental thugs. The more intelligent of them want power, because they want power. The others just like killing people. I spend my time persuading them to kill Germans, rather than the set of elemental thugs on the next mountain."

"It sounds hairy."

"They've had me in front of a firing squad only once, and that wasn't serious. They wanted to see how easily I scared. Things are more comfortable now. We've brought off a couple of useful operations, saved each other's lives a few times, and so on. But it doesn't mean that if things took a certain kind of wrong turning, it mightn't be the firing squad in earnest."

He stopped, having heard the movement on the stair before I did. Farzi's daughter and her younger sister brought in peppermint tea and served it solemnly. Gerry looked out at the yellowing sky and I studied him. His file had been more detailed than I'd implied. One of the operations he'd referred to had been the complex ambush of an armoured column, with three feuding partisan groups having to be persuaded to cooperate. The risks, not only from German bullets, must have been appalling. It was clear that to achieve anything, the liaising agents had had to lead from the front. One of them had died. Gerry didn't speak again till the girls' soft tread had fluttered down the stair.

"Let's get it over before we start on the wine," he said. "What else do you want to know?"

"Nothing specific. Only if you come across anyone who you think is likely to have influence and whom we could in the long term trust."

His laugh was a snort.

"Someone bright enough, you mean, to perceive interests beyond his inherited feuds and alliances, honourable enough to keep his word to us, naïf enough to believe that we will do the same for him?"

"That's about it, though it might always be in our interest to keep our word. I see you've gone native."

There was always a tendency for agents of his kind to see things—their local campaign, of course, but also the war at large and global politics beyond—from the viewpoint of the people with whom they were sharing their lives and dangers. Indeed, that was pretty well a precondition of their acceptance among these people. It merely made their individual reports trickier to assess, and skewed the attitudes of the outfits they worked for.

"I must have been born native," he said. "I find I understand these people a good deal better than I understand my own."

"Natural enough," I said. "Did you ever finally get rid of your doppelgänger, speaking of the incomprehensible?"

He was puzzled a moment, then laughed.

"Not utterly," he said. "An occasional document pursues me from the War Office, so he still has his dusty existence among their files. I have a fantasy that someday I may find him useful. I suppose I should feel uncomfortable to continue to have two existences when others have ceased to have even one. Tommy Havers, I heard."

"Yes. He trod on a mine at Alamein."

"I'm sorry. I expect you miss him."

"Yes and no. That bit of Kipling you quoted applies. Even a serious friendship becomes somehow less real."

"I don't know that I have any serious friends. A couple of my thugs, maybe. Otherwise there are just people I happen to know. Heard anything from Blatchards?"

As it happened, I had. One of the odder phenomena of the desert war was an ambulance group set up by the formidable wife of a senior general. The medical staff were Free French, the orderlies British conscientious objectors—mostly Quakers of scholarly disposition—and the drivers a group of girls who before the war would have been parading themselves at the posher end of the marriage market. These last used to swirl into Cairo on leave, treating it as an exotic extension of the London Season—dances, dinners, gossip, riding. With their family connections and rarity value, they could command almost any escort they chose. A colleague of mine was besotted on one of them, who, on one of her leaves and (I guessed) because some more amusing engagement had fallen through, agreed to dine with him but, to forestall a tête-à-tête, told him she was bringing a friend and he must bring one, too. I was his, and Harriet Vereker was hers.

"Hello," she'd said at once. "You came with Gerry one Sunday, didn't you? And didn't he look dire in that uniform?"

We'd hit it off rather well, though not in any romantic fashion, my affections being then fully engaged by my Armenian, and later in the evening Harriet had deliberately separated us from the other pair as we were moving off to find somewhere to dance.

"I think he's rather sweet," she'd explained. "And Sue's a

greedy little so-and-so. She just wanted a free meal. I think we should give him a chance to get his money's worth."

This, incidentally, was typical of Harriet, a severe judge of character and a great arranger of other people's lives. My colleague's evening went well, apparently. He lived in a daze of content for weeks and was convinced I had arranged the separation for his benefit. Harriet and I had found a French-run café with umbrellas on the pavement and had drunk Pernod and sweet muddy coffee into the small hours while she talked eagerly of Vereker doings. Thus I was now able to bring Gerry up to date.

"Blatchards has been taken over by some kind of Signals show—at least Harriet says it's sprouted aerials all over the home paddock and motorbikes roar down the drive at three A.M. Lord and Lady Vereker are living in the stables—"

"In loose boxes? She'd like that."

"There's some kind of groom's accommodation they've done up. Lord V. has learnt to cook. Harriet says he's rather good."

"He couldn't conceivably be worse than Mrs. Chad."

"I only experienced tea. Harriet says Lady V. tried and she *was* worse than Mrs. Chad, and that's what stirred him into action. The tradespeople take pity on him and try to slip him extra rations, but he won't have it. Not, Harriet says, out of high-mindedness, but because he's interested in the challenge of creating edible meals with what he's allowed. Like not cheating at patience. But he's talking about opening the stables as a restaurant after the war."

"Mighty are the changes time hath wrought. What does Lady V. find to do?"

"She seems to have fallen in love with Joe Stalin. She rides round the county bullying Mothers' Unions into churning out mittens for the Eastern Front. Do I have to be careful talking to you about Uncle Joe?"

"A fetish of inconceivable savagery whom my people happen to worship. It will please them to know that they have a sister cult in Suffolk. Come to think of it, they have a noble horsewoman among their folk heroines. She led cavalry charges against the Turks."

"I'll tell Harriet. Maybe it will be good for a parcel of mittens."

"You won't, will you?"

"No, of course not."

"After the war, perhaps. What about the girls?"

This was uncomfortable ground, but there was nothing for it.

"Nancy's a WAAF, a flight lieutenant, Harriet says. Not that she flies. She works in the Air Ministry, in charge of a gang of women who shove toy aeroplanes around on vast map tables so that the brass can see where our bombers have got to."

"Any men in her life?"

"I'm afraid so, in fact she's engaged to a ludicrously rich American called Dick Felder. Or is it Fedler?"

He nodded as if he'd been expecting it.

"Harriet described him as rather a good egg. Do they all use that sort of Woosterish vocabulary?"

"About things that matter to them, yes. Where does the money come from?"

"Lumber, apparently. His grandfather was the ruffian who amassed the loot, his father multiplied it umpteenfold, and now Nancy is proposing to use it to put new lead on the Blatchards roof."

"Yes, of course. In Nan's case that is a sine qua non of the marriage contract. Is there any evidence whether she loves the chap?"

"Harriet discussed the question. She thinks Nancy herself isn't sure. If he can afford the upkeep of Blatchards, then she is effectively forced to love him. I met a few Americans of that general sort in my last job, and I can't imagine any of them adapting to life at Blatchards in anything like the style the Verekers seem to have evolved."

"That's also in the marriage contract. A secret clause. I think even Nancy may not be aware of it. Superficially attractive, but not easy for outsiders for more than a brief visit, I'd have thought."

"Mine was too brief to judge."

"You seem to have liked Harriet."

"Very much, and rather to my surprise. I wouldn't have expected us to have a lot in common."

"I know what you mean. There's something of the noble savage about them. The noble savage is not an open book—indeed the springs of his nobility might well appal the civilised mind. No chance of seeing Harriet here, I suppose?"

I explained about the ambulance unit. In fact I was due to meet Harriet again in ten days' time, when she'd be in Cairo on a forty-eight. She had told me bluntly that she preferred me (to, presumably, a dozen possible escorts) because my Armenian entanglement meant I could be relied on not to make a pass at her. (Naïve, but in my then situation correct.) She wanted none of that sort of thing till after the war. She was on the other side of Kipling's mirror. Nothing that happened here and now was real.

We discussed the remaining sisters. Lucy had started as a Land Girl on the Home Farm but had used her evenings to teach herself shorthand and typing. She had then attracted the attention (Harriet had said she was "a stunner, these days") of one of the senior officers running the Signals operation in the main house and was now working not there but at some kind of hush-hush sister operation near Hemel Hempstead. Janet had left school and was working on the Home Farm while she waited for call-up. Ben was still at school.

Harriet's account had been very full, and Gerry wanted every detail, so our meal was ready before we'd exhausted the subject.

He then began to talk more openly than before about his own doings, rather as though he felt he now owed me something for what I'd told him. I learnt a few things that might be useful to me in my job, but what I most remember is Gerry's own attitude. He was performing a delicate balancing act manoeuvring among groups of fighters whose motives and passions he could sometimes adapt and channel to his own purposes. He endured periods of tense tedium interrupted by great physical hardship and danger. It became clear to me that he was better at the job than I could imagine anyone else being, and I sensed the same knowledge in him, together with a huge exhilaration at being so stretched, so tried, and still finding no limit to his own capacities. As the master at the cricket match had said, there seemed to be nothing he couldn't achieve. To know that of yourself might, paradoxically, become a source of self-distrust. What are these unbelievable talents for? For the moment the narrow purposes of war seemed to have provided an answer.

He drank two glasses of wine, slowly, and I offered a third.

"Better not," he said. "I'm about on my limit, and I see your point about not wishing to wheel me home."

"How do your partisan friends react to this, um, defect in you?"

"At first with ridicule, now as an eccentricity. It is more of an asset than you might think. There are times when I need, as it were, to hide, while remaining physically present. What is it, by the way? I've never tasted anything like it."

"Chateauneuf is all I was told," I said. "There was a bedridden old Frenchwoman I had to interview about something. She wanted news of her nephew, who was supposed to be doing something with the Free French. I broke a few rules and found out that he'd volunteered to go back into France, where he'd been caught almost at once and executed. She just nodded and rang for a servant, who went and got a half crate of these. No labels on any of them. She'd been keeping them for the nephew. Now they were no use to her and she wanted them out of her house. She said they were Chateauneuf, but the vineyard and the year didn't matter, as I'd never drink anything like them again."

"And she was right. How much is there left?"

"A bit under a glass each. I'll withdraw my caveat about wheeling you home. Or maybe the last couple of years have given you greater tolerance."

He shook his head but let me share the last of the decanter between us, and continued to sip slowly as we talked, still giving no sign that the wine was affecting him. There were longer silences. At one point he said, "Remind me what your family consists of."

"Minimal," I told him. "Father, mother, self. No aunts or uncles. My English grandparents died before the war. I had grandparents in Vienna. My father tried to get them out but they refused to come. I should think Adolf's murdered them by now."

"Do you believe all that?"

"Oh yes. It suits a lot of people who should know better to play it down or dismiss it as crude anti-Hunism, but it's happening. I'm a Jew, remember. News comes out to us. In fact I think it's going to turn out to be a good deal worse than anyone imagined."

Gerry nodded.

"We stopped a train," he said. "We thought there was a staff officer on it, but we were wrong. There were German guards, SS, all the same, and we couldn't think why till we opened up a couple of cattle trucks at the rear. They were full of children from a Jewish orphanage. They'd had nothing to eat or drink. Some of them were dead already. Any of them could have been me."

"You've lost me."

"If your family is minimal, mine is null, void, a blank."

"I thought you had an aunt. The one with the Marmite sandwiches."

"The appellation is honorary. She taught at my orphanage, decided I had possibilities and took me into her house, but being a maiden lady with a strong sense of the proprieties, didn't adopt me. It would confuse the issue, she said."

"Her own joke?"

"Of course. She died last year in an air raid on Leeds. There aren't many people around whom one can readily admire."

We sat in silence, I haunted by the thought of the children in the cattle trucks. To exorcise them, I said, "Are you going to try and trace your own parents?"

He shook his head.

"My aunt looked into it," he said. "I was literally a foundling, newborn, unwashed, wrapped in a bloodstained petticoat in a public lavatory in Leeds."

I seemed to have replaced one haunting by another, less obviously dreadful but individual, personal, unique in its own pain. I tried again.

"Family life, as exemplified by the Verekers, must have been something of a shock to you."

"Shock?" he said. "Revelation is nearer the mark. A new heaven and a new earth."

In fact he spoke the line in Greek, and I had to ask my boss next day for the reference. I couldn't ask Gerry, because at that point he fell asleep. I had been watching the half-moon rise above the tumbled rooftops while I puzzled out the gist (my Greek was still up to that then, but as a Jew the Apocalypse was not part of my scriptures) when I heard a faint thump, turned, and saw that he had passed out, neatly and with dignity, after placing his not-quite-finished glass on the wicker table beside him. When I shook him, he remained inert. I waited a few minutes and tried again, without result, then telephoned a setup we used for the more physical aspects of our work, bodyguards and frighteners and so on. They sent a couple of men with a car, though not for over an hour, during which I made several useless efforts to rouse Gerry with cold water. He never once stirred, nor had he by the time I was able to deliver him into the care of his own people, sometime after midnight. They were not pleased, and nor was my boss when I told him next morning what had happened, but no long-term harm was done. Gerry continued to have a "good" war and survived unscathed.

Lucy

THREE

1942

I'm not sure that this is such a good idea after all. Something funny's happening—not to me, to Paul. He shows me what he's written when he's finished a chunk. I asked. Of course I was interested. But then he said he didn't want to listen to what I'd been putting on these tapes. I was a bit miffed about that and said so, but he said he was sorry, but he was afraid it might "contaminate his own recollections." He feels that intense about it. And in the evening, when he puts his pen down, he just sits there as if he was in some kind of trance he had to swim slowly up out of, like divers in case they get the bends.

Paul isn't like that, for God's sake! He just doesn't get obsessed about things. But now he's sneaking off at odd times of the day when usually he'd be out in the garden, getting it all down on his word processor. He doesn't want to talk about it either, and I daren't have a scene with him because that will bring on my shakes and it isn't fair. But honestly, the only time I remember him at all like this was just before that last week-end at Blatchards when he was absolutely burying himself in work, trying to get his company floated, and then . . .

No, I'll come to that later. I've got to keep things in order.

Well, I had a good war too, though the other way round

from Gerry's. I mean, I was like Harriet. For me it was time out, when nothing was real, and everyone was just waiting for it to be over so that we could start our proper lives again. Only when someone you knew got killed, then you'd find it was real after all, for a bit. But soon you'd forget.

I was lucky. I was just the right age. If there hadn't been a war, what would have happened to me? Finish my dreary school, probably go and live with a family in France for a bit to get a good accent, come home, do a season if Father could afford it, have some sort of nonsense job, I can't think what— we must have been pretty well unemployable. But as it was, because of Blatchards being taken over by an ESIU—sorry, that's short for Enemy Signals Interception Unit—and me meeting some of them, when I got called up, I wangled a really interesting job, code breaking, not at Blatchards but a place called Halford Hall, near Hemel Hempstead.

As soon as I say code breaking, you'll think I'm talking about the Enigma code at Bletchley, because that's what everyone knows about. We were trying to do the same sort of thing, yes, but in a quite different way. The simplest way to say it, though it sounds quite mad, was that we were trying to do it by telepathy. I started out as just one of about thirty girls who typed out endless lists of numbers, but a couple of times I noticed something about a number that just seemed wrong to me, I didn't know why—we'd been told to ask about that sort of thing if it came up—and I was right, so after that I was one of the people who went through the lists actually looking for joeys (that's what we called them). The women were much better at it than the men, and I wasn't bad. After a bit I could remember whole pages of numbers, not to recite straight off but enough to say "There was something like that a few columns back." I had no idea what the somethings meant. That needed absolute superbrains.

It sounds unspeakably boring but I was happy. I knew I'd got the job first off because of my looks, but it wasn't long before I was sure they'd still have wanted me there if I'd been plain as a boot. That made life easier for me in another way. It's difficult for people to realise now what a big thing losing your virginity used to be, especially if you'd been brought up the way I had, with our whole purpose in life—no one told us this, of course, but even then I had a good idea that that was what it was all about—our whole purpose in life being like some sort of missile, like a whaling harpoon, and what we had to do was go and hunt for the right man and skewer him and reel him in so we could have more sons and daughters who could start all over again. It wasn't for us, it was to keep our kind of world going.

But now it was different, a different sea, full of all sorts of terrific fish threshing around—oh, I'm not going on with the harpoon idea or I shall get muddled. The point is that there were plenty of men at Halford Hall, and far fewer women, most of us young and unattached, so there was a lot of pressure on us. Specially on me, because I was—let's call it officer class—and so were the superbrains we worked for, and what they were doing was very hard work, vitally important to the war effort, and mostly pretty frustrating because they spent a lot of time not getting anywhere, so there was a sort of feeling that it was our patriotic duty to help them relax. I learnt pretty soon that even cuddly old dons with photographs of their children in their wallets can't help hoping for the sort of adventure that will make them feel young and glorious again. So it was a help to me that I could do more than look decorative and just do the sort of work anyone else could do.

My best friend was Dora. We worked together. Her father was a milkman in Darlington. She had eleven brothers and sisters. She was nothing to look at, dark and square. You could tell she'd be really fat by the time she was forty. She was three years older than I was and she'd been experimenting with men since she was fifteen. That was the main thing about Dora. She was incredibly randy, and she liked to talk about it. I was shocked at first, but I soon realised that she was really a good, kind, happy person, and in the end I liked her a lot and I was sorry when they gave me a commission and put me in charge of a different section and I couldn't talk to her the same way anymore. But that was later, after I'd lost the knack of spotting joeys. You could do that for a few months only, and then it left you. Difficult to explain.

I'll try, though. We worked in a cubbyhole of our own, side by side at a trestle table, and the messengers would come in with the sheets of intercepts, and we'd sit and read them. Each sheet had five columns. Each column had thirty-six numbers. Each number had eight figures. It sounds completely impossible. For the first half-hour it usually was. Sometimes it was all day. But most days, after a bit, the numbers began to speak, and we knew we'd got hot. That's how we talked about it. You got hot and the numbers spoke. It really was like that. The numbers became like a sort of language to us. It wasn't a language we could understand, mind you, not a word of it, but we could hear it somehow in our heads, a bit like voices, and what's more, we could hear that the voices were making sense to themselves. And that way we could somehow spot when one of them said something that didn't make sense in the language. We had absolutely no idea how we did this— we couldn't explain it even to the superbrains, and of course it didn't work all the time, and a lot of the joeys we spotted weren't joeys, but enough of them were. There really did turn out to be something wrong with them.

I think the most extraordinary thing was that we needed each other, Dora and me, to do this. We'd be sitting there, reading slowly down the columns, sheet after sheet. We had two copies of each sheet, and we taught ourselves to read at the same speed so we could be pretty certain we'd be reading the same number at the same time, and nothing would happen and nothing would happen and then, both at the same moment, we'd feel the tingle of the numbers beginning to speak.

We didn't have to look at each other. We knew. And next, just as if our hands had been connected by a wire, we'd reach out and ring the same number, our first joey, me in green and Dora in blue. I forgot to say there was a board between us so we couldn't see each other's sheets.

We'd go on for about a dozen sheets, usually, like that, and then the voices would fade and the numbers would just be numbers and we'd know it was time for a break. Dora would light a fag and I'd have a couple of puffs and she'd start telling me in a dreamy, happy way about some adventure she'd had until she'd finished her cigarette and we'd go on. If we timed it right, we could keep going like that for a whole shift.

There was one terrific morning when we spotted five joeys in two sheets. That simply didn't happen. One in three sheets was good going, but we were so singing sure that we sent them out and ten minutes later Captain Mantock came in waving the sheets to ask us had we gone mad, while Dora was in the middle of telling me about a tumble she'd had with a Chinese tailor in the back of his shop, all in among the pin-striped trousering. We had a hard time persuading him we hadn't been playing the fool, but it turned out we were right and the coding machine must have been sticking somewhere, and that was a whole piece of the puzzle firmly in place.

Well, naturally, being with Dora such a lot and hearing all the things she'd tried—I'm afraid she had to explain what a lot of the words meant, because pretty well the only sex education Mother had ever given us was all about gelding colts—natu-rally I wanted to try. Bother being a harpoon, I felt, and getting just one whale. I'd be missing such a lot. So the next question was where to begin, and who with. I talked it over with Dora, of course. She laughed a lot, but she took it seri-ously too. She liked the cookhouse staff best of the men at Halford, but they were slobs, she said, and I was too good for them. It had got to be an officer. The next question was whether it ought to be somebody who knew exactly what he was doing, who'd show me how and make sure I had a good time, or somebody who'd be finding out, like me. I was all for the good time, but Dora was in favour of a finder-out. "It's more exciting that way," she said. "Neither of you knowing what's going to happen, and you only get that once in your life so you don't want to miss it." I said how could we be sure any of the men was still only a finder-out, but Dora swore she could tell, just looking at them. We'd pretty well settled on a rather handsome lieutenant who was i/c Despatch Riders— I've forgotten his name—when I decided off my own bat that I wanted Beano.

(By the way, I'm not going to talk like this about all the men I've had what are nowadays called relations with. Just take it from me it wasn't nearly as many as people seem to think. But Beano comes into the story later, and anyway the whole business still makes me smile.)

Beano was David Fish. He was called Beano because of runner beans, I think, but it might have been because he looked like a character in the comic. He was a junior superbrain—there's no way he could have been given a commission otherwise; he was the most hopeless officer you could imagine. But some of the work was the sort that even superbrains are best at before they're twenty-five, and after that their minds harden or something and they can't do it anymore. Beano might have been six foot four if he'd known how to stand straight, but he didn't. Perhaps he was too thin. There's a little tree called *cytisus battandieri* that drives Paul mad. It has silky leaves and yellow flowers a bit like lupins that reek of pineapple, and you have to grow it against a wall because it's so floppy, but Paul wants it where there isn't a wall, and however he stakes it, it still manages to flop. Beano was like that. He drove CSM Barnett mad.

CSM Barnett was in charge of the weekly parade, which we all had to turn out for in proper uniform and be inspected by the CO and march past him and so on, to remind us that we were in the army. The rest of the time we were pretty slack. The superbrains dressed any old how, battle-dress trousers and carpet slippers and a Fair Isle cardigan with holes in it. Other ranks like me did wear uniform, but for instance Dora got away with far more makeup than she'd have been allowed in the proper army, and I wore my hair down a lot of the time. But not on the weekly parade, my goodness no. CSM Barnett would have exploded. He was an enormous man with a face like a ham and a ginger moustache that he could make bristle, the way a dog can make its hackles stand up, and he'd put his face six inches from yours and yell in a voice you could hear on the other side of the parade ground. He would yell at the officers, too. That's how I found out about Beano having gone to Eton.

"And where were you at school, Mr. Fish, sir!!?"

Mumble mumble.

"Well, you're not at bleeding Eton now, sir! You're in His Majesty's Armed Forces, sir!! And in His Majesty's Armed Forces . . . we . . . stand . . . up . . . straight!!! SIR!!!"

The "sir" was the most insulting part. Out of the corner of my eye I could see Beano making a huge effort and drawing himself up to six foot two. I'll try him, I thought. He might know Gerry.

Dora wasn't at all keen on Beano. "He'll make a mess of it," she said. But in the end she agreed it was better for me to try with someone I wanted than with someone I didn't and she got her friend Sergeant Hattersley in Transport to fix things. Beano was due a forty-eight-hour pass, but there was a hitch and the pass wasn't ready so he didn't get away with the main transport and Sergeant Hattersley said he'd fix him a spare truck. At that point I turned up with my own forty-eight, and of course I'd missed the transport too, so the obvious thing was for me to go in Beano's truck, only it was still in the workshop having something done to its engine. Sergeant Hattersley swore it would be along, and he'd drive it himself—he was having a lovely time, winking at me behind Beano's back and then keeping a straight face for Beano—but it didn't come and it didn't come until there was only one train left we could catch, and then it did at last, but it sounded pretty sick and halfway to the station it conked out. Sergeant Hattersley just managed to get it to chug off the road into a by-lane beside a wood—I'd picked the place a couple of days before—and then he said he'd go and get another truck. He said he'd be about an hour, so we still ought to make the train.

It was a lovely May evening. We sat in the driver's cab. I asked Beano if he'd known Gerry, and it turned out he'd been in College too, but in the election above, so he hadn't known him very well.

"Besides," he said, "I was a maths specialist, and I was useless at games."

It got dark. We found some other people we both knew to talk about. I yawned and said we'd obviously missed the last train, and I was going to see if there was anything to sleep on in the back of the truck. Of course there was. Beano pretended he was happy to sleep in the cab, but he didn't need a lot of persuading that he'd be much more comfortable in the back.

The birds woke us before it was properly light, making the usual racket. I lay quiet, feeling extremely pleased with myself. Dora had been right about David being a first-timer, but wrong about him making a mess of it.

"Did that really happen?" he asked in a dreamy voice. "And if so, how?"

I hadn't realised he was awake. I'd already decided I was going to tell him. I didn't want him falling in love or anything. He lay there, thinking about it. Then he laughed.

"But why me?" he said.

"I heard CSM Barnett yelling at you for being at Eton," I

said. "So I thought you might know Gerry. It was a sort of introduction, I suppose."

He laughed again, differently.

"Good Lord," he said. "Who'd have thought I'd ever owe something like that to Gerry Grantworth?"

"I can't remember all that. It would be much better . . . Look, what are you doing this week-end?"

"Not much, as far as I know."

"Couldn't you come down? Mother and Father will be back, and Nan and . . . and in fact everyone except Harriet. They'll all want to know. We're moving back into the house, you see, and we need all the hands we can get."

I hesitated. Ben, I calculated, must be about fifteen. What was her authority to issue such an invitation, though she seemed to take it for granted? On the other hand I was tempted. I had missed Harriet in the last few months, especially since my Armenian had met and fallen in love with a young journalist who wanted to marry her. We had both agreed from the first that our relationship would belong to the unrealities of war. She had no wish to settle in England, nor I in Egypt. Still, there was a vacuum in my life, not that I expected to fill it at once, and the prospect of spending time among presentable young women was attractive.

"You can catch the same train as Nan and Dick," said Ben. "I'll get Nan to ring you and tell you which one. Have you got a number?"

That was a way through, and indeed when Nancy did call, she proved just as insistent as Ben. She asked whether I'd seen anything of Gerry, and I told her yes.

"We'll all want to hear about him, too," she said, not seemingly embarrassed by her marriage to Richard Felder, on which I'd already congratulated her. "You really must come. That's an order."

It was a joke, of course. I was senior in rank to her by some way. But she spoke like someone used to giving orders.

We recognised each other on the platform, among the three-deep ranks waiting for our train to come in. It wasn't so difficult for me. We were both in uniform, and a strikingly pretty WAAF officer heading towards Bury on a Friday evening had every chance of being her, but she picked me out at once,

Paul

FOUR

1944

In 1944 I was back in London for several weeks. The desert
war was over. Harriet was driving in Italy with a different unit,
but had asked me at our last meeting to telephone Blatchards if
I got home before she did and give them her news. (For all
their closeness as a family, the Verekers were among the most
perfunctory letter writers I have ever known.) My own job was
in transition. The Balkans, Greece in particular, looked like
becoming a raging chaos of feuds, murders, and betrayals. At
the same time the probability of communist regimes taking
over in the area, and the nature of the problems we might ther
face, was becoming more apparent. My boss sent me hom
ostensibly to brief relevant officials on the current mess, bu
with private instructions to investigate the possibility of ot
organisation being moved to London in an expanded form
continue its work after the war was over.

When I called Blatchards, Ben answered. I explained w
I was, and that I'd been seeing a bit of Harriet in Cairo.

"Oh ho!" she said.

"Neither 'Oh' nor 'Ho,' but she asked me to ring
parents and give them the news."

"Which is?"

I began to tell her, but she cut me short.

too. (Later I learnt that this was a Vereker trait, not merely the memory for faces and names, but the genuine interest in the lives and concerns of people they met.)

"So glad you could come," she said. "We need everyone we can get on our side, to stop Mother making a mess of things. She has an absolute genius for discomfort, and Chad always does exactly what she tells him even when he knows it's madness, so that he can shake his head about it when it goes wrong."

I knew from Harriet that Mr. Chad was the general handyman at Blatchards, husband of Mrs. Chad, notorious for her cooking. Nancy was standing tiptoe, craning back along the platform.

"Sorry if I look a bit distrait," she said. "I'm keeping an eye out for Dick. He doesn't understand why trains can't just wait till he gets here. I bet you he'll come bellowing onto the platform just as we're steaming out."

She was right. The train arrived and the mob surged aboard. Being commissioned officers in uniform we were compelled to travel first class, but the crush was just as bad as in third. We were lucky in that there was a door immediately in front of where we stood, so I nipped in and took a corner seat, expecting to be able to give it to Nancy and myself stand for the journey, but she insisted on staying at the door so that she could crane from the window. By the time the train moved out, only forty minutes late, we were crammed five a side, with six standing between the seats.

"Dick! Dick!" yelled Nancy, leaning far out and waving.

She ducked back in and opened the door. Someone was pounding along the dim platform. Already we were going far too fast to be boarded in safety. Then, effortlessly it seemed, he was on the step and inside and closing the door behind him with one hand while with the other arm he lifted Nancy off her feet to give her a long, unabashedly tongue-touching kiss, clean contrary to good order and military discipline.

He was huge, easily the biggest man I have ever met. His uniform was the finest available cloth and clearly tailored for him, but only partly because it had been cut taut-trousered in the American fashion, it still looked as if it had been made for someone a couple of sizes smaller. Nancy introduced us when at last he put her down. He beamed down at me, an affable ogre dim against the single shaded light. I had risen, expecting Nancy to take my seat, but she said, "Dick can put me on the luggage rack," so he reorganised the cases and swung her up, a convenient arrangement for both of them as her face was now level with his and they could whisper and kiss during the frequent unexplained stops, leaving me to gaze at his portentously muscled buttocks.

Bury is about sixty miles from London. The journey took nearly three hours. Lady Vereker met us at the station driving a sort of carriage drawn by two horses, with six-foot-diameter wheels behind and smaller ones in front. I sat beside her while Dick and Nancy canoodled on the backseat as we trotted briskly along dark winding lanes. (Lady Vereker, multifariously incompetent, at least knew what she was up to with horses.) We reached Blatchards well after eleven. Lord Vereker had a cold supper ready for us at the Stables and hovered by while we ate, so as not to miss one syllable of praise for his cuisine. It was past midnight and had started to rain when Nancy, Dick, and I carried our bags down a weedy drive to the back door of the main house, let ourselves in, lit candles, and climbed the bare servants' stairs to the top floor. I was extremely tired.

Not wishing to mistake my door among the dozen others along that side of the blank, sparse-carpeted corridor, I left it open when I went to the lavatory. Returning with my candle in my hand, I was in the room and closing the door when a voice behind me said sleepily, "Who's that?"

I turned and saw it was the wrong room. The occupant of the bed was beginning to lift herself onto an elbow.

"Don't go," she said, interrupting my apologies. "You're Paul, aren't you? You came with Gerry and I was rude to you at tea."

"I don't remember the rudeness. We collected eggs, though."

"Did we? I was so fagged I went to bed early, but I left the door open so I should hear you come, only I didn't. Nan says you've seen Gerry. And Harriet, of course. Where's my dressing gown? You're probably dying for sleep, but do just tell me quickly."

I picked the dressing gown off the floor and gave it to her, then put my candle on the washstand and pulled up a rush-seated chair. Lucy cuddled the gown around her and sat like a child with her arms wrapped round her knees. Harriet had partly prepared me for her beauty, but it was still astonishing. The candlelight shadowed sideways across her face, leaving the further half almost in darkness and glinting off the loose waves of her hair. The elfin look was much less marked than I'd remembered, but still there, though not at all fey, and her manner was down-to-earth, direct, a bit too challenging for some tastes perhaps. . . .

And she was no fool. She understood, for instance, presumably from her work at Hemel Hempstead, my difficulty in telling in detail much of what Gerry was doing; but at the same time she clearly grasped the nature of it, and of my work too, things that many people, including experienced soldiers, often completely mistook.

"You said Gerry knew about Nancy and Dick?" she asked.

"I told him they were engaged. I don't know if he's heard about the marriage."

"How did he take it?"

"Just accepted it, as far as I could see. I thought he was a bit depressed later that evening, but it could have been anything. When people under stress go on leave . . ."

"Yes, of course. You know, I'm not sure Gerry really wanted to marry Nancy. Not like that. I mean, it's not as simple as that makes it sound. He wants something, he wants it very much indeed, something to do with Nan, and all of us, and this house. . . . Of course it may all be different now he's been through a war and seen so many other things. . . . What about Harriet? No, don't tell me, I can see you're dropping. It can wait till tomorrow. Thank you for staying awake this long. I put the hotties in the left-hand bed. Don't try the right one, it will be sopping. Yours will just be a bit damp, I'm afraid."

Next morning she woke me with a tea tray.

"You don't get this every time you come," she said. "It's to make up for last night. The jug's to shave with—there doesn't seem to be any hot water on this floor. It's either the ram or the gas, probably."

This was my first taste of the high standard of discomfort one came to regard as the norm at Blatchards—damp beds were a commonplace of wartime. The water supply depended on a "ram" at the bottom of the grove, whose working, because the drop that supplied it was not sufficient, needed endless fine-tuning by the general handyman, Mr. Chad. Hot water in turn depended on a private gas plant (Victorian, like the ram), which ran off a particular sort of coking coal, not often available. Not only the hot water but all the heating of the house—mainly ancient gas fires—was run off the plant. There was never enough gas. If one turned one's own fire on, those in neighbouring rooms were liable to go out, an effect so dangerous that most of the guestrooms had their gas taps locked into the off position. There were also a number of huge radiators downstairs in the passages and state rooms, but the only time I detected one at higher than room temperature was once in July, when Mr. Chad had taken it into his head to test the system.

Lucy put the tray down and was leaving, but she turned in the doorway.

"By the way, do you know Bobo Smith?" she said. "He was at Eton, but he may have been before you."

"Unless there's more than one of him, he was Captain of Games in my house when I was a lower boy. He flogged me several times."

"Oh, dear. I'm afraid he's coming. Do you mind?"

"Water under the bridge."

"Mother asked him to help with the sofas . . . she says. She's got it into her head that it's her duty to present us with suitable young men. Do you mind if I use you as a defence?"

"It is my task in life to interpose myself between the Verekers and their admirers."

"Harriet, too? Why you? You don't look totally safe to me."

"In general I'm not, but it happens that in Cairo I was. What does Bobo make of your mother's plans?"

"Too keen for comfort. Breakfast's at the Stables in twenty minutes. Don't be late. Father will sulk if you keep his scrambled eggs waiting."

I enjoyed the rest of the week-end, at first because of the malicious pleasure of thwarting Bobo Smith, to whom I had taken a renewed dislike. He was in the Coldstream, had seen a good deal of fighting and won an MC, and was now on sick leave after a fairly serious shrapnel wound in Italy. The loutish air he'd had at eighteen had now been replaced by run-of-the-mill blue-eyed, tow-haired good looks. He got on well with Dick Felder, both playing the game of male competitiveness hard, with much abuse and laughter. He was polite with Lord Vereker but had no idea how to deal with Lady Vereker's anticapitalist tirades, interspersed as they were with material from different fields. A local Master of Foxhounds was a particular enemy of hers because as a coal owner he was an oppressor of the workers and as a hunting man he was not cooperating with the hunt with which she herself rode. Bobo would have preferred to ignore my presence but was unable to because of Lucy's ingenuity (aided by Janet and Ben) in seeing to it that there was always an adequate reason why she and I should be doing one thing while Bobo used his greater strength and reach elsewhere.

Later the nature of the pleasure changed. At least, something happened between us, though I made no attempt to give it expression in conscious tone or gesture, let alone touch. Her beauty was a bit inhibiting, not merely because of my aware-ness that she must get a lot of almost automatic advances made to her and might welcome a respite, but also—this is going to sound banal and ridiculous—a feeling on my part that she was too good for me, out of my class, a showpiece, as if with a little tasseled rope round her and a notice saying "Do not sit on this chair."

(This feeling was to endure. For most pairings the exigencies of wartime accelerated affairs, but with us it took twenty-one months, by which time I was out of the army, and even then Lucy made the running:

"Do you want to sleep with me?"

"Only if you yourself really want to. Not just out of kindness to me."

She looked at me for a while under the dimmed light of the passage. Beyond its arch crumbs of snow were falling through the moonlight.

"Not just for that," she said, with a twitch of a smile. "Come in."

Later she tried to tell me that all she'd meant had been that she was getting cold.)

The two other girls had appeared in the course of Saturday, Ben in midmorning, having slept in because it was still the first week of school holidays, and Janet for lunch, having finished her morning stint on the farm. Janet took after her mother, bouncy, horsy, and given to strong opinions that were difficult to discuss, let alone refute, because the reasoning on which they were based was impenetrable. Ben was already different from the other four, though she had some of Lucy's features, the high cheekbones and teardrop eyes, without more than ordinary good looks. She was long limbed, determined, quiet, but with a knack—one that she retained throughout her life—of breaking valued objects. She had already made up her mind she was going to be a professional dancer.

The Signals outfit that had occupied the main house had left a few weeks earlier, and Lady Vereker and the girls were insisting on moving back in. Lord Vereker made a show of reluctance, how genuine I was unable to decide—he probably enjoyed the diminished responsibilities of life at the Stables. Lady Vereker had decided during her exile on certain improvements, or rather rearrangements of inconveniences, in the way the house was used, which the girls now set about thwarting, Nancy because she had better ideas and the other three because they wanted to restore everything as far as possible to the exact state in which it had been on September 2, 1939. The damage caused by the soldiers had been moderate by military standards. (I know of another house where complete rooms of Jacobean panelling, as well as banisters and doors, had been stripped to feed the men's fires one cold winter.) Still, alterations had been made, doorways blocked or opened, partitions built, and so on. It rained drenchingly most of the time. Bobo and Dick would trudge down from the Stables carrying, say, a tarpaulined chest-of-drawers, having been told by Lady Vereker which room she wanted it in. At the front door Nancy or one of the others would countermand their orders, so they would dump it under the porte-cochère, and Lucy and I would lug it into the house. Then Lady Vereker would arrive, dishevelled and shouting for one girl or the other, her voice echoing away down the corridors, and fresh disputes would erupt. The whole move took place in an atmosphere of delighted disagreement, an infectious communal excitement in which my own increasing exhilaration with Lucy's company probably went unnoticed.

An interesting struggle began for the soul of Mr. Chad, out

of which I got extra enjoyment because he reminded me strongly of my boss back in Cairo, with the same large suety face, small sharp eyes, and slow movements and speech. He was mostly engaged on tasks such as removing the unwanted partitions, but would stop at once when asked by Lady Vereker to tackle some chore she'd just thought of (probably trivial, certainly secondary) until Nancy discovered him at it and sent him back to the partitions. If anything, he seemed rather to enjoy his role as moral battleground.

I found Nancy impressive, if alarming. She had a clear head for details, and a combination of charm and willpower that allowed her to get away with what, in someone else, might have been an intolerable level of bossiness, but I have to say it crossed my mind to wonder how Dick Felder would cope with this when he was back on his home ground.

By Saturday evening the bulk of the carrying was done. Lord Vereker had spent the afternoon in the kitchens preparing a celebratory supper, greatly to the resentment of Mrs. Chad. Furthermore, he had unlocked the cellars and brought out several bottles of 1926 Chateau Beychevelle, astonishing by Blatchards standards. The Signals people had decided that the ancient wiring of the house was inadequate for their purposes and had installed their own generators, which they had taken with them, leaving the electricity disconnected, so we ate and spent the rest of the evening by candlelight. Lord Vereker dozed by the fire while the rest of us played cards, vingt-et-un for matchsticks first and then racing demon—not at all my kind of activity, though it turned out I was no worse than Dick and Bobo, we three regularly scoring minuses while the girls and Lady Vereker, in a frenzy of competitiveness, notched up thirties and forties. Because none of them would trust the others, I kept the score. Bobo and Dick became irritable, Dick because he wanted to take Nancy off to bed and Bobo because he didn't enjoy not winning. They began to disrupt the game by playing the fool, and blatant cheating.

The second time this happened Nancy said, "If you can't play properly, you'd better not play at all."

It was a moment of ice, of exclusion. Dick shrugged, not understanding.

"Why don't you two see if the billiard table's still all right?" said Lady Vereker, in tones she might have used trying to distract small children.

They left, taking with them the bottle of scotch Dick had brought as a house present. Lucy glanced at me.

"I'll just score," I said, happy to be wherever she was. "You can tear each other's throats out."

In a lull of shuffling the packs between the intensities of play, Janet said, "I say, there's eight of us, not counting Father. We could play The Game tomorrow!"

"Oh, yes!" said Lucy. "But Father's got to, too. First time back."

"I'm afraid I've asked Teddy Voss-Thompson for luncheon," said Lady Vereker.

"Oh, Mother!" said Janet. "He's dire!"

"And he'll be bringing a friend."

"Oh, Mother!"

The friend turned out to be a shy, busty, scarlet-lipped young woman. Edward Voss-Thompson, whom I got to know later, while he was married to Janet, had had TB at Winchester and walked with a swinging limp. Even then he gave an impression of the quiet but relentlessly questioning intelligence that was to become his stock-in-trade. He was also clearly very ambitious. Having escaped conscription because of his hip, he had broken the Wykehamist mould by refusing a scholarship to New College and joining *Picture Post* as a trainee journalist. He was short on small talk but in no sense dire, Janet's protest having been her normal response to any guest invited by her mother.

Despite his hip he was a better games player than I, so they played five-a-side while I scored and refereed. There are several accounts of The Game in memoirs, so I shall not describe it here, apart from reminding readers that it was played in the Long Gallery, originally designed for the second Lord Vereker for pictures he proposed to collect on his Grand Tour, which he never aroused himself sufficiently to embark on, and eventually used to house the trophies of big game shot by the girls' grandfather. The noise made by a wooden polo ball and the Verekers in those echoing acoustics was unbelievable, and at the same time expressive of the rather pure but inward-turned enjoyment the Verekers derived out of their mutual activities.

Lucy had a complex bus-and-train journey back to Hemel Hempstead and left in midafternoon. We tried to find some way of meeting before I returned to Cairo (she seemed as interested in doing so as I was) but were unable to make it work. I managed to telephone her once before I left.

My mission had been a success, and almost as soon as I got back to work, preparations began for our transfer to London. Then my father died, and I was able to apply for early demob, to keep the business going, so I was never involved in the actual move. Of course, as soon as I was in London again, I began my long, slow courtship of Lucy, but was soon aware that I was one of a number of contenders whom, for her own purposes, she preferred to keep on an equal footing with each other. I found this irksome but understandable, and was forced to accept it.

Lucy

FOUR

1945–47

Well, this is absolutely extraordinary! I had no idea. We've never talked about that sort of thing, but it must have been the same man. Paul's boss, I mean, and mine. It's not as much of a coincidence as it seems because of what was happening around then, and it wasn't a very big world. Intelligence, I mean.

I'd better go back to where I left off, looking for joeys with Dora. After a bit I lost the knack. Actually Dora lost it first, and I couldn't get the same whatever-it-was with anyone else, so I gave up too and they sent me off to get a commission and put me in charge of training other girls to do it. Only by then, the people over at Bletchley had really got their machines going and shown that was a better way of doing things than the way we'd been sweating our guts out over, so we all got shifted over to what they called information analysis. The superbrains left and the language nuts arrived, funny foreigners with chips on their shoulders about their countries being given away by Churchill and Roosevelt, and if I'd been them, I'd have been just as furious about it. It meant enormous mounds of paper that had to be sorted and filed and cross-referenced. The cross-referencing was the really important bit, because it was all a matter of linking one bit of information from one place with another bit from another place. For instance, there was this Russian everybody was pretty sure was some kind of KGB expert, only they didn't know what he was an expert at. He kept getting posted to embassies in Eastern Europe for a few months and then leaving. Easily my best filing clerk was a girl called Sylvia—I'll talk about her later. She didn't even know that the people upstairs were specially interested in this man, but off her own bat she spotted that three not-very-important people—communist officials the Russians were supposed to be friends with—had died of scarlet fever while this chap was there. And then of course we found other places where it had happened.

I've shot on. That was later, after we'd moved to London, when the system was really working. It was my system. I set it up. Filing doesn't sound at all glamorous, so when we were making the changeover they just said, "We'll need a lot of women to do the filing," and because I happened to be in charge of a lot of women, I was put in charge of filing, and luckily I got it right. Then, of course, they found how vital it was, just about when I was due for demob, so they asked me to stay on. In fact I pretended to get demobbed and told everyone I was getting a job in something called the Anglo-Balkan Exchange, which arranged trade deals with places like Budapest and Sofia—we actually had a department that did that, for show.

They moved us to London, into an old linen warehouse near the Elephant and Castle and teamed us up with another lot of Balkan experts who'd been working on our sort of thing from Egypt. My job was to finish setting the system up and then keep it going and pick people who could do it—almost all women—and train them and fight like hell when anyone from outside thought he—it was always a man—knew a better way of doing it.

Then in the evening I'd go back to my flat, which I was

sharing with Ben, who was in dance school now, and just mug in front of the gas fire with a book, or go out with some man, or go to one of the dances that were just starting up, with almost nothing to drink and half the dresses made of furnishing fabrics because clothes were still rationed. There were social diaries in *The Tatler* and *Queen* and gossip columns in the dailies so I sometimes got photographed, you know, "sharing a joke," and all my people in Files were thrilled when that happened. Almost as good as knowing Princess Margaret, one of them told me.

We had Open Files and F Block Files. The Open Files were about things like timber exports and politics and so on, and anyone upstairs could requisition them. But there was tight security on the F Block Files, which we kept with the F Block clerks in a locked cage, which of course we called the Zoo. If someone upstairs wanted one of these, he had to send down a green tag countersigned by his section chief, and I took the tags into the Zoo myself, and then I collected the files when they were ready and took them up myself to get them signed for. We all thought the system was very tight. I'd been on the working group that had set it up, and it hadn't struck any of us that there was one weak link in it, and that was me. I would trot to and fro holding these precious things and fret about getting them back. (B Section could be as careless as a small child. I remember laying into the B Section chief at a Thursday Meeting about it. He wasn't used to being talked to like that by a woman, and young enough to be his daughter, what's more, so he got pretty huffy, but he was wrong and I was right, so I didn't give a bean.)

One day the lift stuck with me in it. It was four hours before they got me out, and it was terrifying. The workmen would bang away and the lift would judder down a few inches and stop with a jerk and I got more and more certain that next time it was going to the bottom with me in it. It was a closed box, like a coffin. They'd yell at me was I alright and I'd yell back yes, but I wasn't. To stop myself going mad, I started to read the files.

They were about some different groups of resistance fighters in Yugoslavia and Albania and what they'd been doing in the war. It actually was rather thrilling, because some of the papers were sheets torn out of notepads with handwritten reports by the British officers who'd been liaising with them. You could almost smell the danger. There was quite a bit I didn't understand, of course, with all the different initials of different groups, and the political parties and so on, but it did take my mind off what was happening to the lift. I read right through the first file and started on the second. I'd hardly begun when I turned a page and realised I was looking at Gerry Grantworth's handwriting. It was signed "G. Gissing, Capt.," but it couldn't be anyone else's. I knew it as well as I knew my own. When I'd had my original crush on him, I used to find excuses to write to him and I'd carry his answers round tucked into my bra. He had beautiful writing, very square but flowing and easy—I've always envied it. And now I actually felt I had him there in the lift with me and I wasn't frightened anymore. How old was I? Twenty-three? Grown up, anyway, sensible, trusted, in charge of thirty other women. It sounds ridiculous, but it was like that. When they got me out, I was calm and smiling and everyone said how brave I'd been.

I haven't really got an excuse for what happened next. I suppose I was getting a bit fed up with the job by then, without realising it. I'd taken it on because I'd started it and wanted to see it through till it was really working, and it was now, and there wasn't anything else special I wanted to do, and Father couldn't afford to give me an allowance I could live on in London, and besides it was a real job. It felt important. I was good at it.

But then, somehow, it began to get dingy and pointless, at least to me. The people changed—even if they were the same people, I mean. I think it was because of the secrecy. If you'd asked them, I suppose they might have said they were becoming more professional, but looking back, I think they'd got too caught up, obsessed. It was their little world, and they were the only people who understood it, and everyone else was an outsider. For instance I remember a row at the Thursday Meeting, which we had so that all the section chiefs knew what the others were up to and didn't get in each other's way. That was the theory, but of course they all wanted to tell as little as they could and find out as much as they could. The row was about something that was happening in Romania, and my enemy from B Section and the D Section Chief started accusing each other of being the reason why something out there had gone wrong. (I know I signed the Official Secrets Act, but it was a long time ago, and I'd better explain that by then some of the sections were running their own agents in these countries. They weren't supposed to, but they did.) B was a large untidy man who put on an old-buffer act and took snuff, but was really pretty sly. D was an exercise fanatic with the brightest blue eyes I've ever seen. He always returned his files same day, in perfect order. He had a way of speaking in a slow, absolutely level voice, which made him sound as if he was the only reasonable man in the whole world. It was maddening. It certainly got B's goat that morning, and at one point he stood up and snarled, "Why don't you go over and work for the KGB? You'd really feel at home there!"

The director made them simmer down, but looking back I think B was right. Perhaps it was because of the war being over. The normal people wanted to do proper peacetime things, and left, so the ones who stayed weren't quite normal. Anyway, I suppose I was vaguely aware of feeling things weren't quite as good as they'd been, and getting restless and wondering why I'd agreed to stay on in the first place. People seem to think I'm a rather happy-go-lucky, slapdash, impulsive kind of person, but that's mainly because my hair never wants to stay in place and I tend to dress any old how because . . . well, I suppose it was a sort of defence against them thinking of me as "a beauty," as if that was all I was. And it's true that sometimes, with important decisions (not just men) I'm apt to shut my eyes and jump in (because I'm scared, really) but with everyday things I like to know exactly where I am. When I was a small girl I enjoyed folding my clothes and keeping my room tidy, and in the same way in my job I was an absolute stickler for the rules. That's why Files worked so well. So it wouldn't have crossed my mind to see if Gerry had a file if I hadn't already been pretty demoralised.

Because that's what I did. It was easy. I had the green tags because I kept the Security stationery in the F Block safe. They only had to be accounted for after I'd issued them. I filled one in for Gissing and faked old B's scrawl on it and took it in with a batch of others to the Zoo. There were two ways of asking for files. If the people upstairs knew the file number, that was easy, but much more likely they'd ask for anything on the Bulgarian commissar for light industry, or something like that. That depended entirely on how good the clerks were, not just looking up the commissar's number and getting his file out but going through it for cross-references and getting those files out, and sorting out anything else that might be useful. Naturally this took a bit of time, so I went back to my cubbyhole and got on with other things. Then about twenty minutes later I suppose, Millie from G Block came bustling along to tell me I was wanted in the Zoo. (The girls in the cage weren't allowed out without going through a security hoo-ha, even for a pee, so usually they called to someone in E or G for anything they needed.)

I found F at a standstill with Sylvia in floods of tears on a stool and the others crowding around trying to comfort her.

"We've lost a file," someone whispered, "and Sylvia thinks it's her fault."

Sylvia was an extraordinary girl, about my age, plain and

pasty. She seemed to have decided quite early on that she wasn't any good at anything and nobody would ever love her or value her and she was doomed to go on like that till she died. Then she'd been sent down to me from Personnel with a note to say she wasn't any use at shorthand or typing but she'd got a good memory and I'd given her my usual tests and found it was true. More than good. Absolutely phenomenal, it turned out. She could have been in a circus, only she wouldn't have had the self-confidence. She really loved working for us, hidden away where almost nobody could see her, burrowing through the files. Anything odd or difficult, anything we didn't seem to have a scrap of stuff about, we'd ask Sylvia and she'd brighten up as if we'd flicked a switch and say, "Oh, yes. . . ." She'd pause for about three seconds while the machinery clicked and then she'd start to rattle off file numbers. Computers can do that sort of thing now, though I don't believe even a computer could do some of the weird sideways leaps Sylvia came up with. She was obsessive. I don't believe she wanted any life outside F Block. Annie, who shared a flat with her, used to tease her by saying that if we put her in a trance and dumped her in a cupboard at night, she'd have preferred that to going home.

There was nowhere in the Zoo to be alone, so I took her off to the stationery store and told Di, the F Section head, to stand guard. I settled Sylvia onto a file box and pulled another over and sat with my arm around her waist while she blubbed about it being all her fault, not noticing before, only she wasn't supposed to open the contam cabinet without a requisition and she was sure it was there last time but that was weeks ago, and so on. My heart sank. There wasn't anything that could have been a contam among the tags that had come down from upstairs. Sylvia blubbed on. It was a lovely file. Lots of crossrefs she'd found and entered . . .

I'm sorry, I'll have to explain. A contam was a contaminated source—somebody who'd been sending us information and now we thought might have been got at by the other side. And about the cross-refs—when someone upstairs reading the file found a connection with some other file, there was a special sheet inside the cover where they entered the other file number, and a note about it. And that's what I'd trained my people to do. When stuff came down for filing, they read it and thought about it and put in the cross-refs, and if they hadn't got anything else to do, they just read files and did the same. That's what Sylvia was so good at.

Of course by now I was desperately worried. It didn't matter that the idea of Gerry being a contam was totally ridiculous, I was still in serious trouble. *Any* missing file, let alone F Section, let alone a contam, I had to report. Even B Section would eventually work out they'd never sent down a requisition. Anyway, the first thing was to try and get Sylvia out of her hysterics by giving her something to do, so I asked her if she could remember any of the cross-ref numbers.

The sobs stopped. The machinery clicked. She started to rattle off numbers.

"You'll have to write them down," I said. "Don't worry if you can't remember them all."

"Oh, I can!" she said, and went rattling on.

"You're extraordinary," I said, still trying to cheer her up.

"It was a nice easy name," she said. "I don't like Robinsons. But George Gissing—he was a writer, you know. My father read him all the time."

I ordered a file check, though we didn't misfile, ever. There was no card in the card index. I told Di to check Sylvia's cross-refs while I took the other files upstairs. While I was there, I looked in on the director's secretary and asked for an urgent appointment. When I got back, Di told me that three more files were missing, and so were the cross-ref sheets in the other ones Sylvia had remembered. They'd all got something to do with Yugoslavia. Sylvia, of course, was in tears again.

I felt cold all through. Once, years later, my flat was burgled. There'd been some stuff about me in the gossip columns, with pictures, and hints about my private life, so people knew who I was and thought they knew the sort of person I was. This man—it must have been a man—didn't just come in and take my jewellery. He'd brought a packet of condoms and written little notes to go with them and hidden them round the flat for me to find. It was horrible. After I found the third, I decided to move. It was a nice flat, but I couldn't live there anymore. But before that, whenever I found one, I immediately remembered how I'd felt looking at the files in the Zoo that morning.

I rang the director's secretary and told her I had to see him at once. She said he was in a meeting, but I said I was coming up now and she had to get him out. She didn't like it at all, but she did it. I told him what it was about and he went and cancelled the meeting and came back. I told him the whole story. I suppose I could have said I'd asked for the file in order to test the system, but he'd have been bound to smell a rat. He just sat there looking at me with his little piggy eyes, exactly the way Mr. Chad used to look at Mother when she was making her madder suggestions. (That's how I'm so sure it must have been the same man as Paul's boss. They weren't twins, but there was a terrific family likeness. They could easily have been brothers.)

The director was ill by then. He'd had something wrong with his blood that winter, and his skin was blotchy and yellow and his lips were blue and his voice sounded exhausted, but he was still one of the cleverest people I've ever met.

"This girl," he said. "What does she do outside?"

"I don't know. She shares a flat with one of the other clerks, Annie Dunwoody."

"Send up her personal file," he said. "We'll have to run a check on all of them, but we'll start with her. I should have known about her earlier."

I didn't understand for a moment. Here I was coming up

with the appalling news that someone had got into the Zoo and taken several files from the contam cabinet and removed a lot of cross-refs from other files, and on top of that that I'd been forging green tags, and he was worrying about Sylvia's personal life . . . then I got it. It was just that I was so used to Sylvia that I hadn't thought about it before. She didn't have to take files home. She carried them around in her head. And if somebody outside realised . . . They'd only need to be kind to her, pretend to be fond of her, cuddle her. . . . But *she* couldn't have taken the file. I was absolutely certain it had been a terrible shock to her when she found it was missing. . . .

The director was on the telephone, arranging an emergency meeting of section chiefs. I would normally have come to that but he looked at me and said, "I think you'd better go down and do some further checking. I'll let you know if I need you."

Down in filing I found two things. Sylvia was having hysterics again and saying she'd lost her memory. And Annie Dunwoody had disappeared. Just about when the first panic had started, before I'd even shown up, she'd said she needed to go to the loo—I've explained about this being a nuisance—and she hadn't come back. I checked with main security and found she'd left the building, getting on an hour before. I reported up to the director's office and next thing there was a team of men down in Files, poking around and questioning everyone, and I had to explain how everything was supposed to work, and answer questions over and over and over. They kept us there till after ten at night, except Sylvia, who was in such a state, I made them send her home with an escort. As soon as she thought she was alone, she turned on the gas oven and put her head in it, but the man who'd stayed to keep watch on her realised what was up and got her out in time.

I only heard about that, because people stopped telling me things and I didn't go to the Thursday Meetings anymore, so I don't know if they ever found out how Annie had smuggled the files (we found several more were missing) out of the Zoo.

Looking back, I suppose the security might have got a bit slacker than I realised. That's always the trouble with systems. The people who set them up assume they're working the way they're supposed to, while the people who're actually in them are taking shortcuts.

Anyway, next thing I knew was rumours about a terrific power struggle upstairs, and the old director resigned and the D Section chief—that was the blue-eyed maniac—took over. Almost the first thing he did was send for me.

He didn't ask me to sit down. I had to stand in front of his desk while he stared at me as if he was trying to hypnotise me.

"I have some further questions about the security lapse last month," he said. "Grantworth, alias Gissing, is a friend of yours?"

"He's a friend of the family," I said. "Mostly my older sister's, I suppose."

"Were you previously aware of his wartime activities?" he asked.

"Somebody told me he'd been doing something hush-hush in the Balkans," I said.

"Somebody?" he asked. "Mr. Paul Ackerley?"

"As a matter of fact, yes, but . . ."

He interrupted me. His dead-level voice was getting on my nerves. It made the most obvious, innocent things sound sinister.

"Another friend?" he asked.

"He used to be more a friend of Harriet's," I said. "She's another sister. But I've seen him several times recently. In fact, I'm having supper with him tonight."

"Has either of them ever asked you for any information about your work here?" he said.

"I always say it's too boring to talk about," I said. "I mean, looking after the filing in a trade—"

He interrupted me again.

"That is not the answer to my question," he said. "Has

either of them ever asked you for information about your work here."

"I don't think so," I said.

"What about your sisters?" he said.

"No, not them, either," I said. "They know I work around here because I sometimes meet them for lunch and things. And I wouldn't dream of talking about it at home because my mother is mad on Joe Stalin."

That was a bad mistake. He really stared now.

"It's just like a schoolgirl crush," I said. "On Gary Cooper or someone. She got it during the war when he was on our side. It doesn't mean anything."

It was no use. He was the kind who thinks everything means something. It was maddening, so maddening in fact that I decided I'd really give him something to think about. Gerry had told us the story once when he came over to Blatchards from Bury.

"Anyway," I said. "It probably wasn't Gerry at all. It was probably his doppelgänger."

"His doppelgänger?" he said in that stupid machine voice.

"When he was called up, they turned him into two people. You know, two army numbers, and a double set of pay books and so on, and then they posted him to two places and tried to arrest him for being a deserter from the other one, and last I heard, they still hadn't got it sorted out. You see?"

I think he knew I was teasing him, but there was something behind those mad blue eyes which told me I'd touched a really raw nerve. It was a sort of spy-hunter's nightmare, I suppose, the idea of an enemy agent who can somehow turn himself into two people and actually get into your filing system like that and stay there.

"And Ackerley?" he said at last.

"Oh, he's different," I said. "He didn't exist at all, and they made him up."

He'd got hold of himself by now and nodded as if he understood what I was talking about. He kept me standing there while he made a couple of notes. Then he looked up.

"Very well," he said. "You can go. In the circumstances you would do well to cancel your engagement this evening."

Now it was my turn to stare and have to get hold of myself. As soon as I was out of the room, I ran downstairs, grabbed a typewriter, and wrote out my letter of resignation. Before I could take it upstairs a note came down from the director's office telling me that my services were no longer required, that I must be clear of my desk by that evening, that I'd get a month's pay in lieu of notice, and so on, and reminding me, underlined, that I'd signed the Official Secrets Act. While I was clearing my desk, a man called Parry came down to ask me more questions and tell me what I could and couldn't do without getting sent to prison for breaking the act. I used to think he was a bit of a friend, but he wasn't now. I didn't mind. I was absolutely furious.

I knew I was going to be followed, so I deliberately walked the whole way home to give the man blisters. It was trying to snow, fine icy crumbs, coming on for a really cold night. The hell with them, I thought, thinking they've got a right to tell me how to run my life! I'll show 'em how much I care! And he can bloody well wait out on the pavement all night!

Paul

FIVE

1948

I suppose the next significant forgathering for me was the party to celebrate Harriet's engagement to Bobo Smith in the summer of 1948. Characteristically the central event was a cricket match, Blatchards *v.* The World. The World could raise only two women prepared to have a go, but all five sisters played for the house. There were no restrictions in favour of the women. The men in the Blatchards team were Lord Vereker, Bobo, and three workers from the estate and home farm. Dick Felder was to have played but at the last minute refused to make the trip and, I believe, wanted to prevent Nancy from doing so. Lucy had already hinted that the marriage was in an uncomfortable state. She rang to ask if I had any suggestions for a replacement.

"I could try Gerry again," I said.

"Oh, yes. Perhaps if you tell him . . ."

"Of course."

Gerry was up at King's on a scholarship. He'd won a cricket Blue in his first summer but had switched from classics to economics for his second year (he was on a short course), effectively cramming three years' work in the new subject into one. That had meant no cricket till after the Tripos. Though that was by now done with, he hadn't wanted to commit himself to playing regularly for the rest of the summer. Tommy Seddon, a county neighbour of the Verekers who was captaining The World, had already asked me to approach him about playing, but Gerry had made his excuses, letting me understand that it wouldn't much amuse him to stay at Seddon Hall and merely come over for the match and the party, while Dick was installed with Nancy at the house itself. Lucy, of course, knew all this, and indeed as soon as I spoke to Gerry, he jumped at the offer, though it meant cancelling an engagement to play elsewhere.

Mr. Chad and Lord Seddon's head gardener umpired. My unofficial position as Lucy's lover was recognised by my being appointed scorer for both teams. The match was enjoyable, with an excitingly close finish. Ben, bowling a lively medium with a pleasant loose-limbed action, took three good wickets, one of them Michael Allwegg's, a stocky aggressive hitter, of whom more later. Gerry opened for the house and was still there when Lucy, going in last "because someone has to," joined him with a dozen runs still needed. This was apparently a repeat of a similar ending in the last match before the war, and there were great hurrahings when she hit the winning runs with a neat square cut. A beautiful late-June day turned into a mild dusk and starlit night.

Despite problems at home, Dick was still being generous about money, so Nancy was able to subsidise the party well beyond the Blatchards norm. Harriet, insisting that it was *her* engagement, had taken over the arrangements, limiting Lady Vereker's genius for discomfort to a few minor awkwardnesses—the coats of guests could not, for some reason, be stored anywhere near the front door but had to be carried through the crowded inner hall to three different locations, and thus were almost impossible to find when guests wanted to leave. An uncle of Bobo's in the wine trade had bought a large parcel of prewar champagne at an auction, cheap because the occasional bottle was past it. With the import restrictions then prevailing, one glass of champagne at a party was a luxury. Enough to supply over a hundred guests well into the small hours was a miracle. The band was Tommy Kinsman's, pretty good still. We danced in the Long Gallery.

Lucy and I had been lovers long enough for me to be able to bear seeing her in someone else's arms, and with so many of the guests being old friends, her card quickly filled. I was curious to dance with Ben, who had turned out far too tall for classical ballet and was now living in Paris and working in the chorus line of the Moulin Rouge. She had kept the angular coltish look and made it part of her style (in her fifties she used to lounge in teenager poses). She had, though, acquired a cool, amused, watchful manner, which I guessed was largely defensive. We waltzed, and she was indeed good—for some reason I specially enjoy dancing with partners taller than myself.

"Can you tango?" she said as we finished.

"Reasonably."

"I'll get them to do one."

"It's not on the card, and how many people—"

"The hell with them. What's the point of being the daughter of the house?"

As I'd guessed, the floor largely cleared, apart from a few incorrigible shufflers, but enough other pairs at first made a go of it for me not to feel as if we were behaving antisocially. Ben took charge. Apparently there was a tango number in that year's show. I merely kept my end up, but it was still very exhilarating. There is something about that particular combination of discipline and panache, of drill precision not simply mastering and controlling but actually expressing the prime sexual urge, which . . . I don't know. Before long the other couples seemed to be dropping out until only one pair were still dancing along with us. I was too busy keeping up to Ben's standard to do more than register that they were Nancy and Gerry, but when we'd finished and the spectators were applauding, Ben turned laughing to Nancy and said, "You've been taking lessons."

Nancy was excited, bright eyed. Up till that moment, though she had made no parade of her feelings, she had seemed to me rather depressed, presumably by her problems with Dick.

"Not me," she said. "Gerry did the dancing. I was a passenger."

"Not in a tango," said Ben. "Can't be done."

I looked at Gerry. He seemed as nonchalant as ever, but he caught my eye and gave a minimal nod of satisfaction as we moved off. (Later that evening, incidentally, the floor was cleared again and Ben, in costume, did a can-can for us. It was clearly the real thing, but the applause hadn't quite the spontaneity our tango had elicited.)

I was due for the next dance with Lucy. I'd apologised before taking Ben off to tango, but she'd simply smiled indulgently and said, "Go ahead. Have fun." Now I found her mysteriously cross.

"I want some air," she said.

"Can't we dance first?"

"No. Let's get out of here. Have you got a fag?"

She practically never smoked, knowing I didn't like it, but I found her a cigarette, and we went out into the warm night and strolled past the weeping beech into the heavy shadow of the cedar. When I put my hand in hers, she twisted her fingers tightly between mine, but when I turned her and reached to put my other arm round her bare shoulders, she lifted it away.

"Oh, God," she sighed, and started to weep.

I had nothing to say. I tried to let go of her hand, but she clutched my fingers tight enough to hurt.

"I'm sorry, Paul," she whispered. "I truly am sorry. I've been telling us both lies."

"No, you haven't. You've never said you loved me. Not once."

"You've kept count?"

"It isn't difficult to count up to one."

We walked for a while more, holding each other close in a useless attempt at comforting.

"Stay with me tonight," she said as we made our way back to the house. There was a convention by which we slept separately when staying at Blatchards. I didn't feel like breaking it on those terms.

"Please," she said.

"All right, but change your mind if you want to."

She disappeared for the rest of the evening, leaving the rest of her partners in the lurch. I got through somehow till the last guests left, around three in the morning. We still had double summertime then, so it was getting light by the time I stole along to Lucy's room. As I was closing her door, I heard a movement behind me. I waited, watching through the crack, and saw Gerry go past towards where Nancy slept.

Lucy was awake. We held each close, like children, until after a while she dropped asleep as if she'd been drugged. I lay on my back until there was a reasonable chance of breakfast, when I slipped back to my room, dressed, and shaved in cold water. I found Harriet in the breakfast room, looking typically healthy and kempt. I was fond of her since Cairo and felt that because of those days we enjoyed a sort of alliance different from either friendship or love. We could be entirely open and trusting with each other. She showed me her ring, platinum, from Asprey, an aggressive diamond in an uninteresting setting.

"Bobo chose it," she said. "I didn't get a say."

"Do you mind?"

"Not really. I don't suppose I'd have chosen much different. You know, about getting married and putting up with someone, I think it doesn't much matter not having the same kind of good taste—I mean preferring baroque to gothic or

something. But you've really got to have the same kind of bad taste. If one of you likes damask lampshades with gold tassles, then you've both got to."

She studied the ring.

"At least it makes it pretty definite I'm engaged," she said. "One likes to be clear about these things. I don't know I could cope the way you and Lucy manage."

"It's tricky, certainly, at times."

"Are you coming over to Seddon Hall for luncheon? Tommy asked me to ring him with numbers. He's a fusser."

"I don't know him that well."

"You should make more effort. He's going to be foreign secretary one day. Everyone says so."

"I'd have thought if you went in for that sort of ambition, you'd aim for the top."

"He can't be prime minister because when old Lord Seddon dies, he'll inherit the title. Tommy's got less sense of humour than anyone I've ever met, but otherwise he's all right. Bobo can't stand him."

"One of a fair-size list, I imagine. I suppose it includes me."

"I'm working him round."

"Why are you marrying him?"

"Because I'll know where I am with him, I've decided. I don't want to fall properly in love—it only seems to make people unhappy."

"When it's going well, there's nothing like it."

"But then, whoops, and you're miserable. Aren't you, Paul?"

"Things don't look too good at the moment."

"I'm sorry. What about luncheon?"

"I don't want to wake Lucy—I think she's going to sleep in. Find out what Nan and Gerry are doing, and if they want to go, we won't, and vice versa. Then you'll have the same numbers regardless."

At this point Lady Vereker rushed in.

"Just the two of you?" she said. "You're early. I was just going to go and tell everyone they didn't have to get up."

"No, mother," said Harriet.

"I thought it would be friendly."

"You are going to wake everyone up to tell them they don't have to wake up?"

"Then they can go back to sleep."

"Not after you've been round shouting at them. Will Father mind if I fry my own egg?"

"Provided you take one from the left of the box. Oh well, in that case I might as well go and clean tack for a bit."

Neither Lucy nor Nancy went over to Seddon Hall. Lucy, despite her stated need for me the night before, could now apparently hardly bear to be in the same room as me, not, I guessed, out of revulsion but out of distress at her own behaviour to me. As for Nancy's motives, anyone's guess is as good as mine. So both Gerry and I were needed to make up the numbers.

Petrol rationing still being in force, eight of us crammed into Bobo's Riley, which he then deliberately drove to elicit as much by way of screams and protests as he could. At one moment, coming down to a humpbacked bridge, he was on the edge of being out of control when a child on a bicycle wobbled up from the far side. Everyone yelled. The car spun as Bobo braked. We almost overturned but finished up facing the way we had come, with our rear mudguard jammed against the stone parapet. While the child watched, quivering, we heaved the car clear, and Bobo and Gerry managed to wrench the mudguard out to a point where it no longer rubbed against the tire. After that we drove on more sensibly.

Seddon Hall can legitimately be described as a gothick pile. *Ivanhoe*-inspired, it might have been an architectural sampler built to display all the possible variations of turret, battlement, and machicolation available in the 1820s. Lord Seddon was on the steps waiting to greet us—not, it turned out, for the pleasure of welcoming three pretty, if dishevelled, girls under his portcullis, but because he was anxious whether Gerry was in our party.

I had met Lord Seddon the day before, when he had spent some time at the scoring table. He was small, wiry, bright eyed, and weirdly inarticulate. I never heard him reach the end of a sentence. Often he stopped short of the main verb. Since his thought processes were routine and his sole interest was cricket, I had found conversation with him not too difficult. Now, though, when he took me aside as soon as the party had assembled for sherry in the Solar, he lost me for a while.

"Grantworth, er . . . ?"

"Yes, sir. I've known him several years."

"First-class, eh?"

"I should think he'll get one, pretty certainly."

"Eh? No, no. Yesterday . . ."

"I've seen him play much better bowling just as well."

"Got his Blue, but then, I say, why . . . ?"

"He had to work, sir. He was doing a three years' course in one. Even so, as I say, I should think he'll get his First."

Lord Seddon vented a rasping snort. There was no point in my explaining that for a penniless undergraduate a Cricket Blue plus a First in economics might offer better job prospects than a Blue alone, but both poverty and work were probably concepts beyond Lord Seddon's imagination.

"Happen to know where . . . ?"

"He was at Eton with me, sir."

"No, no, where . . . ?"

"At his prep school, I imagine, sir. He has no family to—"

"No, no, no. I mean, where . . . ?"

I worked it out. Lucy had already told me that Lord Seddon, though living entirely in Suffolk, maintained another house near Ripon, where all his children had been born and most of his grandchildren too, at his insistence, so that they should have birth qualifications to play for Yorkshire. In the event, only three of them had been male, none anything like good enough to represent the county, and he was now, according to Lucy, waiting with some impatience for the next generation. I remembered what Gerry had told me about his being found in a public lavatory.

"Leeds, I believe, sir," I said. "Would you like me to check?"

"Very good of you. Very good of you."

I went over to ask Gerry if he had Yorkshire qualifications, but Lord Seddon came tripping eagerly at my elbow, so I simply introduced them and stood back to watch Gerry mastering the art of supplying both halves of a conversation, which he did with ease. Lord Seddon was clearly delighted.

I spent most of lunch in silence. We ate, parsimoniously but with vast gaps between courses, at a long black refectory table in the Great Hall. "Not enough girls to go round," Bobo had announced gloomily as we went in. I found myself sitting next to him towards one end of the table, and naturally enough he was more interested in the female houseguest on his far side. Janet, on my right, was soon absorbed by her other neighbour's account of how he was keeping his dairy herd free of mastitis by installing in the cowshed a special box that picked up beneficial vibrations from the planets. Time passed for me extremely slowly. After a while I noticed Gerry and Michael Allwegg in animated conversation some way down the other side of the table.

My feelings about Gerry were not straightforward. I didn't at all understand Lucy's attitude to him. She had said, once, that she wasn't in love with him, but I was aware that what had happened last night had much more to do with him and Nancy than it had with my obvious relish in tangoing with Ben. I couldn't blame Gerry for taking advantage of the dance, and the champagne, and Nancy's disaffection from Dick. None of these were things that he'd set up or worked for. He'd simply taken his chance as deftly as he'd take a catch at short leg. But this didn't make it any easier for me not to feel that he had somehow betrayed me, his friend, and at the same time angry that he should be, however unconsciously, the cause of Lucy's unhappiness. I wondered whether there was any way I could explain to him the effect he was having on two people, both of whom, I assumed, he valued.

Perhaps my perceptions were oversharpened, but after a while I seemed to perceive that there was something unusual about the conversation he was having with Allwegg. I've had difficulty conveying Gerry's normal conversational style. On paper it looks rather on the florid side, formal and self-conscious, but one wasn't aware of this when talking with him as he did the trick so easily that with him it seemed no trick at all. He was well mannered about it too, listening, accepting interruptions, finding something interesting with which to reply to banal or dim remarks, and so on. Still, without apparently wishing to do so, he usually managed to dominate any conversation. This didn't seem to be the case now, though. It was Allwegg who was doing most of the talking, while Gerry was listening with what looked like eager attention.

I never knew Allwegg well, nor wished to. It is difficult for me to be fair to him, in the light of later events. The most obvious thing about him was the combination of charm and intelligence with striking physical ugliness. Dark coarse hair, harsh eyebrows flaring upward at the outer ends, brownish pocked skin, full mouth, a jowly look even then, he appeared in that company much more of an outsider than Gerry, or even I (the two genuine outsiders) probably did, though I believe his family was perfectly acceptable, minor squirearchy from the Welsh borders. I was aware of the charm, but I have to say it is not the sort I find charming, too blatant, too willed for my taste. Will, in fact, was for me his most marked characteristic, more so even than his appearance. Some people seem to possess a sort of psychic force, stemming perhaps from a self-validating conviction of the rightness of all their beliefs and actions, which is very hard to resist. Hitler was an obvious example. They are madmen who contrive somehow to act sane, perhaps until a sudden crack-up, perhaps for all their lives. Allwegg had at least a touch of that. He was, by the way, a goodish cricketer, having captained Winchester, but had just missed his Blue. His father was a High Court judge, and he himself was reading law at Pembroke. Most of that, of course, is later knowledge. All that I really noticed then was the effect that he seemed to be having on Gerry.

I wasn't the only one. As we were settling into the car to return to Blatchards, Ben, squeezed in beside me on the front passenger seat with Janet across our knees, twisted her neck and spoke over her shoulder.

"What on earth were you talking to Michael about, Gerry? It must have been rivetting."

Gerry laughed. Crushed though we were, without touch or eye contact, I sensed the electric tingle of satisfaction in him. The obvious thing was to put it down to his night with Nancy, and the possibility of more such nights, but it seemed·in the context to be more a response to Ben's question.

"How to become millionaires," he said.

Lucy

FIVE

1948

I've been listening to what I said last time, and thinking about
it, and wondering. Wondering, I mean, why almost at once I
started to behave as if none of that had ever happened. The
easiest thing is to say I just *knew* there couldn't be anything
wrong about Gerry. Perhaps that was the hidden reason why
I was so furious with them. I don't know. I'd got plenty to be
furious about, without that. And you've got to remember that
without me realising it, I'd got pretty browned off about the
kind of thing we were doing. Telling the madman about
Gerry's doppelgänger was the final straw. It made me start
actually thinking what a nonsense it all was.

And then, oh, I suppose it was a few weeks after I'd left the
Exchange, I got asked to a ball at Greenwich, in the Painted
Hall—terrifically glamorous, except that marble's such hell to
dance on. Of course almost all the men were navy, and at the
dinner before the dance, two of them had been talking about
Greece. Greece was in a frightful mess just then, with communists and anticommunists killing and torturing each other, and
us trying to stop Stalin getting his hands on yet another
country. Both these officers had actually been there, one after
the other, first when we were trying to keep the peace and
then when we were trying to boot the communists out. I

pretended not to be listening, but actually I knew quite a bit about what they were talking about, because we'd got a lot of files on Greece and were always having to get them out and update them. There was a man called Mizikouros, who was head of an anticommunist group on Euboea. I knew his name well, because he had a blue-tagged file, which meant he'd been checked and rechecked and he was absolutely reliable, but neither of these men had a good word to say for him. According to them he was a total liar and a complete savage. One of them told a story about what he'd done to a village that hadn't come up with as much food as he'd wanted, though the villagers were pretty well starving already. It sounded just as bad as anything the Germans had done. Of course we always knew in the Exchange that nothing on the files was dead certain— intelligence work isn't like that. But even so. I mean, Mizi- kouros had a blue tag!

And it seems funny now that I never talked to Paul about it, either, but it didn't then. It was past, over, part of the war, unreal. I didn't want to know it anymore. I remember having breakfast in his flat one morning—I should think it was several months after the Greenwich party—and he was reading the *Telegraph*, but suddenly he flung it on the floor and said, "Oh, honestly, how stupid can you get! They've arrested Anwal!"

I knew about Anwal. He was Sonia's husband. Sonia was the girl who'd lived with Paul in Cairo. Only a few weeks before, they'd written to Paul asking if he'd be their new baby's godfather. He was terribly pleased.

"What's he done?" I said.

"Written some articles critical of the government. That makes him an agitator. If he's an agitator, then so is Anthony Eden."

"Is he a communist?"

"You don't have to be a communist to think the unspeakable Farouk isn't fit to rule your country, any more than you have to be a fascist to make a speech like Eden's last, saying much the same thing about Attlee. Of course there'll be raving Red-hunters in the security services who'll point out that Anwal's been to meetings where a lot of communists happen to have been, too. I've done that kind of work myself. You actually know so little for sure that you're always persuading yourself that shadows are solid."

"Is there anything you can do?" I said.

"Write a few letters," he said. "At least try and see Sonia's alright."

That was an obvious chance—I mean about how wrong security people can be—but I don't think I even thought about it. Somebody'd persuaded Annie to steal a lot of files about Yugoslavia, and one of them was Gerry's, which obviously shouldn't have been there in the first place. That was all. And there was another chance a bit later, because soon after that Paul's flat got burgled. At least we were pretty sure someone had been in, though nothing was taken. It was just that Paul's so neat about everything that all his papers are always in a particular order, and they weren't. And after that we noticed there was sometimes something funny about the telephone. This was long before people started to make all the fuss about phone tapping, but Paul thought something like that might be happening.

"My fault for writing those letters," he said. "Now I'm a Red under the bed, too."

He didn't take it very seriously, and they let Anwal out again quite soon, but thinking about it now, I wonder whether it was just that. I mean, just imagine how it must have looked to my blue-eyed madman. I was a friend of a contam, and so was Paul, and Paul had worked in the Exchange before it was the Exchange, and when he'd told me not to go out with Paul, I'd deliberately done just the opposite, and now I was living with him, and he was in cahoots with this agitator in Cairo. . . . Oh, yes, and of course I'd been in charge of the security in Files and I'd hired Annie, so perhaps I'd arranged the whole business of the files getting stolen, and then pretended to find out about it so as to persuade everyone that the Exchange files were hopelessly compromised. . . . That's how that kind of madman thinks.

I'm not going to say much more now. I tried to do too much last time and I had a really bad day next day, so I've got to be careful or Paul will stop me doing it at all. But I'll just tidy up to where he's got to, from my side. I had a good eighteen months (was it?) with Paul. I was happy in a restful kind of way. At first I didn't have enough money to go on paying rent, so I moved in to Paul's flat and Ben found someone else to share with. Then I got my first modelling jobs. I was lucky. I started at the top. A cousin of mine was working for Norman Parkinson, and he needed two girls who might be sisters, and since we had an obvious family look, she suggested me. That's how the money started coming in again. Please don't think I only left Paul because I could pay the rent again now. It would have happened anyway. We both knew we were just marking time. But I did know he was going to mind a lot more than me. That made it difficult. I really don't like hurting people, even when they've earned it, and he hadn't.

Several times in my life I've had to say "Look, I'm afraid that's it" to a man, and I've never enjoyed it. (Alright, I've had it said to me, too, and that's no fun, either.) Long before Harriet's party I'd vaguely known it was coming. I didn't know what I wanted instead of Paul, only something stronger and wilder than his tidy, gentle, battened-down way of living. I didn't think about it then and there, but going in last again with Gerry and scraping home with me scoring the winning run—while it was happening all I thought was how terrific, as if we were back where we'd started and everything was fresh and new and I was being given my time all over again. . . . But it's never like that, is it? Try to have the same happiness twice over, and it always goes sour on you. All evening I seemed to be getting edgier and edgier. I knew something was going to happen to spoil what ought to have been a perfect day, like the one before. That bloody tango. Ben. So young, just starting, like I used to be. I absolutely loathed myself for feeling so jealous. Yes, jealous. And not just about her being the one who was starting at the beginning when I couldn't anymore, jealous about Paul. This may surprise you, because of what I've just been saying about him not being all that exciting, but suddenly he was with Ben. I don't imagine for a moment that she wanted to go to bed with him, or he with her, but there she was, in the middle of the Long Gallery, saying these things with her body, yelling them almost. And Paul answering her. They were only acting them, of course, but they were acting wildness, danger, passion—things we couldn't do for each other, me and Paul. God damn it, we couldn't even *act* them for each other!

And then Nan and Gerry joining in. Gerry *making* her tango. Nobody could make Nan do things, but he bloody well hypnotised her into dancing that effing tango with her, and everybody saw them, and I had to sit there looking as calm and sweet as the fairy on the Christmas tree and clapping when it was all over. God, I was miserable! I was sick at Ben and Paul and Gerry and Nan and myself more than anyone! Paul, of course, couldn't have behaved better when I gave him the push. I do think he might have sulked and snarled a bit. That would have made life easier.

Paul

SIX

March 1956

Lord Vereker died, appropriately, of food poisoning. I was in
two minds whether to attend the funeral until Harriet telephoned and asked me to drive two ancient cousins down from
Hampstead. Both could barely walk, but they proved jovial
and talkative passengers, artists, who had known not just the
obvious people (Sargent, Epstein, John) but others such as
Gaudier Brezska and Duchamp. So I had no time to brood
about the prospect of meeting Lucy, now Lady Seddon. Though
we had parted, without quarrels or recriminations, immediately after the week-end just described, I had kept up with
Vereker affairs by becoming godfather to Harriet's first child,
a girl. I would spend a week-end with the Smiths in Dorset
two or three times a year, and see something of them in London
too, as Bobo had a tiny house in Pavilion Road, just off Sloane
Square.

My views on Bobo had changed, and apparently his on me.
Our earlier incompatibility had been partly the effect of our
different speeds of moral and social development. Thanks perhaps to my foreign blood, I was an early maturer, effectively
an adult at seventeen, whereas Bobo remained an adolesecent
lout into his late twenties. Marriage ripened him, and Harriet
managed him with great skill, apart from the occasional over-

bossiness. I never became a close friend of his—we still had too little in common—but we got along well enough. Though not intelligent, he had a very shrewd instinct for anything to do with money, and not only invested in some of my ventures but provided me with valuable contacts in the financial world. He was a stockbroker and did well for himself and his firm, cajoling older partners into fresh approaches. He, in a sense like me, was one of those who caught the tide.

Harriet enjoyed her domesticities, the county round, and local Tory politics. It is mildly interesting that alone of the Vereker girls, and from such calculated beginnings (to judge by our breakfast conversation after the cricket match), she achieved a marriage that worked and continued to work right up to the day when Bobo, in one of his occasional relapses into his earlier style, contrived to drown them both in an idiotic sailing accident off Corfu. But that was not until the late seventies.

Lord Vereker's funeral was in March, the church dank, the service vapid. We sang "Fight the Good Fight" and other hymns equally inapplicable to the deceased. Not being a believer, I tend to notice the meanings of the words I find myself singing, but the point for once struck others. While we were milling out through the porch, clasping Lady Vereker's hands and muttering the ritual inarticulacies, I heard someone at the back of the family group say in a too-loud whisper, "Pity they didn't make it 'Feed Us, Heavenly Father, Feed Us'!" I saw Ben giggle and Janet frown, then realised that the speaker must be Edward Voss-Thompson, at that time married to Janet, choosing this moment to live up to his reputation as the speaker of tasteless truth.

It's hard these days to remember how new and thrilling television then seemed to be; how sane and busy citizens, for instance, would cancel other engagements and drive half across a county to attend a sherry party because Malcolm Muggeridge might be going, too. Voss-Thompson, though half a generation younger than Muggeridge, was somewhat in that mould, and in other ways a forerunner of David Frost, though less heavy-handed. He specialised in a sardonic tone of question that could rattle all but the most experienced flannelers and wafflers. For me there had been the extra curiosity of seeing for the first time the effect that TV exposure can have on a previously reasonable character. Not that I knew Voss-Thompson well, but I'd spent a week-end at the Smiths when he and Janet had also been there, met him again at a couple of dinner parties at Pavilion Road, and run across him elsewhere, at Glynde-bourne, for instance, both of us being assiduous opera-goers. I had liked him then and came to do so again later, but at the period of the funeral, I have to admit that I found him rather a pain in the neck, with his assumption that he was the centre of attention, and a tendency during the normal disagreements of conversation to slip into his TV style, adversarial and domi-neering.

In my turn I condoled. Lady Vereker, I could see, was barely holding herself together, answering every remark with a toneless "So glad you could come." I think someone may have given her a stiff Scotch to get her through. Beyond her were further millings, and umbrellas adjusted to meet the drizzle. I was considering how to get my two charges to my car without their having to hobble too far through the murk when a voice beside me whispered, "You are allowed to look at me, you know."

She slipped her hand into mine, as if nothing had ever changed between us. She was smiling slightly, her face pas-sionless, but I was aware that she was at least as shaken as her mother, and that what she needed from me, from anybody, was comfort. I put my arm round her shoulders and drew her against my side. Someone was watching us. Michael Allwegg. I didn't care.

"You're coming to luncheon," she said.

"I told Harriet no."

The thought of meeting Lucy as someone else's wife, or merely glimpsing her across a roomful of chatterers, had seemed unbearable, so I had invented friends a few miles away with whom I'd said I would be lunching, and picking up the cousins afterwards.

"Please," she whispered.

I nodded and she let go. I helped the cousins to my car. On the drive to Blatchards I found them extra-animated by the possibility of meeting Voss-Thompson. (To do him justice, he spotted their potential and later that year did an interview with them in their studio, hardly intruding himself at all, but allowing them to be themselves. The result was enchanting.)

The catering was below Lord Vereker's standards, but otherwise the lunch went well. There must have been at least sixty guests, almost all of them relatives and connections, who took the opportunity to bring each other up to date with family news. Such gatherings always make me realise that members of truly nuclear families like my own miss out on a large and enjoyable area of human fulfilment simply because they are not part of such a network. The food was laid out in the Dining Room, and most of us perched in the Saloon or Library to eat. I fetched plates for the cousins and left them deep in prattle with one of their coevals. Loading my own plate, I found Nancy beside me. Unlike Lucy, she seemed not to be stricken by the event.

"Paul!" she cried and kissed me warmly. "It's been far, far too long. How are you? What are you doing? Isn't this fun? Funerals are much better than weddings for this sort of thing, don't you think?"

She was more changed than Lucy, pretty still, but wearing too vivid makeup for such an occasion. Though she had acquired no trace of an American accent, I think I might have guessed from her manner and appearance that she had spent a good deal of time in the States. I knew from Harriet that she and Dick had made a serious attempt to mend their marriage, and in the process to produce an heir to the Felder fortune. That failing, they were now divorced. She had come back to live at Blatchards, and to avoid death duties Lord Vereker had handed on most of the estate to her. In the last year or so, Harriet said, Gerry had become rather more than a frequent visitor to the house.

"You've heard the big news?" said Nancy.

"I don't know. Have I?"

"Look at Ben's left hand."

Ben, in the severest black, with a delicious little veiled pillbox hat, was a few yards away, talking with a lot of body language to someone I couldn't see. She raised her arm, twisting the hand back at the wrist, in a gesture of dismissive scorn. A sapphire flashed on her ring finger.

"Good Lord!" I said. "Who's the man?"

"Michael Allwegg."

"Good Lord again."

"What do you imagine it cost? And that neat little black number, too?"

The answer in both cases was clearly a lot. I was amused that Nancy, till recently mistress of colossal wealth, should not only be impressed but be prepared to say so in such a frankly vulgar fashion.

"Do I congratulate her?" I said.

"If you want to. It isn't announced yet, because of Father's death. In fact she oughtn't to be flashing that ring about, really. You'll want to see Lucy. I don't know where she's got to. And I'm sure Gerry will want to see you. I'll find him."

We talked a little more and separated. Lucy wasn't in the Dining Room, so I went to congratulate Ben before searching elsewhere. Ben kissed me, Continental fashion, a quick peck on both cheeks. Her whole appearance was almost ferociously sophisticated, but she seemed genuinely happy to see me and accepted my congratulations with a laugh. She was by now one of the senior dancers at the Moulin Rouge, with her name on the posters. I'd been to one of her shows on a trip to Paris the year before, sent my card round, and gone backstage, to find her in a tiny dressing room which she shared with another girl, whose admirer had sat glowering in the corner while we talked.

"Are you going to give up dancing?" I asked.

"So Michael seems to think. I'm going to give it a rest, anyway. I've been a bit too long at the Mill. I've got a message for you from Lucy. She's not feeling well and she's gone to lie down for a bit, but she says you're not to leave till she's seen you."

"What's the matter, do you know?"

"She's the one who minded most about Father. Of course we all did, funny old thing. But ripeness is all, you know. Except Lucy doesn't think so. She's always wanted to eat her cake and have it still."

(I've forgotten to say that part of Ben's style was to converse in such proverbial scraps and nanny lore, giving them apparent edge and freshness because she herself looked so decidedly not ordinary. I have sometimes wondered whether she took after her father, whose brisk, intelligent glance may have been almost totally deceptive.)

After that I wandered about, talked to a few people, took the cousins' finished plates away and brought their second courses, and so on, until Nancy found me again.

"Gerry's probably up in the Yellow Room," she said. "That's his kingdom now. Do you remember the way?"

"I think so. Anyway, I'll find it. Don't bother to show me."

"Might as well," she said. "See he's behaving himself. Did you find Lucy?"

"According to Ben she's not feeling too well and went to lie down."

"Bet she's just miffed with Ben for flashing that ring around. It's not Ben's fault. Mother pretty well made her. Hang on a mo'."

She darted aside to settle some minor problem, and though when she came back, I tried to tell her again that I could find the Yellow Room without help, she still insisted on coming. In fact I got the impression that she really wished to use the excuse to check up on Gerry in some way. We crossed the Central Hall, turned right down a long corridor past the Drawing Room and East Room, and then at the Billiard Room turned left into the short East Corridor, past the Gun Room to the East Stairs. These led only to the two rooms above. The first was a stately but underfurnished and never-used chamber called King William's Room (nobody knew why, or to which King William it referred) with double doors at either end and four tall windows looking out over the East Lawn. Beyond the further doors lay the Yellow Room.

Once inside the Yellow Room, one realised that one had not in fact come up a full storey, as compared with the rest of the house, in climbing the East Stairs. It and King William's Room occupied a sort of half-storey, because the rooms below not only lay lower than the rest of the ground floor, but also had lower ceilings. Don't ask me why. Many of the internal arrangements at Blatchards were like that, botchings and improvisations connected by strange little stairways and angled corridors behind the bleak, symmetrical facade. The room had not been yellow for at least a generation. The Verekers were disappointed if newcomers failed to remark on its obvious greenness, thus depriving them of the chance to haul out some bound copies of *Horse and Hound* and expose the ancient saffron wallpaper behind. The books on the shelves, unlike most of those in the Library, had been bought to read at some time or other—D. K. Broster and Dornford Yates most recently, and even some Charles Williams at the upper limit of Vereker taste—and the furniture was slackly comfortable. Furthermore, the gas fire really worked. Unlike the other fires at Blatchards, with their feeble supply from extended circuits, for these two rooms at the top of the East Stairs Mr. Chad had at some point installed a separate run of piping so that this was the one place in the house where one could be reasonably sure of getting warm. The other peculiarity was that whereas the two windows on its east side matched those in King William's Room, the ones on the south side began at floor level and reached only halfway up the wall. They were in fact the top sections of the end two of the line of tall windows that ran the length of the south facade, and were bisected at this point by the Billard Room ceiling. In the northwest corner of the room, behind a false bookcase, a twisting stair led to the first true storey of the main house. These contrivances gave the Yellow Room a feeling of concealment, a private lair tucked into the apparently nonexistent spaces between the other rooms of the house, like a priest's hole, though it was in fact a good-size room.

Perhaps it was this that led Nancy, when she opened the door and disclosed Gerry, Tommy Seddon, and Michael Allwegg slouched round the fire with a bottle of Hine on the table before them, to laugh and say, "Hello, it's the Yellow Room Conspiracy. Next stop, Traitor's Gate."

The men had stopped talking and risen as we entered, so there was indeed a mild sense of some cabal being interrupted in its schemings. Seddon smiled at her remark, Michael guffawed, and Gerry paid no attention to her but waved a greeting to me and gestured towards a chair. Nancy, still apparently determined to make her mark, strode into the circle, picked up the bottle and sniffed it.

"That smells like good stuff," she said. "I didn't know we had any of that."

"We don't," said Gerry. "Michael brought it."

There was a roughness about his tone for which Harriet had half-prepared me. "Gerry stands up to her," she'd said. "She used to like it, but now I'm not sure. The trouble is, neither of them is prepared to manage the other one, you know, getting their own way without seeming to, that sort of thing. You've got to have a bit of that in a marriage." Gerry's "we" was not a surprise, either. I had seen little of him over the past few years but knew he was an associate of Allwegg's and had a flat north of Hyde Park, where, Harriet said, Nancy sometimes spent the odd night, while he came down to Blatchards at weekends. The only reason they were not formally married was that Nancy would then forfeit her alimony from Dick Felder, and without that Blatchards would have ceased to be viable.

"Have some," said Michael, stretching for the bottle.

"Which is Gerry's glass?" said Nancy. "Heavens, he's not going to drink all that. I want him on his feet to say good-bye to people."

Without waiting, she picked up the glass nearest where Gerry had been sitting—it indeed held a hefty tot but looked as if it had not so far been touched—and took a good swig, quite obviously not for enjoyment but as if asserting her rights to do so.

"You can put some in a tooth mug for me," she said. "And I mean it about Gerry staying on his feet—Mother's had it, and so's Lucy, blast her. See you later, Paul."

We settled as she left. Michael poured me a lavish brandy and accepted my congratulations with a shrug. He had put on a lot of weight, but this seemed to have improved his looks somehow, or perhaps his facial ugliness seemed less extreme on a grosser body. His business world, mainly the acquisition and development of rundown urban property, didn't impinge on mine, but I had heard that he was doing well, and Ben's ring and dress seemed to confirm this. At other times I might have been more interested to meet him, but as it was, what with Lucy's pressing invitation to me to come to the house followed by her apparent decision to hide from me, and now finding myself expected to converse with her husband, I was in some confusion.

I knew Seddon no better than I'd done seven years earlier. Incidentally, there was something about him, even before he had inherited the title, that made one inclined to think of him by his surname. The Vicky caricatures—to my mind one of that overrated cartoonist's better efforts—invariably showed him as a ballet dancer, no matter how inappropriate the dress might be for the activity portrayed, with the lean, handsome but somehow shrewish face always in profile, the blond forelock flopping over one eye. I thought him a vain, clever, empty, ambitious man, a sort of lightweight Lord Curzon.

"We were talking about Egypt," said Michael. "Do you still know anyone there, any Egyptians in particular?"

"Well, yes," I said, relieved to be able to talk about comparatively public matters. As it happened, I did have a regular and knowledgeable correspondent. The Armenian with whom I'd lived in Cairo was now married, with three daughters, to the eldest of whom I had stood godfather, the husband being broadminded enough not simply to accept the situation but to make me his friend. He was a journalist and novelist, politically active—twice, in fact, in prison under various censorship laws. The whole family had stayed with me on a London visit only a few months earlier. It strikes me now that Seddon might possibly have been aware of this. My friend was well enough known as an anti-imperialist of pinkish leanings to have been watched by our security forces. In fact I believe my telephone was tapped for a while following an earlier incident involving him. I assume that Gerry had told Michael about my work in Cairo.

"Do your friends believe that Nasser is anything more than a populist windbag?" said Seddon.

(There is nothing for it. Anyone of my generation will think it merely amazing that literate and intelligent people can have no more than the vaguest notion of the events surrounding the Suez Crisis, but I'm afraid this is so. I will do my best to be brief:

Suez was the British Vietnam, the farce before the tragedy for once, misconceived, inept in execution, deeply shaming, and demonstrating to the world that we were no longer either fit or able to claim any kind of world leadership. The British protégé in Egypt, King Farouk, had been ousted by a group of radical officers, inspired and soon led by Nasser. He established a charismatic hold not only on his own people but on most of the Arab world. The British authorities detested him from the start. The Americans first attempted to buy him with dollars and, when this failed, to bully him by withholding them. Nasser refused to be bullied, the dollars were cut off, and Nasser was forced to accept help from the Russians [who, of course, found him no more amenable]. With his modernising projects stalled for want of funds, he needed new foci for his revolution, so he started a furious propaganda war against Israel, with military buildups along the border, and nationalised the Suez Canal Company, jointly owned by Britain and France.

The British, French, and Israelis contrived a secret scheme under which Israel was to make a preemptive strike against Egypt, and Britain and France were to invade, on the pretext of protecting the canal as an international waterway, not telling the Americans of their plans but assuming that the fait accompli, after a swift and effective military operation, would evoke a few expressions of public disapproval accompanied by private thanks. Of course it didn't work. The military operations, apart from Israel's, were a fiasco; Nasser scuttled ships in the canal and blocked it for a decade; he remained in power, his charisma in Arab eyes enormously enhanced; the Americans expressed genuine outrage and backed it with monetary threats which would have seriously destabilised the pound; and even before our troops had begun to withdraw, the shaming details of our collusion were emerging. The prime minister, Anthony Eden, resigned on the grounds of ill health, and Harold Macmillan, who had been a hothead at the start but, as soon as he saw that the thing wasn't going to work, contrived to present himself as a moderating influence, took over.

In parallel with all this, the Hungarian uprising against hard-line communism and Russian hegemony was taking place, and the Russians were able to use our invasion of Egypt both as cover and excuse for sending in the tanks to crush the dissidents. They would presumably have done this anyway, but the Western powers were in no position to object to their bully-boy tactics.

That is a very crude outline. The conversation in the Yellow Room took place some three months before the nationalisation of the canal, but several months after an arms deal between Egypt and Czechoslovakia by which Nasser had signalled his refusal to become wholly the creature of the West.)

"It depends what you mean by a windbag," I said. "He's certainly more than that in Arab eyes."

"A windbag is one whose threats and promises are without substance," said Seddon.

"I.e., what will the beggar do, if anything?" said Michael. "Attack Israel?"

"Not if he can help it," I said.

"Why not?" said Michael. "It would be pretty popular with your average wog-in-the-street, wouldn't it?"

"The idea might be popular. But Nasser is a soldier. He probably has a better idea than most politicians of how the Egyptian army would match up against the Israelis."

"Are these your own notions?" said Seddon. "Or are they direct from your friends?"

"Notions, hell," said Michael. "There's the whole bloody FO mentality pregnant in a single word. When was the FO last right about anything, tell me?"

He managed to combine geniality with considerable aggression, but Seddon smiled, unruffled. I had in fact discussed all this with my Armenian's husband during their visit. Though he was by no means a natural Nasserite and was scornful of the possibilities of Pan-Arabism, he was on the whole sympathetic to Nasser himself, but I had no reason to tell either Seddon or Michael anything at all about what he said or thought. Michael saved me the trouble of prevaricating.

"A revolution's like a bicycle," he said. "If you don't keep it moving, you fall off."

"The Aswan Dam will keep him going for a couple of years," I said. "Provided we've got the sense to give him a bit of slack."

"Slack?" said Seddon. "He's a pretty slippery customer."

I was starting to say that so were we, no doubt, when Michael broke in.

"That's all balls," he said. "We aren't going to give the bugger the slack, because Eden's going to lose his rag with him and try and smash him direct. He'll cook something up with the French and find an excuse and wade in. What's more, he won't tell the Yanks, and they aren't going to like it. Neither Eisenhower nor Dulles can stand him, I gather. They'll jump at the chance to slap his little wrist and send him blubbing home to Nanny."

This was typical of his style, both the brutal interruption and the coarse forcefulness of his views, which, however, seemed to me sensible and based on good information. And his bullying tone was largely mitigated by his manner of listening, with intelligence and attention, which seemed somehow to licence him to cut one short. He and Seddon continued for a while to discuss the question, or rather, two questions: whether the Americans would not be secretly glad of Nasser being brought to heel; and what, if they didn't like it, they could do about it.

Gerry, meanwhile, said nothing at all. He seemed to have gone into a doze over his brandy until, to my relief, he rose, put his almost untouched glass on the table, and stretched.

He had thickened out, I saw. He must have weighed at least a couple of stone more than he used to, but he still gave that impression of lightness on his feet that I remembered.

"I need some air," he said. "Come and see what I've been doing in the garden, Paul."

"I haven't got any clothes."

"I'll find you some gumboots and a mac. We're not going through brambles. Thanks for the brandy, Michael."

We had no need to reinvolve ourselves with the other guests as the Gun Room lay immediately below King William's Room. It did, rather surprisingly, contain guns, a couple of twelve-bores, a .22, and an air rifle at one end of the huge rack, which had once housed the sporting weapons of the previous lord, the best of which had been sold before the war, and the remainder given to the Home Guard. Now the room was a sort of utility room for outdoor activities, containing tennis rackets, croquet sets, old hockey sticks, and of course cricketing gear, trugs of handtools for Lady Vereker's sporadic gardening forays, a shelf of nostrums for horses (I remember Lucy saying there was one labelled "Old Gipsy's Gall-poultice—doesn't work"), and saws, bill hooks, hatchets, and paraffin for the Verekers' main winter activity, bonfires. Lord Vereker's gumboots were the only ones that fitted me. I felt reluctant, but Gerry laughed and told me to put them on. He found me a macintosh and waterproof hat and we tramped out into the drizzle.

There was little at Blatchards of what most people would consider a garden, no more than a few dreary beds around the house. But out beyond the stable block (prettier, and more sensibly arranged, than the house itself) there was a biggish area of woodland and open spaces, with three small lakes, and paths winding around. Gerry showed me a vista he'd had cut through a wood, and a slope down to one of the lakes where he was clearing out a jungle of old rhododendrons, revetting the bank and replanting with more desirable varieties, I don't remember what—my passion for gardening had not yet struck, and anyway, living as I do on chalky soil has let me off having to cope with the whole azalea family, I'm happy to say.

I was really much more interested in Gerry himself. Inside the house he had not made much impression, apart from his brief response to Nancy. Perhaps he had been cramped by Michael's presence. At any rate he now seemed to expand, to move and breathe freely, and to be actively excited, despite the dismal day, by his plans. I had never seen him like this before. He had always seemed to me to think of himself as somehow futureless, to have come from nowhere and to be going nowhere, and so to rely on his extraordinary speed of reaction to take advantage of whatever the instant might hold. Now he was actually talking about both past and future with relish.

"*This*," he said, waving at the fresh-cut vista, "was actually suggested by Repton. He never did a Red Book for us, I'm sorry to say, because he realised pretty early that Lord Vereker—the second baron—was going to jib at the fees. But a sketch exists, and I've a reasonable idea of what else he might have done. What I'd really like is a cascade, but Suffolk's so bloody flat. My finances are not yet in a state where I can afford to move mountains."

I had been struck by the "us" for whom Repton hadn't done the Red Book. Now he seemed to be inviting me to enquire further.

"You seem to have progressed beyond the molehill stage," I said.

"Not enough, not enough. Nan, or rather Dick Felder, takes care of the house, and I do the grounds. Between the three of us we get by. I imagine you're aware of why we are unable to marry—it seems to be common knowledge."

"Harriet told me."

"I never met Felder. He sounds not a bad chap, but naturally I'd rather not be living on his bounty."

"I doubt if he notices."

"Hitherto that has been the case. Have you heard about this molybdenum thing?"

"Is he in that?"

"Apparently his resources are behind it. His current father-in-law, who is the third to hold that office, has got him to back a scheme to corner the market. Felder is so used to thinking of himself as infinitely rich that he can't recognize that there are some things beyond even his resources."

"It must be illegal, surely."

"Arguably not, as they've set it up. But according to Michael it's not going to work, and before that happens, they're going to try to make it work by shovelling in a lot more money, money that even Felder hasn't got. And then he's going to go broke."

"Actually broke?"

"Well, millionaire broke. He may still have a couple of yachts to rub together, provided he decides to cut his losses in time."

"Will this affect Nancy?"

"Shouldn't do. Her settlement is in trust. Michael's looking into it for us."

"He appears to have his ear to the ground."

Gerry laughed.

"Michael?" he said. "He is Argus eared. He has a limitless appetite for knowledge, and capacity for acquiring it. You remember how secretive old Chad is about his domain—only the initiated priest may be admitted to the central mysteries of the boiler room and the gas plant and the ram? Last time Michael stayed, Chad took him round and showed him everything. And before old Seddon went gaga, he used to sit swapping ancient cricket records with him. He doesn't drive, and he never bothers with a train timetable. He looks through each year's *Bradshaw*, checks on the changes, and that's it."

We had by this time reached the edge of the Blatchards

grounds, a rusty iron gate in what had once been a five-foot wall but was now in a semiruinous state, though I could see its line extending out of sight on either side between the woodland and the fields of the Home Farm.

"That would take some building these days," I said.

"It's three-and-a-half miles long," said Gerry. "Parts of it are not too bad. It goes the whole way round. A sort of curate's eggshell, you might say. Anyway, it's going to have to wait."

"Are you going to have a problem with death duties?"

"Like the wall—parts of it are not too bad. That's to say the old boy made some provisions in good time, and some not. We could have done with him lasting another couple of years. I haven't done the sums yet, but I think we should just about manage. How are things with you?"

Since he had been so open about his affairs, I explained about mine. I had in fact been extremely busy, and looked like being more so. Companies, like most human organisations, are only to a limited extent controllable, and though I still then wholly owned mine and could in theory do what I liked with it, in practice it had its own momentum, which I did my best to guide. For the past year, after a difficult patch, we had been expanding, and we were now at a stage where I knew it was impossible not to expand further, so I was in the process of transforming what had hitherto been a private concern into a public company. I had already been barely able to cope with my work load, and the next few months looked like being a very severe strain. Luckily, having no personal commitments, I could work as many hours as I could stay awake. Lord Vereker's funeral was my first social engagement for weeks.

"Sounds as if you could do with a break," said Gerry. "You can live only so long at that kind of stretch. Do you remember that evening in Cairo, in your flat? I was thinking about it only the other day. It came to me out of nowhere, for no reason, vivid but somehow detached. . . ."

"My whole war now seems a bit like that."

"Yes. In my case it was also an episode outside what I was then doing, so I'm seeing it through a double lens, so to speak. Do you miss that time?"

"Not at all. I had a very comfortable war by most people's standards, but it doesn't belong. It's like a chapter that the printers have managed to bind into the wrong book."

"I don't know when I shall ever feel as alive as I did at times in the mountains."

"I think I can imagine that. Have you kept up with any of those people?"

He stopped and looked around. We were coming back by a different route and had reached what seemed to me a nondescript bit of scrubby woodland. The path was squelchingly muddy at this point.

"The south lake's about there," he said, pointing. "I think there's a spring somewhere under here. The question is, if I opened it up a bit so that you could see through, would I get a pleasing rill, or a stinking bog?"

"A bog's more likely on this soil, I'd have thought. Can we keep going? I promised to take the cousins back before dark, and Lucy left a message for me not to go till I'd seen her."

He grunted and moved on. The path narrowed to single file, so we walked for a while in silence. I don't think it's hindsight to say that I felt uneasy. There was something about Gerry's manner, about his apparently relaxed affability, that seemed forced, calculated. There are some lines of Patric Dickinson about Coleridge, and how his path inevitably lay downward from the clear heights of his early achievement:

> For he was water, though the rock compel
> And shape that first fantastic falling glory.

Gerry as a boy and young man had had something of that. Now he seemed to me more like the cascade he said he wanted for the garden, for which, hidden somewhere, there would have had to be a pump to force the water up to the height from which it would then descend over the landscaped boulders. Perhaps it was the association with Michael Allwegg, perhaps the process of money making for money making's sake, perhaps even the letdown of achieving his heart's desire (and then what?), but I found to my disappointment that I was not actually liking him as much as I used to.

As we came abreast he said, "According to Nan things are a bit sticky between Lucy and Seddon at the moment."

"Oh?"

"That's all I know."

"Thanks for the warning. Apparently she's not feeling too well and went to lie down."

"That's a way of putting it. In fact she went off to her old room in a huff with Ben for being so uppity about her engagement to Michael. Lucy didn't know. Ben arrived only late last night and told us the news at breakfast, and Lucy came direct to the church from Seddon Hall. There'd been a bit of palaver at breakfast about whether Ben should wear the ring. She hadn't intended to of course, but Lady V. got one of her bees in her bonnet and insisted that Lord V. would have wanted her to, but Lucy wasn't appeased."

"I think she may have minded about Lord Vereker more than the others."

"Very likely. What do you make of Michael?"

"You tell me. I hardly know him."

"I'm prejudiced. I suppose I'd have found something to do if he hadn't taken me on, but I can't think what. Schoolmaster? But it's he in a way who's made all this possible. He wasn't at Eton, but if he had been, you'd barely have noticed him. He got a third at Cambridge—wasn't interested in doing any better. If he'd tried he might have scraped a two-point-one. He's not got that sort of brain. But in other ways I should think he's the cleverest chap I've ever met. He's brilliant at people, for a start. He seems to know exactly what they'll stand, what'll make them jib or go along. He can work twenty hours a day, but he never seems stressed or stretched. Suppose you gave us each a complex report to read and then examined us on what was in it, I'd score a good deal higher than Michael on the details, but when it came to the inner significance of the report, and how it related to other information we'd learnt in the last few months, he'd come up with aspects that even the examiners hadn't thought of."

"I wouldn't have thought he was very easy to work with."

"Not too bad, provided you can put up with the occasional tantrum. He's got a remarkable head, don't you think? I keep half-remembering some portrait I've seen—in the Louvre, was it?—Renaissance, anyway. Should be Mantegna but isn't. An unknown gentleman. One of those petty warlords, many sided, dangerous to cross, as straightforward in their aims as they were subtle in their dealings."

"What were their aims?"

"Power, of course."

He laughed and lengthened his stride. We found Lucy and Harriet under the porte-cochère, waving good-bye to a car. As it crunched away across the gravel, Lucy turned to me, not looking at Gerry.

"Where have you been?" she said. "I thought you'd run away."

"Walking the wet woods," I said. "I hope you're feeling better."

"I'm fine. How long can you stay?"

"I have to get your cousins back to Hampstead in time to watch Voss-Thompson perform this evening."

"Don't tell me Ivy and Bella have a set!" said Harriet. "I'd have thought they were far too high-minded."

"I bet they sneak round and watch the neighbours'," said Lucy. "We must meet soon, Paul. It's been far too long. Have you got your diary? I'd better warn you, I'm determined to learn to cook."

"Breaking the habit of a lifetime?"

"Now that Father's dead, I don't feel so threatened. Hang on a mo'. . . ."

Between further farewells we managed to fix a date. It is astonishing how calmly one can conduct oneself under such circumstances. I had a physical sensation as of a force field surrounding me, and another her, not so powerful that we couldn't have broken through and touched, but making that a definite, willed decision, with consequences too serious to risk. The feeling was very unpleasant. Meanwhile the departing guests stood around under the porte-cochère waiting for whoever was driving to fetch their car into its shelter. Curtains of raindrops dripped from its roof onto the gravel. Most of Lucy's evenings were taken up with Seddon's official engagements, and her free ones didn't coincide with mine. In the end I agreed to take time off from work and come to lunch. As we finished and I moved towards the door to look for the cousins, my eye caught Gerry's. He had remained outside, as a kind of honorary host, assisting the farewells. He raised a friendly hand, not actually a thumbs-up gesture, but suggesting one.

Because she couldn't easily oust the cook from the kitchen in Seddon's town house in Eaton Square, Lucy borrowed a flat from a friend. She had prepared a three-course meal, soup, chicken ragout, and apple pie. The soup wasn't bad, but the chicken was too salty to swallow. She looked across the table at me, puckering her brow in mock distress, and then I saw that she was genuinely weeping. We rose. I came round the table. The force fields, barely noticeable on my arrival but establishing themselves at full strength by the time we'd sat down, dissolved.

When we were eating the apple pie, somewhere around half past four, she sighed and said, "I want you to know that I've tried to be faithful. I really have tried."

Lucy

SIX

1949–56

Now I've got a gap to fill. Heavens, it must be seven years! A
mass of things happened, but not a lot that matters anymore—
in fact some of it seems just as dreamy and unreal as the war.
I spent the first half of it being a fashion model. Even now, if
you asked people about that time and what it was like, anyone
who was at all interested in clothes would mention the New
Look, of course, but what they'd actually think about is me. I
was *the* face. I was on the cover of *Vogue* or *Harpers* every other
month, looking untouchably cool and classy in front of the Eif-
fel Tower or Mount Etna or somewhere. It meant I made more
money than I'd ever dreamed of, all for myself. I didn't know
what to do with it, so I spent it having fun in obvious ways.
In fact I went pretty wild for a bit, or at least I tried to. I mean
I kept looking for wildness and not getting there, somehow.
I'm not going to go into details. You can imagine them if you
want to, but just remember this wasn't now. It was the late
forties, a cold, hard time with the war supposed to be over but
all the boring things we'd put up with because of the war still
going on, rationing and shortages and not being allowed to
take any money when you went abroad, and so on. And it was
like that the way people behaved. Things you'd hardly bother
to put in a letter now made newspaper headlines then.

Anyway rackety life didn't suit me and it was bad for my skin, so I settled down a bit. Among other things I began going home more often. Sometime around then, Father finally bit the bullet and handed the main house over to Nan and moved back into the Stables and settled down to try and live for another seven years so there wouldn't be any death duties, but Mother had managed to make the spare room at the Stables so uncomfortable that I almost always slept at the house, in my old room looking out over the park. Nan had divorced Dick Felder by now and come back to live at Blatchards full-time, and it wasn't long before Gerry moved in with her.

It's surprising how little I minded about this. I had the odd sick twinge, just to remind me, like an illness you know might come back one day, but I don't suppose that happened more than two or three times altogether. Actually I didn't see that much of him. He was often away, and I usually ate at the Stables because Father was miffed if I didn't, and so on. Besides that . . . oh, it happens to us all. When you're young, the people you care about seem extraordinary, vivid, different from anyone else, and that's how you go on seeing them, long after they've stopped being like that, if they ever were. And then, when you're quite old, you realise they're mostly pretty ordinary, and some of them are dreadful bores, and what's more they've been that way for years only you hadn't noticed. We were all so used to Gerry being amazing that we still thought of him like that. The trouble was, there wasn't anything for him to be amazing about any longer, so he wasn't really. And I think he knew.

I talked to Paul about this right at the beginning, after that morning in the garden, before we started doing it this way. Paul's idea is that Gerry never knew what he was for, why he'd got all these gifts, and he needed a why, so he chose Blatchards. Only he got it wrong. He thought it was the house, but it wasn't. It was us, our silly family which mattered so much to us. That was what he wanted. I knew Gerry didn't have a family, but I never realised what an utter orphan he was until Paul told me. I suppose that might explain something, in a clockworky kind of way. I don't know.

Then of course there was Nan, who was always a tremendous tough. Partly she was made that way, I suppose, and partly she'd had to learn to stand up to Mother's nonsenses and protect the rest of us from them. Gerry liked acting as if he was master of Blatchards, and Nan went along with him in public, but she wouldn't let him touch anything in the house except the two upstairs rooms in the East Wing, the Yellow Room and King William's Room. Those were Gerry's domain. All the rest of it was hers. That's why he started taking such an interest in the garden, because she let him do pretty well what he liked there, and she wasn't interested. They were a funny couple, come to think of it. I never caught them being lovey-dovey with each other when they thought they were alone. They were like two actors acting a relationship because they need each other—Ginger Rogers and Fred Astaire, for instance—and can put it over like nobody's business when they're on show, but aren't even friends in their private lives.

Anyway I didn't mean to go into all that. What I was trying to say was that I didn't mind Gerry living at Blatchards. I didn't think about it then, but now I suppose that by then I knew in my heart of hearts I didn't actually want Gerry—all I wanted was a sort of *idea* of him—so it suited me having him around but obviously belonging to Nan. He was different. I mean, I usually had a man of some sort or other in my life. I was never any good at living like a nun. In fact I find myself rather boring, alone. I like somebody to be with. I don't mean just to sleep with, though that's important (if ever I start a religion of my own, I'll make Dora a saint), but to talk to and do things with and grouse at. Society, help, and comfort, like the marriage service says, only you don't have to be married to get them. You've still got to work at getting it right, though. Not just a couple of weeks and stop—even if you know they're not going to last forever, they're still commitments, and one of the most important things is to learn to call them off as soon as you realise they're not going to work, before anyone gets hurt. Well, hurt more than you can help.

That happened to me with David Fish. Biddy Trollope had invited a party for Ascot, and David was one of them, looking more Beanoish than ever in a grey topper and tails. He'd never been to the races before, so we had to show him the ropes, and he got terribly interested in the mathematics the bookies used to fix the odds. On the second day he told us he'd thought of a betting system, so we each chipped in a fiver and took turns to put the bets on so the bookies wouldn't realise it was the same person, and by the end of the day we'd turned fifty-five pounds into six hundred and something. It was raining, but we didn't mind. We stood under the awning of a tent, all absolutely hysterical, while people went squelching about outside, telling each other we'd never have to work again. The only person who wasn't happy was Beano. He'd got all the money in his hands, in pound notes, and he was just staring at it and shaking his head.

"It's far too much," he explained. "There must be a flaw in my assumptions. Ah, well, back to the drawing board."

And he hunched even further down into his tailcoat and began peering round as if he was looking for a litter bin to put the money in, and then looking sheepish and surprised at the way we were falling about. Even Biddy Trollope, who'd inherited half a county as well as several coal fields and shipyards and so on, and always behaved as if money came out of the air, was more interested in our winnings than Beano was. She slapped him on the back and said, "Well, if you can't think what to do with it, David, we'll all go out to dinner and cook can have the night off." We finished up dancing at Hatchett's at 4:00 A.M. and I took David home. The trouble was this time he fell in love with me.

At least he thought he did. I made the mistake of assuming because of what had happened at Halford Hall, he'd realise this was meant to be another time like that (it never is) and I didn't spell things out to him as much as I should have. I simply had no idea anyone could be so naïve as he still was. He was living in digs somewhere up by Euston, and Biddy had run across him in a train going north and got talking and asked him to Ascot because she needed a spare man. He'd hired his topper and tails. He had a pretty good job—something complicated to do with foreign currency and how you get round the rules without breaking the law, which was what everyone was trying to do those days—so he was earning plenty of money and he couldn't think of anything to spend it on, which was why he was travelling first-class, which was why Biddy had assumed he was the sort of type she could invite to Ascot, but that was all. There wasn't anything else about him. I mean that. Nothing. Having him around was like having a gawky great dog, which doesn't have any interests in life apart from meals and walks and sitting by your chair with its head on your knees and gazing adoringly at you and drooling. I stood it for a couple of weeks and then I sat him down one evening and talked to him like a grandmother and told him why it wasn't any good. I'm afraid all my friends probably heaved a sigh of relief.

I suppose I've got to say something about Michael Allwegg. I'd known him vaguely for a bit, because he'd been at Winchester with Tommy Seddon and Tommy was a neighbour. He was in the Rest-of-the-World team for Harriet's engagement party, but I'd hardly talked to him then. About 1950, I should think, Tommy had a dinner party before the Hunt Ball, and I sat next to Michael. (Old Lord Seddon was still alive, but he'd gone gaga and was living in the West Wing with a couple of nurses to look after him. He was still perfectly spry, but he kept trying to escape to open the batting for England in the Oval Test.)

The first thing anyone says about Michael—anyone who's met him, I mean—is that he was the ugliest man they ever saw, and the next breath they'll tell you how attractive he was. I once asked him about it. He'd just got up and was wandering round the room, stark naked, scratching like a chimpanzee. He was a very hairy man, but the hair was in strange places, tangled and wiry across his chest and down his legs, but then shorter and almost as thick as a dog's pelt around his crotch and up on either side of his paunch, which was bald. And there was an extraordinary patch like the ace of spades below the small of his back, with the stem running down into the cleavage between his buttocks. His skin was a nasty suety white, like dumplings. He drank a fair bit, smoked at least ten cigars a day, and ate incredible amounts. He always ordered a double helping of anything in restaurants, and often when the meal was over and everyone was drinking their coffee, he'd send for another steak. (Yes, that was still against the rationing laws then, but Michael knew places where he could do it.) He didn't like being fat, so he did exercises, but he still managed to look flabby.

Anyway there he was, shambling round my bedroom, grunting and scratching his armpits. I'd just woken up.

"If your skin wasn't so horrid white you'd look like an ape in the zoo," I said. "What on earth do people see in you?"

I expect I was cross with him about something. I usually was. He was the sort who likes to push you right to the edge and see whether you'll come back, and for a bit you do, even though you know quite well what's going on. He stopped in front of my long mirror and stood there, looking at his reflection as if it was a statue in a museum. Then he laughed, really pleased with himself.

"I am an ape," he said, "and so are you. The challenge is to evoke our primitive nature."

I've run on a bit, but not much. I was going to bed with him a week after the Hunt Ball, and that lasted several months.

He never told me anything about his work. He usually slept
at my flat and complained how poky it was. He had a flat of
his own, one large plain room, with a bit of cheap furniture,
up above a bookshop in the Charing Cross Road, but I knew
he must have somewhere else to live because he had a lot of
good clothes and he didn't keep much there. We nearly always
ate at restaurants or dined with friends. He loved ballet. I
think we saw every new production, some of them two or three
times. Some opera, a few plays, no films.

There's no getting away from it, Michael was a complete
bastard. That's something else everyone will tell you. I've
thought about this a lot, because having an affair with him is
one of the few things I'm really ashamed of in my whole life.
I think I knew from the very first that I was doing something
wrong. The easy way out is to say that I couldn't help myself,
but that's not true. Of course I could. I'd got pretty good at
saying no. It isn't anything to do with looks, or not much,
but some men have something about them that gives you an
impulse to say yes, in spite of yourself, but unless you're
practically feebleminded you don't give in to it. Michael had
as much of that as any man I've ever met, but it still doesn't
explain his effect on people.

I'm not just talking about sex. This is men as well as women.
People actually seemed to want to give in to him. I think he
was right about it being something primitive. He was like one
of those African kings you read about (I never know whether
this sort of story is true) who thought they could feed their
own soul power by eating their enemies' hearts. He turned
people into things he could use, and we let him. Why? I am
not just a piece of decoration with no mind of her own, but
that's how he sometimes treated me. And I let him.

The first time I really understood about this was an extraordinary party Michael took me to, somewhere out in the East
End in a kind of hall like a dreary old barn outside but decorated like a palace in a pantomime inside, and everything lavish

as all get-out, masses of food, lashings of scotch and champagne, long dresses (I never saw so many sequins), dinner
jackets, a twelve-piece band playing jazz and smooch-music,
but everything just a little bit wrong, a bit in the way Holly-
wood high-life films are, but different from those, too. For
instance, the champagne was sweet. Most of the dinner jackets
had padded shoulders and immense lapels. A lot of the women
had orchises sort of appliquéd to them somewhere or other,
and makeup an inch thick, and hair done into enormous con-
structions, which they kept patting. And they had huge busts
with bras that made them stick out like mantelpieces (very
convenient for the orchises). And they were property. They
belonged to the men, who were mostly older than they were,
and short and square and blue chinned and dangerous looking.
They treated me as if I belonged to Michael, and so did he.
He'd brought me there to show them that he'd got a bit of
property just as good as any of theirs.

I danced with some of the men. They held me close against
them, but they were pretty good, and the band was terrific.
One of the men asked me how long I'd known Michael. I said
off and on for years. He said (I can't do the accent), "He's a
good boy. Fine lawyer. Done well for my nephew, well as
anyone could of, in the circs. Just so long as he doesn't get too
clever. You can tell him that, from me."

I did, on the way home, and Michael laughed. He was
pleased.

"Was all that food and drink black market?" I said.

"What do you think?" he said.

Sorry, I've gone astray. It was this business of belonging,
of being a piece of property he could do what he liked with—
why did we put up with it?

Of course he could be charming—I've said that. It got him
off to a good start with people. But it wasn't ordinary charm.
You felt that at once. There was something dangerous about
it, like a purring tiger. He liked talking, and he was really

interesting because he seemed to know such a lot, especially about what was going on, the real underneath reasons of things, money of course, but politics too, and arty things. He gobbled books, the way he ate. He used to lie in my bath with the hot water trickling in to keep it scalding and read a whole novel in an hour, and get out and know what he thought about it by the time he'd towelled himself down. He was interesting in another way too, in himself, I mean. You felt that there was a lot to find out about him but you'd have to be very careful doing the finding.

He threw money about because he liked looking generous, but he could be really mean as well. It all depended on whether he thought meanness or generosity would get him what he wanted, which was usually getting someone else to do something they'd have preferred not to. One time he told me he was tired of my wardrobe and I must get myself everything new. I told him he'd have to pay for it because I was saving up to buy myself a TR2. (He knew this already.)

He said, "Don't be stupid. Just put the bills in the wastepaper basket. There's plenty of dressmakers who'd pay to be able to tell people you're wearing their stuff."

"That's why I won't let them," I said.

I remember how he looked at me. I knew I was digging my heels in and this was something he couldn't make me do. He knew too. And the very next week my agent told me that a series of advertisements for one of the new synthetics had been cancelled. I'd rather been counting on them. They would have been the final dollop of money for the TR. My agent was very angry about it. She said the reasons she'd been told didn't make sense. It just happened that I knew a girl at the advertising agency well enough to ring her up at home and ask her if she knew anything, and she nosed around and rang back and told me that one of the directors had suddenly descended on them, though he hadn't got anything at all to do with that account, and said his wife was tired of my face. This was even more baffling, because I'd actually met the woman at the ballet one evening. Michael had introduced me to her. It was a new ballet company and he was on the board, and so was she. She was a vague-looking fluty-arty old girl, and I thought she'd hardly noticed me because she was so busy loving the way Michael was buttering her up.

At first I thought she must simply have taken against me then, for some reason, but then, well, I'd told Michael about the ads being cancelled and he'd pretended not to be interested, which was usual, but when I told him about the director's wife, I must have caught him by surprise, because just for a flicker of a half-second, he gave me a furious look before he said, "What balls. The man's a shit. He's just making excuses. He probably wants you for himself. I'll ask her about it." And then he was specially nice to me for the rest of the evening.

I still don't know whether he'd fixed the whole thing up to punish me for not doing what he wanted about my clothes, but I think so now. I didn't at first. I suppose I couldn't imagine anyone being that mean, but you live and learn. But even then the whole business of him trying to make me get my dresses without paying for them was one of the things (the women at that party had been another) that were making me feel I'd better stop seeing him, if I could find a way how. That sounds stupid, but to be honest, I was afraid of him. I wonder whether he had actually guessed I wanted to stop, because of the way he behaved when Tommy Seddon proposed.

Before I go on with that, I'd better admit—though you've probably guessed by now—that all this was the reason why I behaved so badly at Father's funeral. That's another thing I'm really ashamed of, or rather it's part of the same thing. It wasn't even that I knew Ben was making a terrible mistake and I couldn't tell her. I'm afraid the fact is I was jealous of her, not just that she was taking on one of my old lovers, and he'd actually proposed to her, which he never had to me, though there was all that. But what I was really afraid of in my heart of hearts was that she'd be able to cope with him, understand him, not just what he was up to but what he was really like inside. She'd be the one who opened the Bluebeard door and got away with it. Anyone else and I'd have been cheering them on, but not Ben.

Well, Tommy proposed. By letter, typically. Old Lord Seddon was dead now. They found him on the West Terrace with his neck broken. He must have been climbing out to try and get to the Oval for his Test Match, though there was snow on the ground. So Tommy was in the House of Lords making speeches about foreign affairs, and everyone was saying he was a coming man. The proposal came out of the blue, though I'd been seeing a fair bit of him, because Michael and he were rather cronies (though you wouldn't have thought they'd got a bit in common, but Michael was like that, and so, I found out later, was Tommy), but he'd given no sign.

When the post came, Michael was on his rowing machine. This was a wooden affair with enormous creaking springs, which he'd insisted on bringing to my flat, where it took up most of the spare bedroom. The letter came in a lovely thick House of Lords envelope, so I picked it up off the doormat and opened it in the passage to see what it was, and laughed aloud.

The creaking and puffing stopped.

"What's up?" said Michael.

"Tommy Seddon's asked me to marry him," I said.

He rowed a few more strokes and stopped again.

"Not a bad idea," he said. "He needs a wife. You'd fit the bill."

"What about me, for heaven's sake!" I said.

"What were you proposing to do with yourself," he said, "wait till you fall in love with someone?"

"That sort of thing," I said.

"Indeed?" he said.

No, he didn't say it, he sneered it, a real lawyer's sneer, the sort that's supposed to make witnesses stammer and contradict themselves. He went on rowing. I read the letter again.

It was rather charming, old-fashioned without being pompous. He didn't say he loved me. I approved of that.

"You actually want me to marry Tommy Seddon?" I said.

"Nothing to do with me," he said.

"If I marry anyone, I'm going to be faithful to them," I said.

"I'm delighted to hear it," he said.

I only just stopped myself from saying something about him being tired of me, which was the sort of barmaidish kind of thing you found yourself saying, almost as if he made you so that he could despise you for it. That's what he wanted, I'm pretty sure, to despise me, and I didn't quite let him. Anyway, he got off his rowing machine and came and stood over me. I knew he wasn't going to hit me—it would have been almost a relief if he had—but it was still difficult not to feel frightened.

"I've told you it's nothing to do with me," he said. "But since you seem to want my opinion, I think you would be extremely stupid not to marry Tommy Seddon. You would be as happy married to him as you would to anyone else. Your style of looks will go out of fashion in a year or two. As Tommy's wife you would have a reasonable certainty of being comfortable."

"I'd have to tell him about you," I said.

"He knows," he said.

Then he went and sponged himself off with cold water and got dressed. I was running my bath, so I didn't hear him leave. When I got back from work that evening, I found his rowing machine and everything else of his gone, and his key on the mat. (I bet he'd had a spare cut, though, before he gave it back.)

I didn't answer Tommy's letter at once. After a few days he telephoned me. I told him I'd been very surprised, and I still didn't know what to say. He asked me to dinner at his club, which was the Athenaeum. I made no bones about how unsuitable I thought I was, and the sort of life I'd been living, though I didn't mention anyone by name. He just said, "I was aware of that. I thought perhaps you might like to settle down."

I told him I'd think about it. We went to a play or two. Our dinners together got less stiff. I heard him speak in the House of Lords, about China. He was extremely good. He showed me his house in Eaton Square, and I went over from Blatchards and spent a whole day (and it took a whole day!) going round Seddon Hall. Outside the absurd downstairs rooms, it was a surprisingly friendly-feeling house, full of ingenious convenient Victorian arrangements. Perhaps it was that that made me say yes. I made him come to bed with me before we announced the engagement, which he disapproved of. He'd never done it before, believe it or not, but we just about managed, and I thought I could teach him. It's funny how easy it is to make that mistake.

The other snag was that Tommy was a Catholic. Apparently the Seddons always were, right back to the Reformation, but they didn't make a fuss about it; in fact old Lord Seddon's real religion was cricket, and most of the time it seemed as if Tommy's was foreign affairs, but deep down inside he'd got sticking points. I was the usual automatic C of E—if I'd really bothered to think about it ever, I wouldn't have believed it— and I suppose Tommy thought it wouldn't be much of an effort for me to switch over to the same sort of automatic RC one day, but all we'd agreed at the time was that though we couldn't have a full-dress Catholic wedding because of me not being one, so in the eyes of the church we weren't really married, in his eyes we still were and he wasn't going to divorce me if things went wrong, but he wouldn't hold me to that—though of course I said "Sauce for the goose" and made the same promise.

So we got married in our church and had a terrific society

wedding from Blatchards (which Tommy paid for most of, though we let everyone think it was all Father), and we settled down and things went rather well for a bit. I got pregnant twice and had a daughter and a son. I'm afraid I was never very interested in them when they were children, but Mother was besotted on them so they spent a lot of time at Blatchards, and Harriet found a jolly nanny for them, who they soon loved much better than me, and quite right too. Years later Rowena told me she used to pray that I'd die of something quick and painless so that Tommy could marry Nanny and they could be a proper family. Actually that might have worked very well.

Paul's unfair to Tommy. He was a really nice man, completely honourable and always fair to me. There've only been two men in my life I felt I could totally trust. Paul's one and Tommy was the other. What happened a few years later was a kind of madness, coming out from deep inside him, from long ago, probably before he could remember. I sometimes think that if I'd been able to love him, it mightn't have happened, but I couldn't, and that was my fault. I've never loved anyone, not like that, except possibly Father. I don't know how. It's a bit like religion. You go to church and you go to church and nothing happens, so you read books about Christ's love for us all and how marvellous it is when you feel it, and you try again and still nothing happens. And then you give up.

Anyway Tommy wasn't like Paul says, and not like the Vicky cartoons, either. I really hated them, because at home he was friendly and funny and not at all pompous. He was good with the children, especially when they were small, and really delighted to have an heir, but for some reason he found the whole business of pregnancy terribly disturbing, and second time round he stopped wanting to come to bed with me. That went on after Timmy was born, but it took me a bit of time to realise he was having to grit his teeth before he could touch me. The Conservatives had won a general election, and

Churchill was PM and Tommy was Lord Seneschal, which is one of those weird leftover offices from the days when kings had proper courts. He didn't have any seneschalling to do, whatever that is, and the only thing I remember about that side of it is that if he visited Warwick, all the church bells had to be rung and the mayor had to present him with a pair of satin slippers (we got them made my size, of course). The real point was that he was a government minister, part of the Foreign Office team, and among other things helped look after FO business in the House of Lords, so he was usually late enough home to have an excuse for sleeping in his dressing room.

Paul

SEVEN

Spring 1956

One of the still continuing tedia of having been involved in the so-called Seddon Affair is the reaction of strangers as soon as they make the connection. Two questions invariably pass through their minds: Did I meet Sammy Whitstable? Was I one of those who made use of her services? Few people in fact bring themselves to the point of asking either question, but I don't think I'm being oversensitive. I am sure that had I been one of these outsiders, I would feel the same curiosity. Notoriety has that effect. It is only human to wish to know how far reality coincides with myth.

The answers in my case are (1) barely, (2) no. I was, however, involved in other ways. Soon after Lord Vereker's funeral, and before my lunch with Lucy, Gerry telephoned. We chatted briefly and then he said, "Look, I don't like doing this, but I'm in a minor fix. If you can't help, or don't want to, which is much the same thing in this case, forget it. That job you did in Cairo, nursemaiding people like me, finding us things to do in the evenings . . ."

"Yes?"

"I take it there were some who demanded rather more exotic entertainment than I did. . . . I'm sorry, old man . . . you may find this deeply unpleasant."

Old man? I suppressed my amusement with a snort, which he misinterpreted. It was somehow typical of him to be so out of his depth in this kind of thing that his embarrassment should result in such false notes. Not that he didn't have cause for embarrassment. As he'd suggested, I might well have told him bluntly that I couldn't help him, but as it happened, there was a wartime acquaintance with whom I'd had to get in touch a few months earlier, for the benefit of an unpleasant Dutchman whose help I needed.

"It's all right," I said. "I know how you feel. One gets stuck with these things. What does the fellow want? Male or female? Not straightforward, I take it?"

"Yes, that's about it. Female."

"Money no object?"

"Not much. I don't know what the limit might be."

"The equivalent of shopping at Harrods, say?"

"That should do."

"Try a woman called Isobel Mudge. You'll think you've got a wrong number—she has one of those Dresden shepherdess voices and a remarkable command of euphemisms, but she keeps her side of a bargain. Incidentally, you'd better keep yours—she's got some pretty tough friends. Tell her Mr. Charles put you on to her. If she can't help, I don't know anyone else."

I gave him the number and he started to thank me.

"Forget it," I said. "These things happen. Incidentally, why did you need to come to me? I'd have thought in the course of your work with Michael . . ."

"I don't want to involve Michael," he said quickly. "But thanks. I'll pay you back someday, somehow."

"You can get me a ticket for the Saturday of the Lord's Test. They've made a cock-up over mine."

"Do my best."

I barely thought about it again, being almost at once taken up with renewing my affair with Lucy. A clandestine relationship, such as ours now needed to be, is much more energy-consuming than a publicly acknowledged one. The expansion of my company, leading to the flotation to which I've already referred, had involved my acquisition of two related businesses when I could only comfortably assimilate one, but I had been forced to take on both or miss the opportunity. I had intended to leave the second one to carry on as it had been doing while I absorbed the first, but I now found that its management had been so cowed by its previous owner, a forceful but erratic autocrat, that they were unable to reach decisions on their own. To make things worse, it was clear that Lucy and I were going to get very few evenings together, as hers were mostly taken up with her public duties as wife of the Lord Seneschal, and her week-ends were tied to Seddon Hall. Her solution was to enrol herself for a series of Cordon Bleu cookery classes. Seddon's chauffeur would drop her at the door every Thursday. She would go in, copy down the day's menu, leave, and catch a taxi to my flat, where we might look the dishes up and perhaps attempt to cook one if I had the ingredients—I have always been a fair cook—but usually we spent most of the time we had in bed.

This was another, and I think to both of us regrettable, difference from our previous affair, which had had time in it for much pleasurable companionship, talk and silences, activities and loiterings, plans and purposes and accidents—all part of the process of being in love. Now all that there seemed to be room for was our time together in bed. That was overwhelmingly necessary—for Lucy, I came to think, even more than for me. She never referred to it, but I soon realised that there must be something seriously amiss between her and Seddon, though she always spoke of him with an odd mixture of warmth and regret. Afterwards she would take a cab to Knightsbridge, do some perfunctory shopping to account for the rest of her afternoon, and so back to Eaton Square. I would return to my desk and work late to make up for lost time, though well aware that my absences were inconvenient for my staff.

No sooner had our renewed affair begun than Lucy telephoned me at work and asked me to come to a formal dinner next day at Eaton Square. Astonished, I demurred, but she begged me.

"Tommy suggested you himself," she said. "He's a terrible fusser about numbers, and someone's fallen out, and we've got this French minister's wife coming who doesn't speak any English and lets everyone know if she isn't enjoying herself, but she'll eat out of your hand. Please."

"I don't think it's a good idea," I said.

"It's all right. I promise. Or I wouldn't ask. I have to do what I can for him, don't you see? Please."

Very uncomfortably I gave in, and found the evening much less dreadful than I had expected. The sheer formality, which was considerable—white ties and stiff shirts, medals, footmen, a partner to take in to dinner on one's arm, seating by protocol, of course—created a complete barrier, or seal, between the occasion and normal life. The minister's wife turned out to be an opera fanatic, which kept us going all evening.

"Tommy was delighted," Lucy told me later. "If it hadn't been you, it would have had to be Colonel Brent, who doesn't speak French and can only talk about breeding pointers."

"Why did it have to be anyone?"

"It's got to be eighteen. $4x + 2$ is the magic formula, so that he can sit at the head and I can sit at the foot with everyone paired off down the sides, and there isn't room for twenty-two and Tommy says fourteen looks mingy. He's a bit obsessive about numbers and things. I oughtn't to tell you this, but it makes me laugh. He has all his socks marked with a red tag sewn into one of each pair, so that he knows which foot it goes on. Some of his socks are made with separate big toes, so it makes sense with them, sort of, but he likes it done with all

of them. Of course sometimes someone drops out at the absolute last minute. There was one poor chap from the ministry
who slipped on the ice outside our front door and broke his
ankle, and Tommy was still grumbling about it at breakfast
next day, saying he could have come to the dinner first and
gone off to hospital afterwards. It was a joke, of course—he's
a very kind man under that shell—but a tiny bit of him meant
it, too."

"How did that evening go?"

"Perfectly well. Even Tommy admitted that. But he still
wasn't happy."

"You must get some pretty odd pairings with all this barrel
scraping."

"Do we not! But he doesn't mind that, in fact he rather
likes it. There's a bit of him, you see, which is in revolt against
all this. I'm not sure that isn't why he wanted to marry me.
He thought I could give him a kind of wildness . . . I don't
know. Anyway, I'm sure it's why he puts up with Michael
Allwegg. The trouble is Tommy says I'm to put you on my
list, so you're going to have to think up some first-rate excuses
if you don't want to come."

"Have you tried Gerry? He's alone in London fairly often."

"He came once and said never again. I'm keeping him till
I'm absolutely desperate."

"How much does your husband know? About us, I mean?"

"He knows about before, of course. We didn't try and hide
it, did we? Not about now."

"Well, I don't like it, but I'll do it if you genuinely need
me. I find I have oddly primitive objections to taking the bread
of a man whom I am at the same time in some sense betraying."

"Do you really? How very strange. I wonder if I'd feel like
that. All right, I won't ask you, though I'm afraid he's bound
to suggest you again."

This turned out to be the case. Indeed, my success with the
minister's wife meant that Seddon had now marked me down

not simply as a possible stopgap but as a useful primary guest, single, cultured, sociable, and fluent in both French and German. I excused myself a couple of times on the grounds of pressure of work, but then Lucy began to worry that it might begin to seem that I had other reasons for staying away, so reluctantly I agreed to accept the next invitation.

The occasion turned out to be even stiffer than the previous one, with minor Balkan ex-royalty present, resulting in a definite air of tension, which I didn't fully understand. The mix of guests contained some obvious oddities. As we settled into our places, I noticed a young man on the other side of the table and two along, slight and decidedly handsome, with an air of swagger, or panache, even when seated and making the first self-introductions to the woman on his left. Neat features, pale face, blue eyes, strong black brows and well-groomed coarse black hair worn rather long for that period. I paid no attention at first, conversing during the hors d'oeuvres with the Austrian on my left and turning formally when the soup was brought to attend to my neighbour on my right. This was a Frenchwoman, the wife of a Greek diplomat, middle-aged, plain featured but svelte, formidable but sufficiently pleased by my speaking French to have unbent a little as I escorted her in to dinner. Now she had hardly acknowledged my approaches before she made a tiny gesture with her head and muttered, *"Le jeune homme là-bas, c'est une femme, n'est-ce-pas?"*

I glanced, took a mouthful, glanced again. Yes. The girl was turned towards her far-side neighbour, so I was seeing her in profile. No doubt she was less conscious of how she might look from that angle, but even so, I don't know that I would have seen through her disguise without my neighbour's prompting.

"Effectivement," I answered. *"Je pense que vous avez raison. Un pari, peut-être?"*

"De la part de qui? Notre hôte un joueur? Il ne me semble pas le genre. Lady Seddon non plus."

I might have expected her to be affronted, but she was clearly amused. Perhaps the intricacies of Greek diplomacy had accustomed her to offbeat events, and it was their emergence at the stuffier end of the British social scene that she found piquant. She dropped the subject and began to question me about how I had learnt my French, then moved on to further probings till the fish arrived and I reverted to the Austrian. By then I had become aware that the Frenchwoman and I were not the only ones to have noticed, and by the time the course was cleared the vague tension of the dinner party had been tightened up a notch along my side of the table, with variations of anxiety, excitement, and amusement. In the lull before the meat, a footman delivered a folded note to the girl. She opened it, blushed scarlet, and was for a second or two very obviously not what she was pretending to be, in fact neither man nor woman, but a child caught out. She recovered herself, spoke briefly to her neighbours, rose, made a stiff little bow to Lucy, and walked towards the door, which was behind Seddon's place.

I had assumed that it was he who had written the note, but he seemed to realise that something was amiss only as she was coming towards him. He too rose, solicitous, perhaps thinking one of his guests was ill, perhaps worried by being about to be one short of his totemic guest number. I'm afraid that we were all watching avidly. One stout bald man with a lot of foreign decorations had half risen from his chair for a better view. Seddon still seemed, as he accompanied her to the door, to be assuming that his guest was a man, but as he opened it for her, she turned to him, put her hand on his arm, and deliberately dropped her disguise. I don't know how she did it, but even from where I sat, there was no mistaking that this was an attractive, indeed seductive, young woman.

Seddon started. His jaw literally dropped. For a moment the whole carapace of his diplomatic manner fell away. Laugh-

ing with teasing glee at his discomposure, she slipped a card
into his breast pocket, kissed her fingers to the company, and
vanished. Seddon resumed his mask of calm as he closed the
door and returned to the table. The rest of the evening was
considerably less interesting. Naturally I asked Lucy, at our
next meeting, about the incident, but she told me she wasn't
supposed to talk about it so I left it alone.

A few days later Gerry rang.

"I'll be sending round your ticket for Lord's," he said.

"Good for you. What did you make of Mrs. Mudge?"

"She wasn't able to help."

"Sorry about that."

"Not your fault. Are you going to the new *Turandot*?"

"I went last night."

"Pity. I've got two spare tickets for the twelfth. Some friends
of Nan fell through. Seddon will be at this Chequers Confer-
ence, so we could see if Lucy's free. Nan would be there to
give the occasion respectability."

Lucy, I already knew, would be free. With Seddon away,
she and I had planned to spend the night together. The offer
was extremely tempting.

"I wouldn't mind hearing *Turandot* again," I said.

"Excellent. I'll get Nan to try Lucy."

The seats, it turned out, were not together, but in two
pairs separated by several rows. Gerry apologised and made
mumblings about how we should arrange ourselves.

"I'll sit with Paul," said Lucy firmly, and as we settled into
our places, she whispered, "I'm sick of creeping around."

At the interval I was rising to join the others when Lucy
pulled me back into my seat and pointed surreptitiously.

"The end box on the right," she said. "Black gloves, bare
shoulders. Seen her before?"

The girl was leaning forward, intending to be noticed. A
mass of dark hair made the face small and perky. The dress

was cut so low that from our angle she mightn't have been wearing a stitch, apart from the long lace gloves. The effect was decidedly erotic.

"Ought I to have?" I said.

"Came to our dinner party dressed as a man."

"That must be a wig, then."

"Can't you see it is? I noticed her because she seemed to be pointing us out to someone as the lights went down."

I had once or twice been forced to take one of those end boxes rather than miss a production, but I'd sooner be right up in the amphitheatre. Your side of the stage is partly invisible from them, and you see out into the wings on the other side. Moreover, the music reaches you unbalanced. Their only advantage, which I'd never needed to make use of myself, might be that unless you leaned forward, you were invisible to everyone except those in the boxes opposite. I was naturally inquisitive about the girl and her companion, but Gerry had ordered champagne for the interval so we had to go and do it justice.

The girl was still there when the performance resumed, but I reabsorbed myself in it and forgot her until the applause for Liu's *"Tanto amore segreto,"* when Lucy whispered in my ear, "I think it's Tommy with her!"

"I thought you told me he didn't enjoy opera."

"He hates it. And he's supposed to be at Chequers talking to the French about how to dish Colonel Nasser. Otherwise . . ."

"Do you want to make sure?"

"I don't know. I suppose. . . . Yes. . . ."

The applause was dying. The best I could think of was to tear a page from my diary and scribble a note to Gerry saying we'd meet him at the restaurant. Luckily he and Nan were near the end of a row, so as the curtain calls began, I was able to barge my way out, reach in to Gerry, and pass him the note. I had seen that the party in the box were also preparing to leave early, but I know my way round the Royal Opera, and Lucy and I were out by the natural exit from those boxes in time to see the other couple hurry out. The man certainly could have been Seddon, but he was wearing a dark hat and a cloaklike greatcoat with big lapels, which he had turned up round his face. I felt Lucy quiver on my arm.

"Are you all right?" I whispered.

"Let's see where they're going."

There were taxis about, waiting to cream off the opera-goers, but the couple ignored them and strode off towards Soho, the girl, despite her high heels, matching her pace to the man's. In those days the streets were nothing like as well lit as they are now, but the two distinctive silhouettes were easy to pick out as they moved from one patch of lamplight to the next. I was never a trained agent and had no expertise in tailing a quarry, but as soon as we crossed Shaftesbury Avenue, the crowds emerging from other theatres gave us cover.

Soho was then a very mixed district, or rather the mixture spilled out onto the streets more than it is allowed to now, with tarts in every other doorway, pimps and bully-boys keeping an eye on them, clients wandering through, boisterous groups emerging from reeking pubs (it was now around closing time), while theatre-goers like us were making their way towards restaurants, and those who had dined earlier were starting home—all, as I say, very ill lit, with passages of deep shadow between the pallid circles cast by the lamps. We were in Greek Street, and the couple seemed to be reaching their destination, with the girl beginning to fumble in her handbag, presumably for a doorkey, when the commotion began.

Most of it happened in shadow. I heard a yelp of alarm—a woman's—cut short. Two or three people were struggling towards a car. I could see the man we'd been following confronting another man who had gripped his coat by the front and was menacing him with his fist while our man made protesting motions with one hand, still holding his lapels over his face with the other. Then a man—and I knew at once from his lightness and speed that it was Gerry—raced past us and flung himself at the group by the car. The impetus of his charge hurled one of the figures against the bodywork. In the same movement he had grabbed the collar of another of the figures, who I could now see had the girl by the arm and was forcing her into the car, and using the man's weight as a brake swung him round, sending the man's legs skidding from beneath him and crashing him into the rear wheel. The girl fell clear. The third man left Seddon and was moving towards Gerry. He had a knife out, but Gerry feinted, dodged the thrust, seized him by the wrist and whisked him over his shoulder and down. The first man was now rising. Gerry kicked him in the throat, picked him up by the collar and crotch and tossed him through the open door of the car as it drove off. The other two men scuttled away. I tried to make a note of the car's number as it drove past, but the plates were illegible with dirt.

Nan joined us.

"What's happening?" she said.

"I think it's over," said Lucy.

She was shuddering. Gerry had helped the girl to her feet and was handing her her wig, which had fallen off. Without it, even in the bad light, I could see that she was indeed the one who'd been at the Seddons' party. She looked white and shaken. The man who'd been with her came up, spoke briefly to Gerry, took her by the arm, and led her away into a side alley.

The street, as I've said, was far from deserted. A dozen people must have seen what happened, and as Gerry came back to us, one or two of them applauded. He responded by raising a hand, rather as he might have done on coming off the cricket field after a successful innings. At that moment an empty cab came by, I hailed it and we climbed in.

"That was extraordinary," said Nan.

"Don't let's talk about it. Please," said Lucy.

For once she allowed her distress to show, so we did as she said. But while she and Nan were "powdering their noses," as we used to call it, at the restaurant, I got a chance to ask Gerry how he happened to show up so opportunely.

"I'm sorry," he said. "I was inquisitive. So was Nan."

"Just as well," I said. "I take it you saw who the man was?"

He shrugged, but his look made it clear that he too had recognised Seddon. At that point the two women returned. Nan had not been in a good temper earlier and was in a worse one now. Lucy was silent throughout the meal, while I merely wanted to be alone with her and discuss what we'd seen. But Gerry was in tremendous form, so to anyone watching us it must have seemed that we were all having a good time.

Even back at my flat, Lucy was unwilling to talk about the episode. During several wakeful patches I was aware of her also lying there, still, tense, miserable. When I moved a hand to comfort her, she held it for a while and then let go, obviously wanting nothing more. At breakfast she said "What am I going to do, Paul? Go on, tell me. You can't make it any worse."

"I'd have to know more, in areas you've asked me not to talk about."

"That's over. Go on."

"Well, for instance, where did the girl come from in the first place? How was she invited to your dinner party?"

The question seemed to steady her, putting her onto known ground.

"UFTFA," she said. "It stands for—let me work it out— oh, yes, Universal Friendship through Folk Art—you know, great festivals of healthy young things in national costume bouncing around to ukulele music."

"Funded by the CIA and riddled with Russian agents, or vice versa."

"I expect so. Somebody told us the princess was interested

in that sort of thing, so we asked the director along. We've had him before. He's rather amusing. He's a Yugoslav called Mikovicz, and apparently he was a frightful thug in the war, but now he's having a lovely time spreading friendship through folk art and wallowing in the fleshpots of London."

"Is he a communist?"

"Officially, I think, but he's a ferocious snob. He wouldn't have minded at all having ex-royals there. They weren't UF-TFA's ex-royals, anyway. Anyway, he rang up pretty well at the last minute and said he was ill and he'd send his assistant along, but it turned out the assistant was a woman and my secretary said it had to be a man because of the numbers, and he wuffled a bit and said all right and he'd send the details round. That's all I know."

"It seems a curious procedure."

"Well, you know what Tommy's like about numbers."

"That's not what I meant. I imagine some enquiry has been made about why the girl was there."

"Officially it was a practical joke, and Mikovicz has promised to sack the chap who set it up. He absolutely grovelled to me on the telephone."

"And unofficially?"

"That's what I'm supposed not to talk about."

"If it was a deliberate ploy to get the girl into your house for some reason, then that would involve someone knowing you would want a replacement for a guest who dropped out. That's what I meant about it being a curious procedure."

"I'm still not supposed to talk about it."

"I'm sorry, but you asked me what you should do, and the answer partly turns on what you believe to be the girl's motives. You see, I have a distinct impression—it was slight at the time but it's grown stronger since—that the object of the girl being at your party was that she should make herself known to your husband."

"Oh! Well . . . Do you really think so? That's not—"

She broke off.

"Not the official theory?" I said. "All I can say is that's what it looked like. He's in an extremely vulnerable position. And if that's what's going on, it must at least affect your attitude, I'd have thought. It's none of my business, except indirectly."

"No. Well, but. You think I ought to tell him?"

"He may already be aware. . . ."

"I still ought to."

Lucy

SEVEN

Spring 1956

I've decided the only thing is to get this over. That sounds a bit grim, though actually I'd be rather enjoying it if I wasn't so bothered about Paul. There's something badly wrong—much wronger than I realised. He's got very silent. If he notices, he makes an effort and starts to chat, but he can't keep it up, and he writes on his knee in the evenings, but I can tell that what he really wants is to sneak back to his word processor and get on with it. Even on lovely sunny days, when he ought to be out—he always says if you don't get things right in the autumn you'll notice all next year—out doing things like taking cuttings and getting at those horrible little spurges before they seed, he shuts himself up in his office and taps away. And *he* isn't enjoying it at all. It's something he's forced to do, as if he was hypnotised. And he won't talk about it, either. He just says, "Let's get it done, and then we can think about something else." So I've got to do my bit.

I'd better explain about the dinner party where Sammy Whitstable showed up pretending to be a man. It makes me sound so stuffy, turfing her out like that. But you've got to remember, it wasn't a private party—it was part of Tommy's job. It was always going to be sticky, because we weren't supposed to be having anything to do with the old Yugoslav

royals in case we offended General Tito but we still were trying
to keep odd sorts of anticommunists happy by pretending to
take them seriously, so in spite of what I've just said, yes, it
was a private party, in case the official Yugoslavs objected. But
we let the prince and his lot make out that it was official by
us all wearing medals and things, so the one thing we couldn't
afford was an Incident, with notes flying to and fro and it all
coming out into the open. But we'd been warned that some of
the anti-Reds were hoping for an Incident, which they could
make a public fuss about, and certainly I'd already found out
before we sat down that the prince was in a decidedly prickly
mood, so . . . well, that's why I decided I'd better ask the girl
to push off. It's not the sort of thing I enjoy. And that's why
I didn't think there was anything odd about Tommy wanting
to hush it up and play it down afterwards. It didn't matter
who'd managed to smuggle the girl in. It could have been
someone on the prince's side, or it could have been someone
on the Reds', because of course all those organisations were
absolutely riddled with agents. But I was so obsessed with
keeping the prince quiet that it never even struck me as possible it might have anything to do with Tommy.

Well, then, talking to Tommy. He really had been at Chequers all day, discussing Colonel Nasser with the French, and
he'd come up for the opera and a few hours afterwards (I
suppose) and gone back in the small hours, so I didn't see him
till we were having breakfast the day after that. Of course I'd
been trying to think of ways of starting in on it, and I was
putting it off by letting him get his post opened and feeling
more and more nervous when he looked up and said, quietly,
"I believe you have resumed your liaison with Paul Ackerley."

I looked back. I couldn't read what he was thinking.

"You saw us at Covent Garden," I said.

Something flickered. He hadn't realised I'd seen him there.

"You were with that girl," I said. "The one who came here
pretending to be a man."

"Yes."

You've got to remember I knew Tommy pretty well. He wasn't difficult to cope with provided everyone kept their manners and stayed polite. Within those rules you could say almost anything you liked, accuse him of all sorts of unspeakable crimes . . . that sounds ridiculous, because of course Tommy wouldn't have known an unspeakable crime if he'd seen one, personally. He was absolutely painfully upright. But in his job people were always telling him how badly Britain was behaving about something and accusing him of going along with it. I can remember how nice he once was to an American Jewish woman who seemed to believe we'd actually wanted the Holocaust to take place and now we were trying to help the Arabs carry on with the job. She was extremely angry about it, but she managed to stay inside Tommy's rules, so Tommy was polite and reasonable, though she wouldn't see reason, and told me afterwards he'd rather liked her. But other people, I mean, there was an Australian who was upset about something he said we'd been doing at Woomera—that was the missile place—and he may have been right but he had a chip on his shoulder about the English, especially ones with titles, and he was so rude and personal that Tommy went completely cold and official and they both finished up loathing each other. . . . So, you see, I knew if I wanted things to work out I mustn't get emotional, or say I thought the girl was a tart, or anything like that.

"I don't blame you," I said.

He slit an envelope and glanced at the letter before he said anything. Then he spoke without looking at me.

"Nor I you," he said. "It is perhaps through my deficiencies that our marriage has failed to function as it should."

"That's not fair," I said. "On you, I mean."

"Let's not go into questions of blame," he said. "They are in my experience invariably jejune. Tell me, for how long have you been seeing Ackerley again?"

about it. Isn't there something you could do to find out without bothering the girl? The UFTFA man would have to be in on it, wouldn't he?"

"David was having a check run on him," he said. "I will see if anything has come of it."

He started to gather up his post.

"We still haven't decided what we're going to do," I said. "Rub along, I suppose."

"You don't want a divorce?" he said.

"I promised, remember? Sauce for the goose," I said. "Anyway, I don't think I could face the fuss."

"Certainly I would be very grateful if we could, as they say, keep up appearances," he said. "I do not fully understand what is happening to me. I find, to my shame, that I am obsessed by this girl, but presumably the infatuation will pass. I have seen it happening to other men and felt nothing but pity and contempt for them. Now it is my turn."

You know, I don't think I'd ever liked him so much. I felt really warm and protective towards him. I wish I could have told him so.

"In that case enjoy it while it lasts," I said. "Have fun."

He shook his head.

" 'Fun' is the wrong word," he said. "The experience is, if anything, painful. Painful but irresistible."

"In that case, be careful," I said.

"Again you mistake," he said. "Obviously one takes superficial precautions, but the risk itself is what matters. The risk to everything I have and am and desire and value. Believe me, I can see my own madness with perfect clarity, and yet I know I shall persist in it."

We were both standing up by now. I went over to him and he let me kiss him and didn't flinch, and then I went and shut myself up in my own room and cried till it was time for my hair appointment.

I have this theory about Englishmen—not all of them, but

"Since Father's funeral," I said. "I don't know, I saw him outside the church in the rain, and I suddenly felt . . . I know you can't go back, it's never the same. But I really had tried to be faithful to you, Tommy. I really had. I wanted to."

"I know," he said, and began to read the letter properly, so as to give me time to get a hold on myself. I'd been almost over the edge, but I managed to pull back. He looked up as soon as I was ready.

"The question is, how shall we now proceed?" he said. "You have been very tactful so far. I take it that your allowing yourselves to be seen so openly together at Covent Garden was not deliberate."

"That was an accident," I said. "Nan was supposed to be chaperoning us, but our seats weren't together."

His head jerked up.

"Nancy was there?" he said. "And Grantworth? I hadn't realised. So you saw the episode in Greek Street?"

"I'm afraid I wanted to be sure it was really you," I said. "We followed you. Paul gave Gerry a note telling him to meet us at the restaurant, but he said he was inquisitive, so he came along behind us. We didn't realise he was there till he ran past. It was lucky he did, I suppose. . . ."

I trailed off, because I could see he'd stopped listening. He was staring at his plate with his head on one side. After a bit he looked up.

"Will you think about this and answer carefully," he said. "I want you to tell me exactly how it was that you noticed my presence at the opera. Were you told I might be there, for instance? Was I pointed out to you by anyone?"

"No," I said. "I just happened to recognise the girl. Do you mind if I ask you some questions about her?"

"In a minute. Go on."

"Well, first I just noticed her," I said. "I mean, she was doing her best to be noticed. Then just as the lights went down, I saw her pointing us out to whoever was with her, and there was something about the way she did it—I don't know what, but it made me think I must have seen her, and after a bit I realised when. Of course I was inquisitive, so I kept an eye on her in the second act, and I saw her say something to whoever was with her, and he leaned forward for a moment and I just caught a glimpse. I still wasn't sure it was you. That's why we rushed round to catch you."

"I see," he said.

"Did she just happen to notice us?" I said. "I mean, there were a lot of other people there."

He smiled at me, charming but sad.

"The fact is, you catch the eye," he said. "My companion is the type of woman who automatically scans a gathering for rival beauties. And of course the moment she'd spotted you, she recognized you."

"You were going to tell me about her," I said.

"Her name is the one she used at the party," he said. "Sammy Whitstable. She has claims to be an actress, but it would not be unfair to describe her as a call girl. She has some education and is not unintelligent."

"Does she wear men's clothes often?" I said.

"For preference," he said, "though not for the obvious reasons."

"Did you just ring her up and say 'Let's meet'?" I said.

"I gave myself the excuse that I was interviewing her," he said. "The morning after the party I discussed the incident with David Pottinger, who felt we should know at whose instigation she had put on that charade. He proposed to send our security people round, but for reasons which you will no doubt think obvious, I decided it would amuse me to talk to her myself. She had left me her card, of course."

"What did she say?" I asked.

"She had done it for a bet," he said. "You'll remember she was supposed to be Mikovicz's assistant from UFTFA. Now

she told me she was simply a friend of his—by which I imagine she meant a client—and he was complaining about the boring functions he had to go to when he could have been spending the time with her. She offered to go in his place."

"They wanted to send a woman at first, but we said no," I said.

"It was her idea that she should come as a man," he said.

"Do you think that's true?" I said.

"Knowing her, quite likely," he said. "At least it seems a more plausible hypothesis than that she was planted there to cause an incident. Don't you think so?"

"I was having such a sticky time with the prince that I can't tell," I said. "But listen—I talked about all this with Paul. I hope you don't mind, but—"

"I would sooner you hadn't, but I suppose it was inevitable," he said. "Well?"

"He was at the dinner party, remember," I said. "He says he got a strong impression that the real reason she was there was to meet you. He says she was sort of seizing her chance when you said good-bye to her at the door."

He'd been opening another letter but stopped.

"She herself wanted to meet me?" he said. "Or some third party wanted her to?"

"I don't know," I said. "Someone else, I suppose."

"Why should anyone want that?" he said.

"Look what's happened," I said. "You've got an awful lo to lose if anyone found out, Tommy. There must be lots c people who'd like to have some kind of hold on you."

"You are suggesting that somebody, some foreign agen say, planted Miss Whitstable at our party in the hope that would become emotionally entangled with her?" he said.

"Not like that, of course. They just wanted you to mee and then it would be up to her," I said. "How else is she goir to meet you? You don't go to ordinary parties. Do just thir

"Since Father's funeral," I said. "I don't know, I saw him outside the church in the rain, and I suddenly felt . . . I know you can't go back, it's never the same. But I really had tried to be faithful to you, Tommy. I really had. I wanted to."

"I know," he said, and began to read the letter properly, so as to give me time to get a hold on myself. I'd been almost over the edge, but I managed to pull back. He looked up as soon as I was ready.

"The question is, how shall we now proceed?" he said. "You have been very tactful so far. I take it that your allowing yourselves to be seen so openly together at Covent Garden was not deliberate."

"That was an accident," I said. "Nan was supposed to be chaperoning us, but our seats weren't together."

His head jerked up.

"Nancy was there?" he said. "And Grantworth? I hadn't realised. So you saw the episode in Greek Street?"

"I'm afraid I wanted to be sure it was really you," I said. "We followed you. Paul gave Gerry a note telling him to meet us at the restaurant, but he said he was inquisitive, so he came along behind us. We didn't realise he was there till he ran past. It was lucky he did, I suppose. . . ."

I trailed off, because I could see he'd stopped listening. He was staring at his plate with his head on one side. After a bit he looked up.

"Will you think about this and answer carefully," he said. "I want you to tell me exactly how it was that you noticed my presence at the opera. Were you told I might be there, for instance? Was I pointed out to you by anyone?"

"No," I said. "I just happened to recognise the girl. Do you mind if I ask you some questions about her?"

"In a minute. Go on."

"Well, first I just noticed her," I said. "I mean, she was doing her best to be noticed. Then just as the lights went down, I saw her pointing us out to whoever was with her, and there was something about the way she did it—I don't know what, but it made me think I must have seen her, and after a bit I realised when. Of course I was inquisitive, so I kept an eye on her in the second act, and I saw her say something to whoever was with her, and he leaned forward for a moment and I just caught a glimpse. I still wasn't sure it was you. That's why we rushed round to catch you."

"I see," he said.

"Did she just happen to notice us?" I said. "I mean, there were a lot of other people there."

He smiled at me, charming but sad.

"The fact is, you catch the eye," he said. "My companion is the type of woman who automatically scans a gathering for rival beauties. And of course the moment she'd spotted you, she recognized you."

"You were going to tell me about her," I said.

"Her name is the one she used at the party," he said. "Sammy Whitstable. She has claims to be an actress, but it would not be unfair to describe her as a call girl. She has some education and is not unintelligent."

"Does she wear men's clothes often?" I said.

"For preference," he said, "though not for the obvious reasons."

"Did you just ring her up and say 'Let's meet'?" I said.

"I gave myself the excuse that I was interviewing her," he said. "The morning after the party I discussed the incident with David Pottinger, who felt we should know at whose instigation she had put on that charade. He proposed to send our security people round, but for reasons which you will no doubt think obvious, I decided it would amuse me to talk to her myself. She had left me her card, of course."

"What did she say?" I asked.

"She had done it for a bet," he said. "You'll remember she was supposed to be Mikovicz's assistant from UFTFA. Now she told me she was simply a friend of his—by which I imagine she meant a client—and he was complaining about the boring functions he had to go to when he could have been spending the time with her. She offered to go in his place."

"They wanted to send a woman at first, but we said no," I said.

"It was her idea that she should come as a man," he said.

"Do you think that's true?" I said.

"Knowing her, quite likely," he said. "At least it seems a more plausible hypothesis than that she was planted there to cause an incident. Don't you think so?"

"I was having such a sticky time with the prince that I can't tell," I said. "But listen—I talked about all this with Paul. I hope you don't mind, but—"

"I would sooner you hadn't, but I suppose it was inevitable," he said. "Well?"

"He was at the dinner party, remember," I said. "He says he got a strong impression that the real reason she was there was to meet you. He says she was sort of seizing her chance when you said good-bye to her at the door."

He'd been opening another letter but stopped.

"She herself wanted to meet me?" he said. "Or some third party wanted her to?"

"I don't know," I said. "Someone else, I suppose."

"Why should anyone want that?" he said.

"Look what's happened," I said. "You've got an awful lot to lose if anyone found out, Tommy. There must be lots of people who'd like to have some kind of hold on you."

"You are suggesting that somebody, some foreign agent, say, planted Miss Whitstable at our party in the hope that I would become emotionally entangled with her?" he said.

"Not like that, of course. They just wanted you to meet, and then it would be up to her," I said. "How else is she going to meet you? You don't go to ordinary parties. Do just think about it. Isn't there something you could do to find out without bothering the girl? The UFTFA man would have to be in on it, wouldn't he?"

"David was having a check run on him," he said. "I will see if anything has come of it."

He started to gather up his post.

"We still haven't decided what we're going to do," I said. "Rub along, I suppose."

"You don't want a divorce?" he said.

"I promised, remember? Sauce for the goose," I said. "Anyway, I don't think I could face the fuss."

"Certainly I would be very grateful if we could, as they say, keep up appearances," he said. "I do not fully understand what is happening to me. I find, to my shame, that I am obsessed by this girl, but presumably the infatuation will pass. I have seen it happening to other men and felt nothing but pity and contempt for them. Now it is my turn."

You know, I don't think I'd ever liked him so much. I felt really warm and protective towards him. I wish I could have told him so.

"In that case enjoy it while it lasts," I said. "Have fun."

He shook his head.

" 'Fun' is the wrong word," he said. "The experience is, if anything, painful. Painful but irresistible."

"In that case, be careful," I said.

"Again you mistake," he said. "Obviously one takes superficial precautions, but the risk itself is what matters. The risk to everything I have and am and desire and value. Believe me, I can see my own madness with perfect clarity, and yet I know I shall persist in it."

We were both standing up by now. I went over to him and he let me kiss him and didn't flinch, and then I went and shut myself up in my own room and cried till it was time for my hair appointment.

I have this theory about Englishmen—not all of them, but

a lot of them. Tommy was just an extreme example. Their absolute top fear, worse than pain or sickness or death or danger or anything like that, is Being Found Out. There's a quotation somewhere about fame being a spur. It isn't fame, it's shame. It doesn't even have to be their own shame. You go to the cinema with them and what really twists them up isn't the dreadful bits, the woman learning her son's been run over or the old black man getting lynched, it's the place where the villain gets shown up in front of everyone. Even men with no imagination at all, you'd have said, seem to be able to imagine that happening to themselves. But then, at the same time, there's something in them which makes them feel they *ought* to be found out. They remember silly things they did or said when they were schoolboys and cry them aloud in their sleep, because they still haven't been found out and punished for them, so they're still being haunted by them. I don't know. I don't understand myself, so I don't see how I can be expected to understand anyone else, but I think I knew what Tommy was talking about when he said it was the risk that mattered. That's one of the things that hurt so much.

Paul

EIGHT

June 1956

Several weeks went by. I remained as busy as ever, with neither time nor capacity to pay attention to anything much outside my own affairs, that is to say, my work and my involvement with Lucy. She told me that she and Seddon had agreed to keep up appearances for the time being, but in private to do as each wished. She told me bluntly that she was not prepared to divorce him for my sake. I had expected this but was still disappointed. We seldom talked about that side of her life, but then she always had a great capacity for keeping different relationships in separate compartments. For instance, when Janet rang and asked me to supper, saying that Lucy would be there, she gave no hint of being aware that Lucy and I had resumed our liaison, let alone that I was expecting the invitation.

I knew Janet least of the sisters—that is to say, I had been in her company least. On the other hand, in the sense of understanding what she might be like as a person, I felt I knew as much as I needed to. She remained markedly her mother's daughter, boisterous and opinionated. The opinions were different, but the refusal to base them on any rational, or even arguable, process was the same.

"I think Teddy married her because she's such a joke,"

Harriet had once said, and indeed on the times I'd seen them together they had conducted themselves as if they were playing the lead roles in a light-comedy musical about a wildly ill-matched couple who yet loved each other. His manner became exaggeratedly solemn and sardonic and hers extravagantly whimsical. I once saw her at a cocktail party plait some carnations from a vase into a chaplet and creep up behind him and crown him with them, and then fling her arms round his neck and whisper in his ear. He had reached back and patted her rump absentmindedly, as one might that of a hound, and gone on with his conversation. If this sounds painful, the sort of behavior one would prefer to take place in another room or, preferably, another county, it wasn't, at least in the early years of their marriage. They seemed so happy with each other that one had to be in a bad mood not to regard what they did as an expression of high spirits, which they wanted us all to share. But by hindsight the joke may already have started to wear thin as Voss-Thompson's TV role, introducing him as it did into the entourages of glamorous and powerful people, presented him with alternative attractions. Outwardly Janet's rowdy domesticities seemed still to suit him, and though he had a small flat near the TV studios in Lime Grove, he made every effort to get back to Hertfordshire for the night, if possible. They had one daughter, and Janet was now visibly pregnant again.

That night we dined at their flat. Lucy and I arrived separately. She had not yet formally told even her close family what was going on, though Gerry seemed to be aware of it and had, presumably, told Nancy. The other guests turned out to be an American television producer called Mary Twill, and David Fish. I had not met her before, but David I had met occasionally, a tall, slight but still somehow rubicund man my own age, already balding, with a manner of stooping towards one and peering through thick spectacles, beaming with interest at whatever trivialities one might have found to tell him. I remembered him by sight from Eton, but knew him mainly as a protégé of a family friend of the Verekers, an enormously rich and tactless woman called Biddy Trollope, one of those characters with a lot of old friends who value them but admit that they need a considerable amount of tolerance to do so, while outsiders, such as myself in Biddy Trollope's case, cannot imagine why the friends bother. Fish was a money shoveller, in his own phrase, expert in shifting enormous sums of currency round the globe in order to take advantage of minimal currency fluctuations. The job is now a commonplace, one for the caricature yuppie, but in those days he was a rarity, and his interest in his work seemed more scholarly than ambitious. I had thought him a dull dog, but he had surprised me once by talking with eager excitement about some of the later Roman emperors.

Despite the smallness of their flat, the Voss-Thompsons had a separate dining room, a cramped space that might have been meant for a child's bedroom but was now largely occupied by a circular table, which we had to edge past to get to our places. The food was then served by Janet going round to the kitchen and passing the dishes through a hatch behind Edward's chair. Despite this awkwardness the meal was well organised, straight Elizabeth David, with some good claret.

I sat between Mary Twill and Janet, with Lucy opposite me between Edward and David. Neither of us got much share of the conversation. Learning that I was not involved in television or films, Miss Twill at once wrote me off as a nonentity, receiving any overtures from me with impatient disdain and snatching Edward's attention at the first opportunity. Edward caught my eye once and made an apologetic gesture, but continued to treat her with a respect just short of deference. I assumed he wanted something from her. On my other side Janet, between her disappearances to the kitchen, seemed to be compensating for her earthy rotundity by a particularly extravagant feyness, interrupting conversations, seizing them like a puppy with a blanket, and dragging them off in unwelcome directions. (She was always capable of getting hold of more wrong ends of a stick than most people.) Fairly early on, she had tried to do this with Edward and Miss Twill and had actually seemed abashed for a few seconds when Edward had shut her up. After that she concentrated on preventing David and Lucy having more than three coherent sentences of conversation together. By hindsight I guess that she was conscious of her marriage being in difficulty and was attempting, clumsily, to exaggerate a role that had formerly seemed to please, and to make herself more interesting, or at least more noticeable.

She needed no excuse at all for these intrusions. At one point, coming back from the kitchen, she leaned over and spoke in a stage whisper into David's ear.

"Be careful what you say to Lucy. She was a spy in the war."

David for some reason blushed.

"As a matter of fact we knew each other in the war," he said.

Janet made her eyes enormous.

"Were you a spy, too?" she said. "How desperately glamorous."

"I'm afraid I just did heavy math on codes," said David.

"Oh, I know all about that," said Janet. "We had that sort of stuff in our house too. That's not spying. But after that Lucy went off to London and was a real spy, you know, seducing ambassadors and things."

David giggled uncomfortably.

"Janet's talking nonsense," said Lucy. "I signed the Official Secrets Act, so I don't talk about it, but—"

"They'd put you in the Tower if you did," said Janet. "Then we could all come and visit you, disguised as our servants, and smuggle you out."

"Provided you were the one who stayed behind," said Lucy.

"Oh, yes, and have Possum born in the Tower!" said Janet.

"I bet you get special privileges if you're born in the Tower, like being allowed to wear odd shoes in the queen's presence. Have you got any special privileges yet, David? Or do you have to wait till you're an alderman?"

And so on. It was a thoroughly uncomfortable meal. At one point Lucy caught my eye and smiled commiseratingly. She was looking especially serene, so I guessed that she too was finding things awkward, though she must have been well used to Janet's style.

In those days it was still not unusual, even at supper parties for as few as six, for the women to withdraw before the coffee was served, leaving the men "to their port." This they did, to Miss Twill's obvious irritation, but we didn't leave them much longer than they would have needed to make use of the bathroom. As we rose to join them, Edward said, "Do you mind going ahead, David? I've got something I have to talk to Paul about."

David shambled amiably off and Edward closed the door.

"I need some advice and possibly some help," he said. "I'm afraid this has got to be confidential."

"I'll do my best," I said.

"You've known the Verekers as long as anyone, and what I need is an objective view. I've come across some stuff in the course of my work which I'm not quite sure how to handle. Have you ever heard of John and Mary Driver?"

"I don't think so."

"Ostensibly they run a pub called The Wooden Leg in Wapping, but that's a front. Really they're the bosses of a thoroughly unpleasant organisation, mostly protection and prostitution. Drugs, of course. They've got several of the local police on their payroll, and there's at least a suspicion that someone higher up in the force is finding it worth his while to look the other way. Driver is an ex-pug and she was a tart. The story is that he fell for her, and she used him to take the pimp who'd been running her off her back. After that they set up together, offering some of her friends in the trade the same service, and simply went on from there. He's not just a muscle man. They've both got brains and ambition, and they're just about as ruthless as each other. They're doing well. They give parties, lashings of champagne these days. Dinner jackets and ball gowns. And they've got the sort of dangerous glamor that attracts a certain kind of apparently successful citizen. We've got a photograph of . . . I'd better not tell you who . . . dancing with Mary Driver. Quite a few surprising people have been seen down that way."

"Anyone we know?"

"I'm coming to that. Straight crime isn't really our line. We got onto them because we've been looking into a housing racket. We started off thinking it was a comparatively minor local scandal which might do to fill out a magazine programme one evening. There was this small company which had bought up a few rundown properties covered by the Rent Acts, full of tenants paying only a pound or two a week, and they'd been harassed into leaving so that the company could do the houses up and sell them at a whopping profit."

"It's bound to happen when you get a market as distorted as the Rent Acts have produced."

"Yes, but what made this different was the nature of the harassment. Usually the victims are only too happy to tell the world their wrongs, but these people were really frightened. It was almost impossible to get them to talk. But we found one brave old biddy who not only told us about the men who'd come round and what they'd said and done, but because she happens to be one of an immense and prolific clan who all live a mile or two apart in a great swathe across North London, she knew of several other places where exactly the same thing was beginning to happen. Even the same men coming round. At that point we got really interested and started putting more people onto the story. We made connections both up and down. First, the frighteners appeared to come from the Driver organisation. Second, the landlords were never individuals but always small companies, recently registered. Their addresses were those of a number of East End solicitors, acting on behalf of clients whose names they refused to reveal. The directors were nominees, never available for interview. That seemed to be a blank wall. The only thing we had to take us further was some research at the Land Registry which showed that two separate lots of properties had been previously owned by Michael Allwegg's company."

"That could be a coincidence. He seems to have bought and sold fairly extensively."

"Yes, but there's one more connection. One of our chaps managed to get himself invited to a party of the Drivers'. They like the attention, you know. He'd been at Cambridge just after the war and was a serious cricketer. He recognised Gerry Grantworth."

I said nothing for some while. I felt I should have been astonished, but wasn't. A few connections formed in my mind.

"I believe Gerry is an old friend of yours," said Edward.

"Yes."

"So what is your line?"

"I shall have to think. Are you going to make these allegations public? If you do, you'll be laying yourselves open to colossal libel damages, I'd have thought. What you've told me doesn't sound enough to go on."

"It isn't. I don't know what the official line will be. I'm taking myself off the programme, for obvious reasons. My own guess is that we won't be able to name names, but that we'll create enough of a stir for the names to start coming out. Look, I'm taking a risk telling you at all. If you now tell Allwegg or Grantworth, then there is a serious danger that they will take out injunctions and prevent the programme being shown. I don't want that. In my view this is a vicious piece of exploitation of helpless people. On the other hand, I need advice.

Allwegg is about to marry Ben, and now Janet tells me that
Nancy and Gerry are to get married at last."

"No!"

"On the same day, Janet says. Nancy rang her up this
morning."

"But what about the alimony?"

"Felder is going broke, and it's no longer being paid. The
details were beyond Janet. Look, I've got to get back to that
frightful woman, before she starts throwing furniture around.
The thing is, if these allegations are true, I strongly believe
that they ought to be made public. At the same time I don't
want Janet's sisters waking up one morning and finding out
what they've let themselves in for."

"Couldn't Janet talk to them?"

I knew as I said it the proposal was ludicrous. Edward merely
shrugged.

"I don't know how close you are to Lucy these days," he
said.

"I'll think about it," I said. "I shall have to think about it
in any case. I've never liked or trusted Allwegg. Gerry is, as
you say, an old friend, in the sense that I've known him a long
time, but we've never been intimate. I may decide I have to
tell him some of what you've told me, but if I do, I'll let you
know first. There's one or two enquiries of my own I can
make."

"Be careful," he said. "These people are extremely vicious."

I remembered saying something of the sort to Gerry earlier,
when I had put him on to Mrs. Mudge. Edward had the door
open and was waiting for me, but the thought made me pause
a moment in my stride. Then we went through and joined the
others.

We found Miss Twill on the point of leaving, outraged by
Edward's ten-minute absence. Edward seemed unperturbed,
switching on charm and pouring her a large scotch. Lucy and

Janet embarked on a discussion, full of Vereker references, thus impenetrable to outsiders, about the care of their old Nanny, who after a lifetime of adapting herself to the whims and extravagancies of her employers was now making up for lost chances by being a disruptive influence in the old people's home where they had placed her. This left David and me together, so I took the chance to ask him whether he knew anything about the collapse of the Felder fortune. Rare metal futures were not his area of expertise, but apparently Felder's wallowings had created upheavals elsewhere, so David knew enough about it to explain that in his efforts to drive the price of molybdenum up, Felder had illegally raided a number of trusts (Nancy's presumably included) where he had sufficient clout with the trustees to make them do as he wanted. I then shamelessly pumped him for his views on the various currencies whose movements might affect my business, until a BBC car arrived which Edward had arranged to take Miss Twill home. She was staying at Brown's, and as David had rooms in Albany he took the chance of a lift. I formally offered to drive Lucy back to Eaton Square, and she kept up the charade and gratefully accepted.

As soon as we were alone, she said, "Gerry's going to marry Nan."

"So I hear."

"On the same day as Ben and Michael. Same filthy cricket match! And I'd been looking forward to it!"

(A fortnight or so earlier I'd received a note from Nancy saying that Ben was to be married from Blatchards early in September, in the morning, so that they could hold a celebratory cricket match in the afternoon and have a party in the evening. I was to come and score.)

"You are not enthusiastic?" I said.

"I could spit! Let's talk about something else."

Next morning I telephoned Mrs. Mudge.

Ten years later, it will be remembered, she was briefly a popular media figure following a police raid and a prosecution for living on immoral earnings. She must by then have been well into her seventies. She had always born a mild resemblance to Queen Elizabeth, the queen mother, and for her court appearances deliberately dressed to enhance the likeness, spoke in much the same voice, and tended to use the royal *we* when referring to herself. Most people assumed she was doing this for laughs, as part of the sexual/satirical revolution that was then in full swing, but I guessed she had begun the act not as a tease but in an attempt to emphasise her own respectability and social worth, though she was then quite bright enough to recognise the effect she was having and to broaden her pastiche into caricature. She was always deeply interested in the doings of the royal family and was known to long to number one of them among her clients. I believe she used to hint that Edward VIII, when prince of Wales, had been at least friendly, which is possible, since in those days she used to run a little smart-sleazy hotel and was a pet, rather in the manner of Rosa Lewis, among some of the raffish rich.

Be that as it may, at the time of which I am writing she had what she called an "agency." I had come across her because at one stage in the war, just before I had been posted to the organisation in Cairo, I had spent an unpleasant six months in London with a section, set up with unwonted prescience by some maverick in the security world, which was attempting to subvert members of legations in what was to become the Eastern Bloc. We had a few successes, all of whom were executed as soon as the communists took power. Mrs. Mudge had supplied us with some of what my colleagues insisted on calling "live bait." She was devotedly patriotic and regarded these activities as her war work, even claiming to be giving us a reduced rate for her services, though no doubt charging as much for them as she thought the market would bear. When

I had got in touch with her for help with my Dutchman, she had seemed delighted to be reminded of "the old days," but now her reception of my call was icy. She recognised my voice.

"Mr. Charles!"

We had all used pseudonyms, and mine, I'm sorry to say, had been Charlie. Mrs. Mudge was not one for that level of informality.

"Got it in one," I said. "I hope you're well, Mrs. Mudge."

"We have nothing to say to you."

"I'm sorry. I don't understand."

"You have let me down very badly. Very badly indeed."

"You'll have to explain."

"You know quite well what I'm talking about, Mr. Charles. You gave a certain person my name. He proved utterly untrustworthy."

"I'm sorry to hear that. I didn't know. He's a very old acquaintance of mine, and he's never let me down. Is there anything I can do to make amends? Are you in a position to tell me what happened?"

"Well . . . for old times' sake, then. There is a very talented child I befriended when she was alone in London, and not yet twenty. How some parents allow that I cannot imagine, and I don't know what mightn't have happened to her if she hadn't come under my wing. When your friend called and explained his problem, she came immediately to mind."

"Can you tell me roughly what it was he wanted, Mrs. Mudge? I'm not asking you to break confidences, of course."

"Oh, I certainly wouldn't normally, but after what he's done! I don't know if you are aware of it, Mr. Charles, but there are some gentlemen who seem to feel that they have not been sufficiently corrected in their youth—"

"I've heard about that. Did he want her to be able to dress as a man?"

She sounded surprised, and immediately suspicious again.

"What made you think that?" she said.

"If it's the same girl, that's how she was dressed when I met her."

"You didn't tell me that you had met her."

"If it's the same girl . . . please, Mrs. Mudge, this really is aboveboard. It involves a very dear friend of mine, and I don't want her hurt. That's all."

"I see. In that case . . . Yes, the girl likes to pass herself off as a young man, but I don't believe your friend made it a requirement."

"What happened next?"

"We arranged an interview, which proved satisfactory, but believe it or not, within days the misguided girl had been persuaded to leave our protection, which was bad enough. But on top of that your friend allowed her to become involved with some very undesirable people."

The shock of what she appeared to be telling me took me off balance and I overdid my response, but she appeared not to notice.

"That's awful. I'm really appalled, Mrs. Mudge. Do you mean to say this happened without any acknowledgement to you?"

"Not even a severance fee, Mr. Charles."

"That's too bad. Would you like me to see what I can do about that? What do you suggest? Fifty pounds?"

"Guineas, please, Mr. Charles."

"I'll see what can be arranged."

"You are most kind."

"Tell me, Mrs. Mudge, have you tried to do anything about this yourself? Persuade the girl to come back, for instance?"

"I asked some friends of mine to reason with her, but they were forcibly prevented from doing so."

(Would she have told me if the men who'd tried to abduct the girl had recognised Gerry? I think so.)

"How unpleasant," I said. "Tell me, these people she is now connected with—are they by any chance involved in the licensing trade? In Wapping, perhaps?"

She hesitated again, but I reckoned she would know that she had not yet given me anything like enough for my fifty guineas.

"Are you sure you are not working for anyone else these days, Mr. Charles? Not you-know-who?"

"Not anymore. I work for myself, and it's not the sort of work we used to do ten years ago. I sell business machines for a living, but as I told you, I'm trying to help a friend. I happened to hear something at a dinner party about these people in Wapping, and put two and two together."

"Well, I have to believe you. Let me tell you that there are certain folk, not a hundred miles from Wapping, and if they were to learn that I'd been passing on tittle-tattle about them to someone who might be working for you-know-who—then, well, I don't know what."

"I quite understand. But you're not going to tell me I'm wrong in my guess?"

"No, I'm not going to tell you that."

"Well, thank you. I won't press you any further. What about the girl, though? What's she like, can you tell me? Apart from being ungrateful and disloyal, of course?"

"Oh, we are most disappointed in her. Such a waste. Such real possibilities. If only she'd played her cards right and followed my advice, she might have done really well for herself, made a good marriage, even. It has happened. . . . You say you've met her?"

"Not to talk to. Sat opposite her at a dinner party, when she was dressed as a man—for a bet, apparently."

"The things they get up to!"

"Otherwise I've seen her once in the distance, in a long dress with a wig. I thought she looked decidedly attractive like that."

"Oh, yes, quite a picture she can be, Mr. Charles. Apart from the lower limbs, poor dear. Too much muscle is not becoming, I always think."

"Perhaps that's why she prefers to wear trousers. Is she intelligent?"

"Far from stupid, and a nice educated voice she can do, too. Her big problem is the way she's got it in for men. Quite a few of them have, deep down, in my experience, and of course there's gentlemen that find that interesting in various ways. . . . Only this girl's got it stronger than most."

"Any idea why?"

"You'd need Professor Freud to tell you that, but it's something that happened a long time ago, when she was a little girl, I should think. It usually is."

"All right. I'll call again in a few days' time, and if you happen to have heard any more, I'd be very glad to know. And I'll see what I can manage about your fee. How would you like it paid?"

"In cash, if you please. Leave it in an envelope for me with the cashier at Culley's in Jermyn Street when you're next passing, please."

"That's the saddler's, isn't it? It will be there by tomorrow evening."

"How thoughtful of you."

"Not at all."

We rang off. I was of course considerably perturbed and distressed by what I seemed to have learnt, but I had no time to think about it for a while, as a Spanish client of mine with whom I was hoping to do a lot of business was already waiting for me. By the time I was able to call Lucy, she had gone out, so I sent a note round asking her to get in touch at once. She sounded cross when she rang, and reluctant, but I insisted on a meeting. We had found a strange little tearoom a few minutes' walk from my office, and the same from Heal's and the British Museum, and other places where Lucy might reasonably get the chauffeur to drop her. It was one of about a dozen small shops around a quiet crossroads—a tobacconist, an ironmonger, a fishmonger selling only three basic sorts of fish, and so on—all having an air of being left over from before the war. The sweet shop looked as if it might still be selling sherbet in halfpenny twists. The tearoom had this aura, too. The middle-aged waitress wore a lace cap and apron, called one "dearie," and brought excellent fresh tea and homemade sponge cake. It was a quietly cheerful place, with a regular clientele, though we never needed to wait for a table. Some of these were in screened booths, so we had a sense of secrecy, congenial to such an affair. That afternoon Lucy stood out in the open, looking round while she removed her gloves.

"Father would have liked this place," she said as she sat down.

"I expect so. How have things been?"

"Just living from day to day. Sometimes I feel I want to go back to when I was seventeen and start all over again."

"You're sure about the seventeen?"

"It'll do. Why?"

"It doesn't cut me out of your life. We'd already met."

Her smile was not convincing. I sensed her unhappiness, but when the waitress came for our order, treating us already as old customers, she made the necessary small talk with apparent pleasure and interest.

"You've got something to tell me," she said as soon as we were alone.

"You're not going to like it. I don't."

"Let's get it over."

I started with what Edward Voss-Thompson had told me at the dinner party. She listened impassively, asking no questions but breaking again into factitious liveliness while our tea was brought. Her only comment on that episode was "Michael is a bastard. Go on." So I told her about Gerry's original request and my conversation with Mrs. Mudge.

When I'd finished, she drank her tea in silence for several minutes. Then she said, "Sorry. I was getting over being furious with you. I wanted to scream at you that it was all none of your business, and you should never have rung that woman and you should never have told me, but I suppose you had to. Now you'd better tell me what you think I ought to do."

"It is still none of my business."

"Go on."

"If you tell Nancy, she'll tell Gerry?"

"Of course, but I don't have to tell her about the programme. I can just say it's something I found out, but I can't tell her how."

"Will she accept that?"

"She'll bloody have to. Let's have another pot of tea. And a lot more cake. The only thing to do when you're really miserable is to eat or drink, and drinking's worse. Then you can tell me what to do about Tommy."

She sat brooding while I caught the waitress's eye and reordered.

"You are not yet prepared to ask him for a divorce?" I said.

"No. Definitely not. He won't divorce me because he's a Catholic. Besides, he's got an idea that what's happening is like some sort of disease he's going to get better from, and then we can go back to rubbing along like we were."

"But you could divorce him."

"He won't give me the evidence, and don't tell me I could use this girl. Just think of it in the papers. It would finish him—and it would be almost as horrible for me. And even if it were someone normal, you know, the sort of woman he might have met at a dinner party and fallen in love with . . . No, I don't mean that. . . . If he'd really fallen in love, of course I would. . . . 'Got besotted with,' I suppose . . . Have you got any idea what I'm talking about?"

"Not much."

"He committed himself to me, because he was a Catholic. He knew what he was doing, that I'd had affairs and so on. I couldn't do less, could I? I promised. I'm not going to break my promise unless he wants me to. I've always known that."

I thought this extremely pigheaded of her, but I could see she meant it, so I held my tongue. Our second tea arrived, but she'd hardly begun on it when she looked at her watch and rose.

"I've got to go," she said. "I'll try to talk to Tommy. And Nan. I don't know about Ben—I sort of feel it's her lookout. I'll see what Nan says. Is there anything else?"

"Yes. Most of this is, as you say, not my business, but Gerry seems deliberately to have involved me, and I've a perfect right to ask him why."

"Oh, please don't. Not yet, anyway—not till I've talked to Nan."

"If you say so."

Lucy

EIGHT

June–July 1956

I'm going to have to do this in more than one go, because
several things happened and I can't remember quite in what
order. There was talking to Tommy, of course, and Nan, and
something else—it'll come to me.

Anyway, talking to Tommy. We hadn't said anything much
since we'd talked after the opera, just carried on as usual.
Tommy was working appallingly hard. He was away quite a
bit, mainly in France and America, trying to get a common
front together against Colonel Nasser. It was all very tricky
for him because Anthony Nutting, who was officially senior
to him at the FO, disapproved of what was going on, and the
civil servants at the FO were desperately pro-Arab, which
meant anti-Israel, and Selwyn Lloyd, who was foreign secretary—I really liked him, and not just because he reminded me
of the man who kept the sweet shop in Bury where we were
allowed to go if we'd been good on shopping expeditions—
Selwyn Lloyd couldn't afford to do too much of the plotting
in case things went wrong, and Eden kept changing his mind
though he really detested Nasser, and the French were impossible as usual, and the Israelis didn't care what happened to
anyone else provided they got what they wanted, and there was
Tommy—cold, honourable, reasonable, frightened Tommy—

having to act like a shifty kind of middleman doing dirty deals and knowing that if it all went wrong he'd be the one who got the blame. And on top of all this, his marriage was a sham and he was infatuated with a call girl.

Not that he talked to me about any of this, either. We'd have breakfast together if we were both in town or at Seddon Hall, and we'd be perfectly friendly—in fact most of the time we felt like good old friends—and if we talked, it would be about the children, or arrangements about cars and dinner parties. Luckily he was too busy for week-end house parties. Of course after what happened, I've always been interested in Suez, so I've read everything I can about it, and even when the books disagree with each other, I usually know enough from being on the fringe of it to have a good guess who's right and who's wrong. But at the time all I knew was that Tommy was away a lot and working much too hard and not enjoying it.

In fact I had a better idea what was going on between him and Sammy Whitstable. If he was abrupt and nervous and finished his breakfast early, then I knew he was seeing her that night, and then next day he'd be extrafriendly and relaxed and wanting to know if I was alright. I was glad it was that way round. I've sometimes wondered, suppose earlier on I'd thought of wearing men's clothes and bossing him around— Paul seems to think they went in for whips and things—oh, how can I know? In fact to be absolutely honest, I've never really understood why men seem to want me as I am. Me, rather than anyone else, I mean. I just feel I wouldn't, in their shoes. Of course sometimes you can see things which seem to make sense; for instance, my own Timmy, instead of messing around and trying things out with different girls the way it's so easy for them nowadays struck up with an art student when they were both only nineteen and stayed with her through thick and thin. Her father was a bricklayer at an ironworks, and she still speaks like that—Staffordshire—though she's

Lady Seddon now. Tommy thought he'd get tired of her and marry someone more suitable, but I'd heard her talking to Timmy the way his nanny used to, as if he wasn't safe to cross the road without having his hand held . . . where was I? Putting off talking about telling Tommy.

There wasn't that much to it, as a matter of fact. We were at Seddon Hall, in the Breakfast Room, which was modelled on that place where Charlemagne's tomb is, but surprisingly cosy despite that, and the sun was streaming in and there were kidneys and bacon and scrambled eggs and mushrooms on the sideboard, so it must have been Saturday morning. I can smell them now.

I said, "I'm afraid there's something I've got to talk to you about."

He just nodded, but he put his paper down, so he must have known it mattered.

"That evening at the opera," I said. "Do you know why we were there? Gerry rang Paul up almost at the last moment and said he'd got tickets to spare, only when we got there, we found they weren't all four together. And Nan was furious all evening, and I think that was because he'd made her come when she didn't want to. Wait. And then a few days ago we had dinner with Janet and Edward, and Edward told Paul he was doing a programme about some nasty property deals, you know, turning old people out of houses, which Michael Allwegg seems to have something to do with, and Gerry works for Michael, and Paul somehow put two and two together and next day he rang up someone he used to know who supplies call girls because he'd given Gerry her number a bit before, and she pretty well told him that Gerry had asked her for someone special and she'd suggested your friend, and then your friend had suddenly stopped working for her and it was *her* friends who were trying to get her back that night in Greek Street—I'm afraid that sounds desperately muddled. Do you understand?"

He sighed.

"Well enough," he said.

"I'm sorry. I know you like Michael," I said.

He made a little gesture with his hand, telling me to stop talking, and then just sat there staring straight in front of him.

"Very well," he said at last. "You were no doubt right to tell me. Now it is my turn. I have three things to contribute. All of them are security matters, so I must ask you not to pass them on to Ackerley. Do I have your word?"

"Yes, but you don't have to tell me. I just thought—"

He stopped me again.

"The first thing is about the UFTFA official who dropped out of the dinner party," he said.

"Mikovicz?" I said. "The playboy?"

"That's the man," he said. "You remember I was going to have him looked into? David Pottinger tells me that he is thought to be a senior agent in the Yugoslav intelligence service. The other two things are more intimate. You'll remember that when we married, you were subjected to a security interview? Other checks were run on your immediate family and close friends, and very much to my surprise I was informed that two of them turned out to be what they called 'semipositive,' that is to say not above suspicion. They were Ackerley and Grantworth."

My mouth fell open.

"I have long regarded the suspicions of most security services as largely paranoid," he said. "So I decided not to pay much attention, particularly as one of the reasons I was given for the suspicion of Grantworth was an obviously bureaucratic bungle involving a double identity."

"His doppelgänger!" I said. "Was it a blue-eyed madman who told you all this? If so, it was me who told him about Gerry's doppelgänger. Good Lord!"

"I share your opinion of the man," said Tommy, "though

he carries a lot of weight these days. However, even madmen can occasionally be correct, and David Pottinger now tells me that Mikovicz was a senior member of the partisan group with whom Grantworth worked in the war."

"Oh," I said. "Anyway, I still think he's potty. His bonnet's all bees. Did he tell you *I* couldn't be trusted, either?"

"Not in so many words," said Tommy. "But that was the third thing."

"And you still went ahead and married me?" I said.

"I chose to," he said. "I felt I needed to. I wish it had worked out better."

"Oh, so do I!" I said. "Do you think . . . ?"

"No," he said. His body gave a little jerk, as though it wanted to jump up and rush out of the room, but he'd managed to stop it.

"I'm afraid not," he said in his Foreign Office voice. "I think we have burnt our boats. I'm sorry."

"I'm sorry, too," I said. I managed not to start crying—he'd have hated that. I thought of telling him there must be ways of building another boat, but then I thought not. So I let him go back to his newspaper and finished my breakfast and just squeezed his hand when I left the room.

I did that yesterday. The upsetting bits are extra tiring. But in the middle of the night I remembered the other bit I've got to get in, about David Fish, so I'll do that before I go on about talking to Nan, which might be upsetting too.

Well, David rang, out of the blue, and asked me to lunch. He sounded really embarrassed about it, but he managed to make it clear that he wasn't just hoping to get things going again between him and me. He said he was in a silly mess and he needed my help. I'd always felt a bit guilty about David, as if I'd used him, twice, without him really having a say, so I agreed. He gave me directions. I had to go to a pub in the city, go through the Saloon Bar as if I was going to the loos, and then up some dark stairs, two floors, where there'd be a door with a "Private" notice on it.

I did that, getting more and more inquisitive. The bar was rowdy with large men lunching off double gins, and the stairs reeked of grease and gravy, but the room was fascinating, with really old panelling and diamond-pattern windows, the real thing with old wavy glass. You could easily imagine Restoration rake-hells getting roaring drunk in there and then going out to beat up any honest citizens who had the bad luck to meet them. David was there before me. He had taken a picture off the wall and was peering at the panelling behind it.

"Shan't be a mo'," he said, but then he made a mess of getting the picture back on its hook and I had to help him.

"The trouble is I don't know what I'm looking for," he said. "I think we'll just have to assume it's OK. Have some lunch— it's all cold—so we don't get interrupted."

He was gabbling, so I sat down and helped myself to cold beef and salad, slowly, to give him a chance to pull himself together. When he was ready, too, I smiled at him, doing my best to look wise and calm and comforting, and said, "Well, how can I help?"

"That dinner party," he said. "Janet, your sister, she said something about what you were doing after Halford Hall closed down."

"Janet gets pretty well everything wrong," I said. "Anyway, I'm not supposed to talk about it."

"I don't want you to," he said. "I'm just hoping you can tell me somebody I can go to, because I'm in a mess."

"What sort of mess?" I said. "I won't tell anyone else. I promise."

"Thanks," he said. "I'd certainly rather you didn't. Actually, I can't think of anyone else I could talk to, because you'll understand. Well, let's get it over. Earlier this year I went to Yugoslavia for a fortnight. I don't know if you remember, but I'm a Roman Empire fanatic, and I didn't just want to go to the obvious places like Split, which they've started to open up. I wanted to get there before they started to spoil things with all the tourists. The trouble was, the Yugoslavs weren't at all keen. They don't like us going where we can't be watched. I wasn't getting anywhere, and I moaned about it to everyone I met, and then, out of the blue, the Yugoslav embassy—not the tourist board—rang me up and said they actually wanted someone like me to go and have a look round at places which they might open up for archaeological tours, because they needed the foreign currency. They didn't just give me a visa and permits, they laid on a courier for me. Obviously that was so they could have me watched, but I didn't mind. I wasn't planning to do any spying, and I just thought it would be nice to have someone along who spoke the language, provided we got on alright. Which we did. In fact—this is what I mean about you being the only person I don't mind telling this to— Anna turned out to be a good deal more than your ordinary courier."

He peered at me slyly through his great thick glasses, waiting for me to laugh, which I did. The funny thing about David was that though he was absolutely not an Adonis and pretty wet in most ways, he was rather good in bed—fairly simple, but enjoying himself a lot and seeing that you did too.

"Sounds like a perfect holiday," I said.

"It was," he said. "At least I thought so at the time. We talked quite a bit about how to get her over to England, and I was going to go back and see her again as soon as I could. I've never felt so happy. I've been purring all summer. Then a few evenings ago a chap turned up at my door and showed me a photograph, just of me and Anna having a picnic. I remembered exactly when it happened. There was this man pushing his bicycle up the path through the olives, and he stopped to chat and we asked him to take our photograph with Anna's camera, so of course I assumed this other fellow came from her."

"Was he a Yugoslav too?" I asked.

"Well, if he was, he was a terrific actor. He looked a bit like an undertaker's assistant, professionally gloomy you know, but he talked a cut above that, like an estate agent in a dingy suburb, or a solicitor's clerk, or something. Of course I invited him in. Then he took out some more photographs. Me and Anna."

"In bed?" I said.

"And other places," he said. "You've no idea how empty that part of the world can be. She found some wonderful beaches. I thought we had them completely to ourselves. She showed me a lot of things you can do which I didn't know. They've got pictures of all that happening, and you can always see it's me. And there's some of us just doing touristy things in front of places you can recognise and see it's Yugoslavia."

"What do they want you to do?" I said. "Spy for them? I wouldn't have thought—"

"Nothing like that," he said. "I don't know anything. But there was this ghastly little man—he had a great big signet ring on one hand, and he kept rapping it with his knuckle and saying, 'Hot stuff, eh, Mr. Fish. Hot stuff. You wouldn't want that coming out, would you?' I asked him what he wanted. I thought it was going to be money, and I'd already decided to tell him to go to hell, but he said, 'Just a little cooperation, Mr. Fish. Just a little cooperation on the international money markets. We're not asking anything illegal.'

" 'No dice,' I told him. 'You aren't going to find a paper prepared to publish muck like this, and it wouldn't do me much harm if you did.'

"I mean, who'd mind? It's not as if I'm married or anything. But the fellow just tut-tutted and tapped his bloody ring and said, 'That's as may be, Mr. Fish. But you wouldn't want Mr. Jules Okers in New York, as a for-instance, finding one of these in his breakfast mail with a note about it all happening on the other side of the Iron Curtain. Would you, now?'

"That shook me. It's no use my trying to explain how I earn my living, but the point is that it all depends on trust. I work on very fine margins, two- or three-hundredths of a point, maybe, and all over the telephone. So you've got to be sure that the chap at the other end will stick to exactly what he's said he'll do, and he's got to know the same about you. Jules Okers is one of the people I deal with in New York. He's an out-and-out anticommunist. Rabid is not too strong a word. I had no intention of letting him know I'd even been the other side of the Iron Curtain, let alone that I'd had an affair with a woman who turned out to be an agent of the secret police. Maybe I could talk Jules round, maybe not, but suppose I can't, suppose he's got even the beginnings of a doubt about me, then I'm in trouble. He'll pass the word round, and it might take me years to get back to where I am now. If ever."

"Where did this man come from?" I said. "How did he know?"

"I've no idea," he said. "I'm just telling you what happened. Well, it shook me when he mentioned Jules, and I let him see it—I'm not much of an actor, I'm afraid. All I could do was ask him again what he wanted. 'Just you sit tight for the mo', Mr. Fish,' he said. 'I'll be leaving you the snaps as a reminder. Nice to see young people enjoying themselves, I always say. If you want copies, we've got the negs, right? And we'll be in touch when we need you. Don't come to the door. I'll let myself out.' And off he went. I haven't heard from him since."

"What do you think he wants?" I said. "Did he really mean it wasn't illegal? I mean, why bother—"

"Good Lord," he said. "I'm sometimes not sure if some of the things *I* do are legal. They haven't been tested in the courts yet. The exchange controls are a total maze, but I do know my way round most of it. That's the point. Suppose you got wind there was going to be a great run on sterling on such and such a date, you couldn't just go to your bank and borrow a few million quid and buy dollars with it, with an option to buy your sterling back the day after the run. You'd have to come to someone like me. You'd need to put some money down—if we're talking millions, a couple of hundred thousand would do it—and then I could put the deal through for you on the back of other transactions in such a way that, provided you took your profit in sterling, the whole thing was still inside the rules. Mind you, I'd have to set it up. The people I deal with are extremely sharp. I can't just ask Jules Okers, say, to take a great block of sterling off me out of the blue. He'd smell a rat at once. I'd need to have been doing things before that which made it look like part of my normal pattern of dealing, and I'd have to have what looked like reasons for that pattern, and so on. I could do it, but I doubt if there are more than half-a-dozen other people in the City who could. They must have known that when they set this up."

"Who are 'they'?" I said.

"The Yugoslavs, I assume," he said. "Probably not their central bank, more likely some security outfit operating on its own. They're always hungry for hard currency. Much more use to them, if they could bring it off, than stealing plans of the latest fighter. Anyway, it's all academic, because I'm not going to do what they want. I don't get angry very easily, you know, but I'm really angry about this. After that bastard had gone, I burnt all the photographs except the one of the picnic, and I sat looking at it and thinking about Anna. There was one particular beach I couldn't get out of my mind. We swam, and fooled around in the water and took our towels up onto the sand, and she made a fuss about choosing a really lucky place—laughing about it, fey, excited—at least that's what I thought, only now I know she was making sure we were in a good light and at a good angle so that the beggar on top of the rocks could get a nice clear picture of us, showing exactly who I was and what we were up to, when all I was thinking was what fun we were having, and it was just us, and just for each other. I'm never going to have another holiday like that, to be, poised and smart and going to dances and looking at least three years older than she really was. That made things easier for the rest of us.

Then the war came, splitting us all up, and then she married Dick and went to America and tried being smart-set rich for a bit (which I bet she did perfectly), and I still used to write pages to her every now and then and she'd always answer. And then she seemed to get bored with that and came back to England and took a deep breath and changed again. It happened just about when she set up at Blatchards with Gerry. At first she used to go up to London most weeks to be with him, but she soon stopped doing that and pretty well only went up to buy things she couldn't get in Bury. She wore practically no makeup and stopped having her hair cut and permed and put it up into a bun and wore polo necks and slacks most of the time, and so on. But she was always clean and neat, and if she had to dress up, she did it properly.

In fact that was one thing about Nan that didn't change. Whatever she was doing or being, she did it properly. She was never mad about horses, like Mother, but she rode really well. And when she came back to England, she brought the Ferrari Dick had given her and drove it incredibly fast, but you felt just as safe with her as if it had been a Morris Minor. And so on. So now she started taking on the sort of jobs we'd always been brought up to believe only Mr. Chad could do, or you had to get in proper workmen for, because people like us didn't know how, and certainly not if we were women.

Father hated change and Mother couldn't be bothered, so when Nan moved in, a lot of the rooms hadn't been decorated since before the First War. She tried a local firm, found out what it would cost, and decided she and Mr. Chad could do it between them, which they did. Then Gerry started complaining about the hot water in the West Wing, which was where they mostly lived because those were the nicest rooms, only the old gas plant, which was right away in the Brew

and now I haven't even got that. They've ruined it. I don't want just to tell them to go to hell. I want to get back at them somehow."

"I bet they blackmailed her into it," I said.

"I've thought of that," he said. "I hope so, but it isn't enough. How can I get them to eat their own dirt, that's what I want to know."

"What about Mr. Okers?" I said.

"That's why I came to you," he said. "I'd still like to keep it quiet, and I'd like those negatives destroyed. But most of all I want to make things hot for whoever cooked up this idiot idea, and I thought the first place to start might be by finding someone sympathetic in our own security setup. Do you know anyone?"

"Oh dear," I said. "It's been a long time. Actually—I don't usually talk about this—I'm the wrong person, because I was sacked. I blotted my copybook and broke the rules and they decided they couldn't trust me anymore. I do know one man who's still there. He's pretty high up now. But I don't like him, in fact I think he's mad, and I wouldn't trust him an inch. How difficult. The only thing I can think of, and I'd have to ask Tommy first because I mustn't go behind his back, is that you could try David Pottinger. I don't know him very well, and he hasn't got any small talk, but I think he's probably alright. He's Foreign Office, but he's the one Tommy talks to about security things. I wish I knew him better. I've a sort of hunch he might be upset about all the sex. You never know."

He thought about it and shook his head.

"Not if it means going through your husband," he said. "I'm sorry . . . nothing personal, but . . ."

I've forgotten to say that during our brief fling after the Ascot party, David kept asking me to marry him. Now I just smiled as understandingly as I could, and told him that was all I could think of for the moment, but if anything came to me, I'd let him know. We talked about it a bit more, and then other things—he wanted to know all about Janet, for some reason—and only when he was helping me into my coat did he go back to the Anna business.

"You won't tell anyone about this, will you?" he said. "I mean, not anyone."

It was the way he said it. I realised he was talking about Paul, as well as Tommy. So he must have guessed. I didn't think we'd been that obvious, or else he'd got much brighter about that sort of thing than when I'd known him before.

This is actually three days later. Paul had to go away, and it was a new nurse came in, one with a button-holey eager look— I bet her lace curtains never stop twitching when she's at home—and I didn't want her listening outside the door while I was rambling on about family things. At least it's a relief having him away doing something else, not brooding and remembering and writing it down all day. The last lot he did, he didn't come to bed till four in the morning. I've tried to get him to stop. I've told him I think it's bad for him. He just said, "I've got to get it over." I feel like that, too, really, I suppose, though I'm not obsessed by it the way he is. Nothing's going to be ordinary again until we've finished.

Well, this bit is going to be mainly about Nan. I'm going to have to back, though. After I got married, I still used to try and get home most weeks—back to Blatchards, I mean. When the children happened, I had the excuse of taking them over from Seddon Hall to see Mother—they adored her just as much as she adored them—though I'd tell myself and anyone else who was listening what a chore it was. But even if they were ill, or Mother was away, I still used to do it, out of habit, really. I don't think I really enjoyed going that much, certainly not every time, and quite often I'd drive away feeling cross with myself, unsatisfied, like one of those dreams where you know something interesting or exciting is just about to happen

and then you wake up realising you've missed it, and you ca even remember what.

Mother got a Shetland pony for Rowena, not a bad litt brute as Shetlands go, only it didn't. I mean it liked standir much better than walking—not that it mattered because R wena was far too small to do anything except perch. So I leave them and Nanny to the riding lessons (in the coach hou if it was raining, which Mother had cleared out much to Na and Gerry's irritation as it meant they had to find somewhe else to store a lot of accumulated junk which no one cou bring themselves to throw out), and I'd go down and see wh Nan was up to now.

I think I've said something about the way people chang and mostly you don't notice, only years too late you realiz that Harry, who you've written down as larky and odd bu worthwhile, because that's how he used to be, has actuall been a bitchy, selfish old nuisance since you don't know wher But some people let you see them changing, almost on purpos as if they were tired of who they'd been so far and now the were going to be someone else, and they wanted everyone t know, like sending out change-of-address cards.

Nan was that sort. When we were growing up, she wa always Top Girl, despite Harriet being the bossy one. In fact because Mother was such a bouncer and flouncer, a sort o perpetual teenage hoyden, I think we subconsciously electe Nan to play Mother instead. She was just much more suitable I was still a junior when Nan left school, and juniors were al sat down to write their letters home after Sunday chapel, so used to write a tidy page-and-just-over to Father and Mothe and use the rest of the time scrawling page after page to Nan and she always answered. (Mother usually forgot.)

Most teenage girls spend half their time longing to be grow up and the other half longing to slink back and be little girl again, but Nan simply was grown up as soon as she decided

House didn't usually produce enough gas for the West Wing
boiler, so the thing about the hot water in the West Wing
was that there wasn't any most of the time. Nan decided to
put in a separate oil system. She got estimates and told Gerry
she couldn't afford it. Gerry went on complaining. (This was
their first real set of rows, at least that I was aware of.) In the
end Nan bought a book and designed her own heating system.
She hired a professional to check it, and then hired a retired
plumber and worked as his mate until he got sick, when she
took over herself—plumbing's dead simple if you've got the
tools, she said—and in the end she put in two new bathrooms
and a spare loo as well as the central heating, hiring the
plasterers and carpenters when she needed them and firing
them if they weren't any good or tried to boss her around.
Then someone found dry rot in the laundry, so she gutted the
building and turned it into a flat, which she let. And so on.

She always had some new project on. It kept her busy. "It
stops me thinking," she used to say. I thought this was a joke
for a while, and then I realised that she meant it, because she
wasn't at all happy.

We got into a pattern. I'd ring up and check she'd be
around, and then I'd bring the kids and Nanny over and dump
them with Mother and go down to the house and get a tea tray
together and take it along to Nan and she'd stop what she was
doing and have a tea break, and we'd talk. She needed somebody to talk to, I decided, and that must mean she couldn't
talk to Gerry.

I remember once I found her with Mr. Chad putting security
catches onto the windows in the Rose Room. (We'd had to do
the same at Seddon Hall because there'd been a rash of big-
house burglaries around, and we actually had things worth
stealing, Raphaels and so on, which Nan didn't.) Mr. Chad
tactfully made himself scarce usually, but this time he was in
the middle of an argument with Nan. I always enjoyed it when
this happened because of the way they went about it, good-

humoured but pigheaded, teasing, scoring points off each other, as though it was all part of a much longer argument that would never properly end until they were both dead, just like a sensibly married couple, in fact. I said so to Nan after Mr. Chad had left, and she laughed.

"Are there such things as sensible marriages?" she said. "How should I know?"

"You and Gerry are as good as," I said.

She just shrugged.

"Aren't you happy with him?" I said. "You don't have to tell me. It's none of my business."

"One doesn't have to be happy," she said. "Either one is coping with one's life, or one isn't. Most of the marriages I know are like that. Husbands and wives are ways of coping. Some work, some don't. Gerry and I have our ups and down, but mostly we seem to work."

"I thought you were besotted with him at first," I said.

"I suppose so," she said. "It's difficult to get oneself back into that sort of state of mind. Yes, I was, but then I wasn't. And he never was. The point about Gerry is that he's besotted with this house, and that's what matters to me. He may let me down, but he's not going to let the house down."

I didn't know what to say. I don't think I've ever heard anyone sound so bleak. Nan lit a cigarette and sat at the top of her stepladder, smoking and thinking.

"I took a chance with Gerry and I've lost," she said. "Of course I didn't think it out like that, but that's what it adds up to. On the other hand, who else was there? I mean, no doubt I could have found some bloke I could stand to live with who'd take me on, but this place? Gerry and I have rows, you know. Pretty savage at times. The one thing he's never come up with to fling at me is that it isn't worth hanging on here. He's as crazy about it as we are. He's genuinely longing for the day when he's made enough of a pile to take over from Dick and marry me and start having kids. You realise that if and now I haven't even got that. They've ruined it. I don't want just to tell them to go to hell. I want to get back at them somehow."

"I bet they blackmailed her into it," I said.

"I've thought of that," he said. "I hope so, but it isn't enough. How can I get them to eat their own dirt, that's what I want to know."

"What about Mr. Okers?" I said.

"That's why I came to you," he said. "I'd still like to keep it quiet, and I'd like those negatives destroyed. But most of all I want to make things hot for whoever cooked up this idiot idea, and I thought the first place to start might be by finding someone sympathetic in our own security setup. Do you know anyone?"

"Oh dear," I said. "It's been a long time. Actually—I don't usually talk about this—I'm the wrong person, because I was sacked. I blotted my copybook and broke the rules and they decided they couldn't trust me anymore. I do know one man who's still there. He's pretty high up now. But I don't like him, in fact I think he's mad, and I wouldn't trust him an inch. How difficult. The only thing I can think of, and I'd have to ask Tommy first because I mustn't go behind his back, is that you could try David Pottinger. I don't know him very well, and he hasn't got any small talk, but I think he's probably alright. He's Foreign Office, but he's the one Tommy talks to about security things. I wish I knew him better. I've a sort of hunch he might be upset about all the sex. You never know."

He thought about it and shook his head.

"Not if it means going through your husband," he said. "I'm sorry . . . nothing personal, but . . ."

I've forgotten to say that during our brief fling after the Ascot party, David kept asking me to marry him. Now I just smiled as understandingly as I could, and told him that was all I could think of for the moment, but if anything came to me, I'd let him know. We talked about it a bit more, and then other things—he wanted to know all about Janet, for some reason—and only when he was helping me into my coat did he go back to the Anna business.

"You won't tell anyone about this, will you?" he said. "I mean, not anyone."

It was the way he said it. I realised he was talking about Paul, as well as Tommy. So he must have guessed. I didn't think we'd been that obvious, or else he'd got much brighter about that sort of thing than when I'd known him before.

This is actually three days later. Paul had to go away, and it was a new nurse came in, one with a button-holey eager look—I bet her lace curtains never stop twitching when she's at home—and I didn't want her listening outside the door while I was rambling on about family things. At least it's a relief having him away doing something else, not brooding and remembering and writing it down all day. The last lot he did, he didn't come to bed till four in the morning. I've tried to get him to stop. I've told him I think it's bad for him. He just said, "I've got to get it over." I feel like that, too, really, I suppose, though I'm not obsessed by it the way he is. Nothing's going to be ordinary again until we've finished.

Well, this bit is going to be mainly about Nan. I'm going to have to back, though. After I got married, I still used to try and get home most weeks—back to Blatchards, I mean. When the children happened, I had the excuse of taking them over from Seddon Hall to see Mother—they adored her just as much as she adored them—though I'd tell myself and anyone else who was listening what a chore it was. But even if they were ill, or Mother was away, I still used to do it, out of habit, really. I don't think I really enjoyed going that much, certainly not every time, and quite often I'd drive away feeling cross with myself, unsatisfied, like one of those dreams where you know something interesting or exciting is just about to happen and then you wake up realising you've missed it, and you can't even remember what.

Mother got a Shetland pony for Rowena, not a bad little brute as Shetlands go, only it didn't. I mean it liked standing much better than walking—not that it mattered because Rowena was far too small to do anything except perch. So I'd leave them and Nanny to the riding lessons (in the coach house if it was raining, which Mother had cleared out much to Nan and Gerry's irritation as it meant they had to find somewhere else to store a lot of accumulated junk which no one could bring themselves to throw out), and I'd go down and see what Nan was up to now.

I think I've said something about the way people change, and mostly you don't notice, only years too late you realise that Harry, who you've written down as larky and odd but worthwhile, because that's how he used to be, has actually been a bitchy, selfish old nuisance since you don't know when. But some people let you see them changing, almost on purpose, as if they were tired of who they'd been so far and now they were going to be someone else, and they wanted everyone to know, like sending out change-of-address cards.

Nan was that sort. When we were growing up, she was always Top Girl, despite Harriet being the bossy one. In fact, because Mother was such a bouncer and flouncer, a sort of perpetual teenage hoyden, I think we subconsciously elected Nan to play Mother instead. She was just much more suitable. I was still a junior when Nan left school, and juniors were all sat down to write their letters home after Sunday chapel, so I used to write a tidy page-and-just-over to Father and Mother and use the rest of the time scrawling page after page to Nan, and she always answered. (Mother usually forgot.)

Most teenage girls spend half their time longing to be grown up and the other half longing to slink back and be little girls again, but Nan simply was grown up as soon as she decided to be, poised and smart and going to dances and looking at least three years older than she really was. That made things easier for the rest of us.

Then the war came, splitting us all up, and then she married Dick and went to America and tried being smart-set rich for a bit (which I bet she did perfectly), and I still used to write pages to her every now and then and she'd always answer. And then she seemed to get bored with that and came back to England and took a deep breath and changed again. It happened just about when she set up at Blatchards with Gerry. At first she used to go up to London most weeks to be with him, but she soon stopped doing that and pretty well only went up to buy things she couldn't get in Bury. She wore practically no makeup and stopped having her hair cut and permed and put it up into a bun and wore polo necks and slacks most of the time, and so on. But she was always clean and neat, and if she had to dress up, she did it properly.

In fact that was one thing about Nan that didn't change. Whatever she was doing or being, she did it properly. She was never mad about horses, like Mother, but she rode really well. And when she came back to England, she brought the Ferrari Dick had given her and drove it incredibly fast, but you felt just as safe with her as if it had been a Morris Minor. And so on. So now she started taking on the sort of jobs we'd always been brought up to believe only Mr. Chad could do, or you had to get in proper workmen for, because people like us didn't know how, and certainly not if we were women.

Father hated change and Mother couldn't be bothered, so when Nan moved in, a lot of the rooms hadn't been decorated since before the First War. She tried a local firm, found out what it would cost, and decided she and Mr. Chad could do it between them, which they did. Then Gerry started complaining about the hot water in the West Wing, which was where they mostly lived because those were the nicest rooms, only the old gas plant, which was right away in the Brew

House didn't usually produce enough gas for the West Wing boiler, so the thing about the hot water in the West Wing was that there wasn't any most of the time. Nan decided to put in a separate oil system. She got estimates and told Gerry she couldn't afford it. Gerry went on complaining. (This was their first real set of rows, at least that I was aware of.) In the end Nan bought a book and designed her own heating system. She hired a professional to check it, and then hired a retired plumber and worked as his mate until he got sick, when she took over herself—plumbing's dead simple if you've got the tools, she said—and in the end she put in two new bathrooms and a spare loo as well as the central heating, hiring the plasterers and carpenters when she needed them and firing them if they weren't any good or tried to boss her around. Then someone found dry rot in the laundry, so she gutted the building and turned it into a flat, which she let. And so on.

She always had some new project on. It kept her busy. "It stops me thinking," she used to say. I thought this was a joke for a while, and then I realised that she meant it, because she wasn't at all happy.

We got into a pattern. I'd ring up and check she'd be around, and then I'd bring the kids and Nanny over and dump them with Mother and go down to the house and get a tea tray together and take it along to Nan and she'd stop what she was doing and have a tea break, and we'd talk. She needed somebody to talk to, I decided, and that must mean she couldn't talk to Gerry.

I remember once I found her with Mr. Chad putting security catches onto the windows in the Rose Room. (We'd had to do the same at Seddon Hall because there'd been a rash of big-house burglaries around, and we actually had things worth stealing, Raphaels and so on, which Nan didn't.) Mr. Chad tactfully made himself scarce usually, but this time he was in the middle of an argument with Nan. I always enjoyed it when this happened because of the way they went about it, good-humoured but pigheaded, teasing, scoring points off each other, as though it was all part of a much longer argument that would never properly end until they were both dead, just like a sensibly married couple, in fact. I said so to Nan after Mr. Chad had left, and she laughed.

"Are there such things as sensible marriages?" she said. "How should I know?"

"You and Gerry are as good as," I said.

She just shrugged.

"Aren't you happy with him?" I said. "You don't have to tell me. It's none of my business."

"One doesn't have to be happy," she said. "Either one is coping with one's life, or one isn't. Most of the marriages I know are like that. Husbands and wives are ways of coping. Some work, some don't. Gerry and I have our ups and down, but mostly we seem to work."

"I thought you were besotted with him at first," I said.

"I suppose so," she said. "It's difficult to get oneself back into that sort of state of mind. Yes, I was, but then I wasn't. And he never was. The point about Gerry is that he's besotted with this house, and that's what matters to me. He may let me down, but he's not going to let the house down."

I didn't know what to say. I don't think I've ever heard anyone sound so bleak. Nan lit a cigarette and sat at the top of her stepladder, smoking and thinking.

"I took a chance with Gerry and I've lost," she said. "Of course I didn't think it out like that, but that's what it adds up to. On the other hand, who else was there? I mean, no doubt I could have found some bloke I could stand to live with who'd take me on, but this place? Gerry and I have rows, you know. Pretty savage at times. The one thing he's never come up with to fling at me is that it isn't worth hanging on here. He's as crazy about it as we are. He's genuinely longing for the day when he's made enough of a pile to take over from Dick and marry me and start having kids. You realise that if

I re-marry, bang goes my alimony? I'm not really supposed to cohabit. Dick's been very good about that, but he'd really mind if I managed a kid with Gerry when he and I couldn't."

"I didn't know," I said.

"So it may never happen," she said. "Not till too late, anyway. I suppose I could leave it to one of yours, or Hattie's or Janet's. Ben's, even, if she ever takes time off from dancing to have one. I don't think it would work. You've got to have grown up here to fall in love with the place before you're sensible enough to realise what's wrong with it. Hattie's and Janet's aren't here enough. Timmy will have his hands full with Seddon Hall. What about Rowena? She seems to like coming here."

"That's because she dotes on Mother," I said. "I don't think she even notices the house. Anyway, she isn't one of us, if you know what I mean. She comes from a different tribe— Tommy's, I suppose. Tommy's a terrific prig, you know. A really nice, kind prig. I'm really fond of him, so I can say that. Rowena's only four, so you can't tell yet if she's nice or kind, but I've known almost from the day she was born that she was a prig."

"I'm not sure children are such a good idea," said Nan. "Hattie seems to enjoy hers, I suppose. Well, all I can do for the moment is soldier on. Lucky I like it, isn't it?"

We talked a bit more, and then she went back to work and I walked up to the Stables wondering if I was being fair to Rowena. Actually I was, as it turned out, but I suppose I couldn't have known, really.

If Rowena was four when we had that talk, then it must have been about a year later that the business with Sammy Whitstable and Tommy and all that blew up, but it was still my usual pattern in spite of everything else that seemed to be happening. I drove over with the kids and Nanny, left them with Mother, and went down to the house to look for Nan, who'd told me that she was trying to get the outside woodwork

along the South Front and the East Wing painted in time for
the wedding party next month. I found her right up at the top
of an extension ladder doing the window of what used to be
Janet's bedroom. I'd put the tea tray down on the iron table
by the arbour and gone over to hold the bottom of the ladder,
which bounced horribly as she came down, though of course
being Nan, she'd got it safely lashed. She didn't seem to mind.

"I couldn't do that," I said. "It makes me sick even looking
at you."

"Don't talk to me about being sick," she said.

"Oh dear," I said. "Trouble?"

"They tell me it's Nature's way," she said. "I must say, I
think Nature could have come up with a better way."

We were just sitting down. I knew at once what she was
talking about. I felt myself go white. She must have been
watching me, on purpose, to see how I'd take it.

"I'm sorry, Lu," she said. "I hoped you wouldn't mind.
You're the first person I've told, except the doctor. And Gerry,
of course."

I didn't say anything.

"I'm sorry," she said again. "I thought you'd got over that
years ago."

"Of course I have," I snapped. "It's . . . well . . . I'm sorry
too. I can't help it. I don't want it. Only it just comes back
and bites me sometimes."

"Ahab's ghost," she said.

That made it alright. It was still a ghastly mess, but that
was all. I could be sane about it, think about it, do my best
to help. I'd better explain. Ahab was a cat from a litter which
had been born at the Home Farm. He was almost wild. Father
got him to deal with a plague of mice in the Gun Room, where
we kept our gumboots. This was when I was fairly small. He
lived under an oak chest in the passage outside the Gun Room
and rushed out and bit you as you went past, but he really did
deal with the mice so Father refused to get rid of him. (Father

wore boots, so he was Ahab-proof.) The chest was on the far side of the Gun Room door, so it was all right about the gumboots, but when we wanted to get to the Yellow Room without going right round and up and back down the secret stair, we had to climb onto a bench on one side of the chest, walk across the chest while Ahab lurked growling underneath, and off onto the stairs beyond. Long after Ahab died (he picked a fight with a visiting Alsatian and lost), we still used to do this. It was because of Ahab's ghost, we told people.

A ghost that still bit you sometimes. It was exactly right. And only one of us would have any idea what she was talking about. I sometimes think, still, that family is the only thing that really matters. Even when you're quarrelling with them, they mean things nobody else can mean. Anyway it was a very important moment. It changed things, changed the way I thought and felt about things, about Gerry. I think I realised, even then, that the ghost was never going to bite me again.

"Just like that," I said. "I'm sorry."

"Forget it," she said.

I poured the tea and Nan lit a cigarette and we didn't say anything for a bit. It was a blissful morning, the last dew just going, pigeons, the sound of the mower from Long Lawn. After a while I said, "I've got something to tell you. I'm afraid you aren't going to like it, especially after what you've just told me, but I think I've got to."

She just nodded, so I started at the beginning and told her everything—everything, I mean, except about it being Teddy Voss-Thompson who'd told Paul—the dinner party Sammy Whitstable had come to, and Paul's talks with Gerry and the Mudge woman, and the opera tickets, and the old people being frightened out of their homes, and so on. Nan didn't interrupt, but chainsmoked, lighting new cigarettes from the butts of the old ones. After a bit I noticed her other hand was pressed across her stomach as if she was trying to hold the baby in place. I stopped.

"Go on," she said. "I think it's alright."

So I finished. She sat and thought for a bit.

"Well, I suppose you had to tell me," she said. "I've heard better news. Bloody Michael. You were keen on him once, weren't you? Gerry told me."

I was appalled. I think I've said my affair with Michael is one of the things I'm truly ashamed of, and for him to go telling his crony about it, and the crony to tell my own sister . . . just thinking about it now, after all these years, it still makes my blood boil.

"Michael's an absolute bastard" was all I could say.

"He's worse than that," said Nan. "He's some kind of monster. He's almost done for Gerry—I've been trying to get him to see it for years. He knows. That's the dreadful thing. He knows. He's always said he's so deep in that he can't get out yet without losing everything he's made. Next year, he's kept saying, or the year after. In the end I lost patience. The day after Father's funeral I told him it's this year or not at all. Of course I didn't know then that Dick was going to go broke, but at least it meant we could get married."

"And have a baby," I said.

"That's the carrot," she said. "It wasn't my idea. He's always wanted one. Not just one, either. He wants to fill the house with a family, *his* family, but like we used to be. Funny, isn't it?"

She didn't make it sound funny.

"There's a stick as well as a carrot, I suppose," I said.

"There better had be," she said. "And by God if this means he's still letting Michael set him up to do all the dirty work . . ."

"Gerry told Paul he didn't want to involve Michael," I said.

"I don't believe it," she said. "Gerry wouldn't have had a clue what sort of a girl would work the oracle. Take it from me. He's still a total innocent about what goes on inside other people's heads. But Michael would have known exactly which switches to press."

She sat still, stroking the round of her stomach. You couldn't see any kind of a bulge yet, but from the way her hand moved, I knew it was there.

"It's funny," she said. "You know, I want this baby. I want it for itself. I started off quite cold-bloodedly, jumping the gun, because I agreed we wouldn't stop at just one, and there isn't that much time. But now it's actually happening, there's a great soft part of me I never knew was there, and all it wants is for the kid to have a life worth living. So for a start I'm not going to get rid of the kid, and that means if poss, I'm not going to get rid of Gerry either. I know he's been behaving like a total shit, but he isn't. Not like Michael. Michael's a shit through and through, and he's taken Gerry with him into the shit heap, but I'm bloody well going to get him back."

I stared at her. I'd seen her once before with that look, when she still had the Ferrari and a blond brute in a Healey cut in on her and waved his hand as he went past, and she sat on his tail for fifteen miles while he tried to get away and he couldn't.

"You can't always make people do things," I said.

"I've got the stick, remember," she said. "The next thing is to make him see I'm ready to use it. I must get hold of some really sharp lawyer, not old Wellow, he's useless. . . ."

She sat there for a bit, brooding.

"What about Ben?" I said.

"I'll write to her," she said, hardly thinking about it. "Ah well, back to work. I've got a paintbrush to rescue. Thanks for telling me, Lu. Don't do anything for the moment, and don't let Paul worry Gerry. I'll deal with him."

She jumped up and strode off to the ladder. I watched her climb it, feeling sick for her again as it bowed under her weight. Then I put the tea tray together and carried it in and washed up and went back up to the Stables.

I found Mother by the mounting block, crouched under the pony with Rowena, explaining how and why colts were gelded. Nanny's face was bright scarlet. This was pretty well all the sex education we'd had, apart from our own Nanny telling us that babies appeared from nowhere under gooseberry bushes and a soppy picture in a book of poems showing the fairies bringing them. A week before and I'd really have screeched at her. Now I just told her to stop talking nonsense, gathered the children up, and took them home.

Paul

NINE

July–August 1956

All Lucy told me about her talk with Nancy was that it had
taken place, that Nancy was now in charge and would deal
with Gerry, and the affair was no longer any business of ours.
I felt it was, but in my case only marginally, and besides I was
now at the critical stage of preparing my company for public
flotation, which involved a series of meetings where I had to
be personally present, decisions only I could take, and so on.
I was glad of the excuse to take no further steps of my own. I
did not ring Mrs. Mudge again.

Seddon was often out of the country, so Lucy had more free
time than usual, but mastering the paperwork for the flotation
often kept me at my desk till the small hours, so we still didn't
manage more than the occasional evening together, and one
night. By unspoken consent we chose not to spoil these occa-
sions by worrying over Vereker affairs. Just before another such
meeting, I returned to my flat and picked up the post from
my doormat. (I had left that morning well before it was delivered, to allow me to get home at a reasonable hour.) It included
a heavy white envelope with a Bury St. Edmunds postmark,
which I opened and found an engraved invitation to a party at
Blatchards to celebrate the marriages of the Honourable Nancy
Felder to Mr. Gerald Grantworth and the Honourable Belinda

Vereker to Mr. Michael Allwegg. "Luncheon, cricket, dinner, dancing," it said. Folded inside was a printed scorecard for the match, Blatchards *v*. Rest of World, with the names of the players on both sides and my own as scorer. I was astonished to see Seddon listed as playing for Blatchards, along with Gerry, Bobo Smith, and Michael Allwegg. There was also a note in Nancy's emphatic, slanting hand: "Counting on you. Keeping a room. *Please* come. For old time's sake!" That was the only suggestion of anything going on beneath the surface appearance of privileged jollification. I felt, as I say, astounded. The date was already pencilled into my diary, but I had naturally assumed that it was now all off. At this point I heard Lucy's key in the door and went out into the hallway to greet her, still holding the card.

She closed the door, turned, faced me, and said, "Ben and Michael were married on Saturday. In Paris."

"Good God!" I said.

"Nan rang and told me. She's just sent out—oh, you've had yours."

"I thought it was off already. It must be now."

"No. And she says we've all got to be there. She's going ahead with marrying Gerry. She's got to. She's having a baby."

"What!"

"What I said. We've got to be there. We've got to express solidarity."

"Ben didn't show much."

"All the more reason why the rest of us should."

"I can think of no more uncomfortable—"

"It's only a week-end, for God's sake! Please, Paul. It's important. She needs everyone there to back her up."

"One of your sisters has just married a man whom we have good reason to believe is criminally untrustworthy, and you are suggesting we should now support another sister in making the same mistake."

"All I know is Nan says it's going to be all right. She knows what she's doing, Paul."

"I will come if you insist."

"No. I want you to come, but I don't want to make you come. We don't do that to each other."

At this point our meal, which I had ordered from a local Italian restaurant, arrived. We ate it largely in silence, angry with ourselves and each other, until Lucy said, "Do you want Nan to ask you herself?"

"She has already," I said. "I think my problem is that I have a feeling of being used. Gerry has been using me, and now Nancy seems to want to to do the same. I don't object to being used, but I need to know how and why."

"I'll get Nan to talk to you," she said. "Is it all right if I give her your office number?"

"Much more chance of finding me there," I said. "I suppose that's best."

After that things eased, and we spent a quiet domestic evening, mostly watching TV. She had her period, which she tended to be squeamish about, so we didn't go to bed. As I kissed her good night in the hallway before driving her back to Eaton Square, I realised with a shock how tense her body still was.

"What is it, darling?" I said. "Is there something you haven't told me?"

"Only that I'm afraid," she said.

Nancy telephoned next day but wrong-footed me as I was beginning to excuse myself for my apparent oversensitivity, when she said, "In a minute, but there's something else first. I want you to do me a favour. You're not going to like it, but it's important."

"I'll do my best."

"Lucy told you about Ben and Michael getting married?"

"Yes."

"I'm pretty mad about it, but it's done now. Still, it's rather spoilt the original idea of our all four going off and getting married on the morning of the fifteenth, and then coming back for luncheon and the cricket match and the party after. So I've talked it over with Gerry and we've decided to clear the decks by getting married the week before. That'll make the fifteenth less of a *thing,* if you know what I mean. Just a cricket match and a party. Do you understand?"

"If you feel unable to cancel it completely—"

"No, that won't do. I'll explain in a minute. But listen. Gerry's got to have a best man, and I'm not going to let him have Michael, which was the original idea. They were each going to be each other's. I know you're not too pleased with Gerry at the moment. Nor, if I may say so, am I. But . . . well, when he asks you, will you please say yes? Are you still there?"

"Yes."

"And wondering how you can get out of it?"

"To some extent."

"Please don't. This is what I mean about it being important. I've got to make him understand that if he breaks up with Michael, he's got friends who'll stand by him. Do you understand? I know it's asking a lot, but . . ."

"Have you fixed a date?"

"Three o'clock on the sixth or seventh, at Bury Registry Office. I'd got all the paperwork done for the fifteenth, but they're letting me shift."

I looked at my diary. Both dates were hideous. I might have excused myself on those grounds alone.

"Shall we make it the sixth?" I said.

"You're a saint. Try and sound surprised when he asks you. Are you there?"

"If you keep springing things on me, you must expect these silences. Do I have to sound pleased?"

and at the same time so healingly, did they embody the ache
of irrecoverable time which I had been feeling that I stopped
to watch. I was in shade, under the down-sweeping branches
of a blue cedar. Four of the sisters were out in the heavy
sunlight practising for tomorrow's match. The contrast emphasised the time gap. I felt myself to be looking out of the
unsatisfactory present into the imagined past—a past in which
their relationship to each other and to the house they lived in,
unencumbered with suitors or husbands or children or business
affairs, had been all that mattered in the world. There was no
place for me in that world. Softly I opened the door, climbed
out, and stood to watch.

They had a net up. Lucy and Harriet were wearing whites,
Ben dark slacks and a yellow Aertex shirt, and Janet a grey
skirt and white blouse. Lucy, properly padded and gloved, was
batting, while the others bowled to her in turn. In the distance,
on the far side of the porte-cochère, I saw Mr. Chad on a
ladder, painting the last of the windows. (Lucy had told me
about Nancy's determination to get the work done before the
match. It looked as if they'd just make it.)

Harriet was the least athletic of the sisters, a stolid bat and
not much of a bowler. Janet was physically gifted, though
erratic, and liable to get herself out with some overambitious
shot before she was really set. She batted right-handed but
bowled left, a decent medium pace with a tendency for the
odd ball to cut away and take the edge. If she'd been able
to control this, she might have posed problems for goodish
batsmen. Ben, I believe, given a boy's strength and opportunities, would have made the first eleven of any public school as
bowler, but was a careless and irresponsible bat. Lucy was a
[ ] bat, though her unthinking grace of movement perhaps
[ma]de her look more proficient than she actually was.

[T]hey were taking their net seriously. I watched Lucy drive a
[ ] from Harriet, play forward to one from Janet, and miss an
[atte]mpted cut when Ben whipped one down off a full run. Some-

"What do you mean?"

"Lucy talked to you about my recent dealings with Gerry,
I think. Have you in your turn told him? That's to say, how
much does he know of what I know and suspect?"

"None of that. All I've said is that he's got to get himself
away from Michael. I'm still working on him, but it's going
to happen. Or else."

"Or else what?"

"Nothing. It's just a way of talking."

"All right. About Michael—you wrote to Ben. How much
did you tell her? Did you mention me, for instance?"

"No. Absolutely not. I just said I'd learnt some things and
I couldn't tell her who'd told me."

"What was her response?"

"A telegram telling me to mind my own asterisk business.
Then she rushed off and married Michael."

"Was that her idea or his?"

"No idea. I've got to go in a mo', but listen. Lu says you're
iffy about the fifteenth. Please, please will you come?"

"For the same reasons that you want me to be Gerry's best
man?"

"Well . . . yes, roughly. Please."

"I'll be there. See you on the sixth. Good luck with everything."

The wedding was functional, not to say bleak. Harriet was
Nancy's witness, and Bobo had come, too, but I had no time
to talk to anyone as I'd been caught in traffic on the way down
and was almost late. Gerry seemed subdued, but pleased to
see me in an uncomfortable, oddly adolescent fashion and tried
to persuade me to return with them to Blatchards, but I said,
truthfully, that I had to get back to London for my postponed
meeting. The only other talk I had was with Bobo as we stood
side by side in the public urinals. I'd been seeing him fairly
frequently as his firm had been handling aspects of my

flotation, but I had not of course said anything about the imbroglio with Gerry, Lucy, and Seddon.

"Surprised to see you here," he said. "I'd have thought you had your hands full in London."

"Full enough," I said.

"How come a wily old bird like you got himself involved in this balls-aching potmess."

I gathered he must know something about it after all. Presumably Nancy had talked to Harriet, who had passed it on, but how much she'd said I had no idea.

"I can't say I'm happy about it," I said cautiously.

"It's that shit Allwegg at the bottom of it all," he said. "And I gather he's going to have the neck to show up at this match. I'll have trouble not shoving his ugly mug in for him."

"You're coming?"

"I wanted to cry off—it's going to be a bloody ghastly wake by the look of it—but Harriet read me the riot act. Thank God I don't have a family—the things you find yourself doing for each other. Gerry been on to you yet?"

"He asked me to be his best man, as you saw."

Bobo grunted dismissively—it hadn't been what he meant—but at that point a drunk came and stood in the next stall, making retching noises as he pissed. We moved out but found Gerry waiting to say good-bye to me, preventing further questions. I drove to London very depressed.

When I saw Lucy later that week, she asked me how the wedding had gone and I told her briefly, but she herself had heard no more from Blatchards and didn't want to talk about it further. I was not due to see her at all in the week before the match, as she was planning to be at Seddon Hall, and going over most days to help with the arrangements.

Having no wish to endure a minute more of the week-end than could be helped, I'd said I would drive down on Saturday

morning, in time for the start of the match, but on the Thursday Gerry telephoned and asked me to come on the Friday evening. He needed my advice, he said. London was sweltering, with that still, choking late-summer heat which feels as if it must relieve itself in thunder in the next few hours, and then doesn't. The road was up, with pneumatic drills, outside my office. The newspapers, with nothing else to report, were full of stories of eight-mile jams on the roads to the coast (those were the days when mass-market holidays meant North-Sea Butlins, not Mallorca or Corfu), with Saturday mornings far the worst. I had only routine work to catch up on. Even with those excuses I think I might have refused, but though I thought Gerry's behaviour almost unforgivably bad, having acceded to Nancy's plea to help her in her attempt to remove him from Michael's influence—and though *redeem* is much to strong a word, there did seem to be some moral princi[..] involved—I now seemed to myself committed to doing [..] could. I agreed and left after lunch on Friday.

The traffic was still atrocious, so it was late afternoo[..] wound along the Blatchards drive with the house, vagu[..] through the heat-haze, coming and going between the [..] of trees. Despite the full-leaved branches and the diff[..] season and my driving a comfortable car rather than [..] in army boots, the effect was extraordinarily simi[..] December afternoon, fifteen years earlier, when I [..] out from the camp with Gerry and first met Lu[..] course come this way many times since then, [..] think, with the same painful nostalgia. I inter[..] The sensation was physical, a clutching tensi[..] chest, and it hurt sufficiently for me to slow [..] whether this could be a premonition of hea[..]

My car was a new Rover, with soft susp[..] running engine. At that drifting speed it [..] the group on East Lawn didn't notice my [..]

thing was said, teasing by the tone of it, and that must have put
Lucy on her mettle, because she took a pace down the pitch for
Harriet's next and hit it on the half-volley with a full swing of
the bat. The ball sailed away over the meaningless group of cherry
trees that partly obscured that end of the facade, out of my sight
behind the cedar branches. Lucy, who had ended her stroke with
the bat theatrically aloft, dropped it and put both hands over her
mouth. The others turned and stood watching. There was a clash
and tinkle of glass, and they all burst into laughter.

I moved into the open. The ground-floor windows seemed
intact. Then I saw the starred pane in the second one along
the upper floor—one of the Yellow Room windows. That
was a considerable shot, a six on most grounds. I must have
completely misread the flight of the ball, or perhaps the force
of the blow, having seen grace and timing but evidently not
having allowed for Lucy's wiry strength.

There was a movement behind the broken window, as somebody climbed onto a chair to reach the catch. In the pause I
heard the sisters still laughing, with the appalled but delighted
laughter of children who have broken the rules. The sash slid
up and Nancy leaned out.

"No pocket money for a month! Any of you!" she called.

Her tone was mock severe, but she too was laughing. My
perception of the scene, I found, had changed. I was now
mostly conscious of its falsity. I felt that the five of them were
making a concerted attempt to regress to an earlier period
when the family was united and happy, and it then struck me
that this might be part of Nancy's scheme for dealing with
Gerry, to suggest that it was still possible for him too to return
to that lost Arcadia and make a fresh start. Well, if so, she
was wrong, and naïvely wrong. Time doesn't work like that,
and if she had summoned the rest of us to take part in the
same charade, we were in for an even more uncomfortable
week-end than I had imagined.

Also, if that was the case, what part was Ben playing? Or

was she perhaps joining in unawares, merely wishing to heal her own rift from the others by this regression?

"Somebody go and get Mr. Chad," called Nancy.

"Coming, coming," he answered, ambling along past the porte-cochère to inspect the damage. "But aren't you girls a bit old for this type of horseplay, then?"

The response was another burst of laughter, still false to my ears.

My move into the open had brought me into Nancy's view. She waved and pointed. The others turned, and Lucy came loping across, mannish in her pads and thus more feminine than ever.

"Wasn't that a terrific shot!" she said.

"Not the best place for a net if you're going to cart the bowling," I said.

"We always have it there. It's the only bit of East Lawn anything like a decent pitch. I'm not facing Ben on a ploughed field, thank you. And Mr. Chad keeps spare panes ready cut. Isn't it hot? It's supposed to thunder tonight, according to the wireless."

"And clear up for tomorrow?"

"Fingers crossed. Nan's put you in Miss Bolton's Room. I hope that's all right."

"Fine," I said.

(Miss Bolton had been a quasi-mythical governess who had educated Lord Vereker's elder sisters. The threat of her return had still been used as an incentive to virtue when Lucy's generation were in the nursery.)

"I wish I could stay, but we've got the Rest of the World to dinner and I've got to go back," she said.

"The Rest of the World and his wife these days, I suppose."

"I'm afraid so."

She sighed, looked at me, ageing right up into the present as she did so, and bent to unbuckle her pads.

*   *   *

The family had already had tea, but Harriet brought me a fresh pot. By the time I took it out onto East Lawn to watch the net continue, Lucy was gone but had been replaced by both Nancy and Gerry. Ben was now batting, and Mr. Chad had his ladder up to the Yellow Room window, where he was already puttying in a fresh pane. I was drinking my second cup when Gerry left the net and came over.

"Glad you could make it," he said. "Tolerable drive?"

"Barely."

"Sorry about that, but it would have been worse tomorrow. Finished? Come and have a look at the lake."

I put my cup down reluctantly and walked beside him towards the Plantations. I had no idea what was going to come up in our interview, but knew I was not looking forward to it. As we passed the Stables, he nodded up and said, "Lady V.'s had another fall. Off a horse, this time."

"Lucy told me. Something wrong with her balance, I gather. She can't be much over sixty."

"Fifty-nine. We're going to have to find someone to be with her all the time."

"How's she going to like that?"

"Not at all. She's still under the impression she's safe to drive. She's got enough energy to power a battleship, only the controls are disconnected."

"It's a worry for you."

"Two worries. First, what to do about it. Second, how to pay for it. What about you? How's your flotation going?"

"Just about ready to slide down the slipway."

"All the shares taken up?"

"Good as. Bobo's people wanted a higher price, but I wasn't going to risk anything being left with the underwriters."

"I imagine you're retaining control."

"For the moment, anyway."

"You'll be a rich man."

At this point I realised that the reason Gerry had wanted me to come down early was that he was going to ask me for money. No doubt this was what Bobo had been about to warn me of in the urinals at Bury.

"Eventually," I said. "If all goes well."

He grunted and seemed to fall into a reverie. The air in the narrow path between the trees was dense and still and swarming with insects.

"Nan is insisting I cut myself loose from Michael," he said. "It's part of the deal."

I made some noncommittal mutter.

"He'll be turning up for supper tonight," he said. "She wants me to have it out with him then. Have you any views?"

"It's none of my business."

"I need your help."

"Last time we spoke about it, you seemed to have nothing but admiration for Michael."

"Things have changed."

We turned the corner and the South Lake stretched before us, dully reflecting the listless woods. Above its surface, in a layer dense enough to look like a band of dark smoke trapped there by the heavy atmosphere, swarmed the midges that had bred from it. The path looked totally uninviting, but Gerry wrenched up a couple of stalks of hog-parsley and gave one to me. We walked on, switching them around our faces.

"Michael and I are not technically partners," he said. "We are merely associates. There are companies we are codirectors of, but in theory we can separate at any time, by either of us expressing a wish to do so. In practice, of course, because we've worked closely together, it's going to take time, which Nan is not prepared to give me."

"Have you already spoken to Michael about this?"

"Not yet."

"What will his attitude be?"

"What do you mean?"

"Lucy talked to you about my recent dealings with Gerry, I think. Have you in your turn told him? That's to say, how much does he know of what I know and suspect?"

"None of that. All I've said is that he's got to get himself away from Michael. I'm still working on him, but it's going to happen. Or else."

"Or else what?"

"Nothing. It's just a way of talking."

"All right. About Michael—you wrote to Ben. How much did you tell her? Did you mention me, for instance?"

"No. Absolutely not. I just said I'd learnt some things and I couldn't tell her who'd told me."

"What was her response?"

"A telegram telling me to mind my own asterisk business. Then she rushed off and married Michael."

"Was that her idea or his?"

"No idea. I've got to go in a mo', but listen. Lu says you're iffy about the fifteenth. Please, please will you come?"

"For the same reasons that you want me to be Gerry's best man?"

"Well . . . yes, roughly. Please."

"I'll be there. See you on the sixth. Good luck with everything."

The wedding was functional, not to say bleak. Harriet was Nancy's witness, and Bobo had come, too, but I had no time to talk to anyone as I'd been caught in traffic on the way down and was almost late. Gerry seemed subdued, but pleased to see me in an uncomfortable, oddly adolescent fashion and tried to persuade me to return with them to Blatchards, but I said, truthfully, that I had to get back to London for my postponed meeting. The only other talk I had was with Bobo as we stood side by side in the public urinals. I'd been seeing him fairly frequently as his firm had been handling aspects of my flotation, but I had not of course said anything about the imbroglio with Gerry, Lucy, and Seddon.

"Surprised to see you here," he said. "I'd have thought you had your hands full in London."

"Full enough," I said.

"How come a wily old bird like you got himself involved in this balls-aching potmess."

I gathered he must know something about it after all. Presumably Nancy had talked to Harriet, who had passed it on, but how much she'd said I had no idea.

"I can't say I'm happy about it," I said cautiously.

"It's that shit Allwegg at the bottom of it all," he said. "And I gather he's going to have the neck to show up at this match. I'll have trouble not shoving his ugly mug in for him."

"You're coming?"

"I wanted to cry off—it's going to be a bloody ghastly wake by the look of it—but Harriet read me the riot act. Thank God I don't have a family—the things you find yourself doing for each other. Gerry been on to you yet?"

"He asked me to be his best man, as you saw."

Bobo grunted dismissively—it hadn't been what he meant—but at that point a drunk came and stood in the next stall, making retching noises as he pissed. We moved out but found Gerry waiting to say good-bye to me, preventing further questions. I drove to London very depressed.

When I saw Lucy later that week, she asked me how the wedding had gone and I told her briefly, but she herself had heard no more from Blatchards and didn't want to talk about it further. I was not due to see her at all in the week before the match, as she was planning to be at Seddon Hall, and going over most days to help with the arrangements.

Having no wish to endure a minute more of the week-end than could be helped, I'd said I would drive down on Saturday morning, in time for the start of the match, but on the Thursday Gerry telephoned and asked me to come on the Friday evening. He needed my advice, he said. London was sweltering, with that still, choking late-summer heat which feels as if it must relieve itself in thunder in the next few hours, and then doesn't. The road was up, with pneumatic drills, outside my office. The newspapers, with nothing else to report, were full of stories of eight-mile jams on the roads to the coast (those were the days when mass-market holidays meant North-Sea Butlins, not Mallorca or Corfu), with Saturday mornings far the worst. I had only routine work to catch up on. Even with those excuses I think I might have refused, but though I thought Gerry's behaviour almost unforgivably bad, having acceded to Nancy's plea to help her in her attempt to remove him from Michael's influence—and though *redeem* is much too strong a word, there did seem to be some moral principle involved—I now seemed to myself committed to doing all I could. I agreed and left after lunch on Friday.

The traffic was still atrocious, so it was late afternoon as I wound along the Blatchards drive with the house, vague-seen through the heat-haze, coming and going between the clumps of trees. Despite the full-leaved branches and the difference of season and my driving a comfortable car rather than tramping in army boots, the effect was extraordinarily similar to that December afternoon, fifteen years earlier, when I had walked out from the camp with Gerry and first met Lucy. I had of course come this way many times since then, but never, I think, with the same painful nostalgia. I intend the epithet. The sensation was physical, a clutching tension in my upper chest, and it hurt sufficiently for me to slow down, wondering whether this could be a premonition of heart attack.

My car was a new Rover, with soft suspension and a quiet-running engine. At that drifting speed it made little noise, so the group on East Lawn didn't notice my arrival. So strongly, and at the same time so healingly, did they embody the ache of irrecoverable time which I had been feeling that I stopped to watch. I was in shade, under the down-sweeping branches of a blue cedar. Four of the sisters were out in the heavy sunlight practising for tomorrow's match. The contrast emphasised the time gap. I felt myself to be looking out of the unsatisfactory present into the imagined past—a past in which their relationship to each other and to the house they lived in, unencumbered with suitors or husbands or children or business affairs, had been all that mattered in the world. There was no place for me in that world. Softly I opened the door, climbed out, and stood to watch.

They had a net up. Lucy and Harriet were wearing whites, Ben dark slacks and a yellow Aertex shirt, and Janet a grey skirt and white blouse. Lucy, properly padded and gloved, was batting, while the others bowled to her in turn. In the distance, on the far side of the porte-cochère, I saw Mr. Chad on a ladder, painting the last of the windows. (Lucy had told me about Nancy's determination to get the work done before the match. It looked as if they'd just make it.)

Harriet was the least athletic of the sisters, a stolid bat and not much of a bowler. Janet was physically gifted, though erratic, and liable to get herself out with some overambitious shot before she was really set. She batted right-handed but bowled left, a decent medium pace with a tendency for the odd ball to cut away and take the edge. If she'd been able to control this, she might have posed problems for goodish batsmen. Ben, I believe, given a boy's strength and opportunities, would have made the first eleven of any public school as a bowler, but was a careless and irresponsible bat. Lucy was a fair bat, though her unthinking grace of movement perhaps made her look more proficient than she actually was.

They were taking their net seriously. I watched Lucy drive a ball from Harriet, play forward to one from Janet, and miss an attempted cut when Ben whipped one down off a full run. Something was said, teasing by the tone of it, and that must have put Lucy on her mettle, because she took a pace down the pitch for Harriet's next and hit it on the half-volley with a full swing of the bat. The ball sailed away over the meaningless group of cherry trees that partly obscured that end of the facade, out of my sight behind the cedar branches. Lucy, who had ended her stroke with the bat theatrically aloft, dropped it and put both hands over her mouth. The others turned and stood watching. There was a clash and tinkle of glass, and they all burst into laughter.

I moved into the open. The ground-floor windows seemed intact. Then I saw the starred pane in the second one along the upper floor—one of the Yellow Room windows. That was a considerable shot, a six on most grounds. I must have completely misread the flight of the ball, or perhaps the force of the blow, having seen grace and timing but evidently not having allowed for Lucy's wiry strength.

There was a movement behind the broken window, as somebody climbed onto a chair to reach the catch. In the pause I heard the sisters still laughing, with the appalled but delighted laughter of children who have broken the rules. The sash slid up and Nancy leaned out.

"No pocket money for a month! Any of you!" she called.

Her tone was mock severe, but she too was laughing. My perception of the scene, I found, had changed. I was now mostly conscious of its falsity. I felt that the five of them were making a concerted attempt to regress to an earlier period when the family was united and happy, and it then struck me that this might be part of Nancy's scheme for dealing with Gerry, to suggest that it was still possible for him too to return to that lost Arcadia and make a fresh start. Well, if so, she was wrong, and naïvely wrong. Time doesn't work like that, and if she had summoned the rest of us to take part in the same charade, we were in for an even more uncomfortable week-end than I had imagined.

Also, if that was the case, what part was Ben playing? Or

was she perhaps joining in unawares, merely wishing to heal her own rift from the others by this regression?

"Somebody go and get Mr. Chad," called Nancy.

"Coming, coming," he answered, ambling along past the porte-cochère to inspect the damage. "But aren't you girls a bit old for this type of horseplay, then?"

The response was another burst of laughter, still false to my ears.

My move into the open had brought me into Nancy's view. She waved and pointed. The others turned, and Lucy came loping across, mannish in her pads and thus more feminine than ever.

"Wasn't that a terrific shot!" she said.

"Not the best place for a net if you're going to cart the bowling," I said.

"We always have it there. It's the only bit of East Lawn anything like a decent pitch. I'm not facing Ben on a ploughed field, thank you. And Mr. Chad keeps spare panes ready cut. Isn't it hot? It's supposed to thunder tonight, according to the wireless."

"And clear up for tomorrow?"

"Fingers crossed. Nan's put you in Miss Bolton's Room. I hope that's all right."

"Fine," I said.

(Miss Bolton had been a quasi-mythical governess who had educated Lord Vereker's elder sisters. The threat of her return had still been used as an incentive to virtue when Lucy's generation were in the nursery.)

"I wish I could stay, but we've got the Rest of the World to dinner and I've got to go back," she said.

"The Rest of the World and his wife these days, I suppose."

"I'm afraid so."

She sighed, looked at me, ageing right up into the present as she did so, and bent to unbuckle her pads.

*   *   *

The family had already had tea, but Harriet brought me a fresh pot. By the time I took it out onto East Lawn to watch the net continue, Lucy was gone but had been replaced by both Nancy and Gerry. Ben was now batting, and Mr. Chad had his ladder up to the Yellow Room window, where he was already puttying in a fresh pane. I was drinking my second cup when Gerry left the net and came over.

"Glad you could make it," he said. "Tolerable drive?"

"Barely."

"Sorry about that, but it would have been worse tomorrow. Finished? Come and have a look at the lake."

I put my cup down reluctantly and walked beside him towards the Plantations. I had no idea what was going to come up in our interview, but knew I was not looking forward to it. As we passed the Stables, he nodded up and said, "Lady V.'s had another fall. Off a horse, this time."

"Lucy told me. Something wrong with her balance, I gather. She can't be much over sixty."

"Fifty-nine. We're going to have to find someone to be with her all the time."

"How's she going to like that?"

"Not at all. She's still under the impression she's safe to drive. She's got enough energy to power a battleship, only the controls are disconnected."

"It's a worry for you."

"Two worries. First, what to do about it. Second, how to pay for it. What about you? How's your flotation going?"

"Just about ready to slide down the slipway."

"All the shares taken up?"

"Good as. Bobo's people wanted a higher price, but I wasn't going to risk anything being left with the underwriters."

"I imagine you're retaining control."

"For the moment, anyway."

"You'll be a rich man."

At this point I realised that the reason Gerry had wanted me to come down early was that he was going to ask me for money. No doubt this was what Bobo had been about to warn me of in the urinals at Bury.

"Eventually," I said. "If all goes well."

He grunted and seemed to fall into a reverie. The air in the narrow path between the trees was dense and still and swarming with insects.

"Nan is insisting I cut myself loose from Michael," he said. "It's part of the deal."

I made some noncommittal mutter.

"He'll be turning up for supper tonight," he said. "She wants me to have it out with him then. Have you any views?"

"It's none of my business."

"I need your help."

"Last time we spoke about it, you seemed to have nothing but admiration for Michael."

"Things have changed."

We turned the corner and the South Lake stretched before us, dully reflecting the listless woods. Above its surface, in a layer dense enough to look like a band of dark smoke trapped there by the heavy atmosphere, swarmed the midges that had bred from it. The path looked totally uninviting, but Gerry wrenched up a couple of stalks of hog-parsley and gave one to me. We walked on, switching them around our faces.

"Michael and I are not technically partners," he said. "We are merely associates. There are companies we are codirectors of, but in theory we can separate at any time, by either of us expressing a wish to do so. In practice, of course, because we've worked closely together, it's going to take time, which Nan is not prepared to give me."

"Have you already spoken to Michael about this?"

"Not yet."

"What will his attitude be?"

"He will try to prevent me leaving him."

"Can he do that? Can he do any more than make things difficult? If you are not even partners?"

"I'm afraid so. To put it simply, I've discovered that some of the things Michael has encouraged me to do have not been legal. I've always relied, naturally enough, on Michael's advice on legal matters, and he himself has always taken the line that it's important to stay inside the law. The trouble is that the richest pickings are just in those areas where the law is obscure or uncertain, so it's those areas we have tended to exploit. Until a few months ago I was perfectly happy about this, but I happened to fall in with an old ruffian in the East End who was an Essex supporter. These people tend to have a sentimental streak, which they use as a substitute for morals, and in his case it's cricket. He'd seen me play a decent knock against the county some years back, and he made a point of taking me aside and telling me he didn't like seeing a good lad getting into bad hands. I asked him what he meant, but all he'd say was that a bent lawyer was a bent lawyer . . . I don't know. Nan had been telling me for months that Michael was using me. There'd been one or two other things I'd more or less shut my eyes to. And this old boy spoke with authority. He's seen it all, as they say. Michael was away, sailing with Ben in the Med. I decided to read up on a particular detail of tax law about which Michael had assured me we were in the clear, and I discovered that we weren't. I took counsel's opinion, and he confirmed it. It wasn't that Michael had been mistaken. He'd expressly misinformed me."

He paused for comment. As far as it went, his story seemed possible, if not plausible. I recalled his difficulty in engaging his intellect with the convolutions of military bureaucracy. He might well have a similar blind spot about the technicalities of tax legislation.

"Did you tackle Michael?" I said.

"As I say, he was away. I checked the files and discovered

that a number of documents were missing, in particular a detailed memorandum from Michael on how to set up a trust structure to our advantage and what and what not to tell our official lawyers to that end. Without it there was nothing to show that the whole scheme was not my idea. I checked more extensively and found that the same thing had happened elsewhere. In fact on any point where we might be in trouble, decisions which I knew to have been joint now appeared to have been made by me alone. All the crucial cheques had been signed by me. I also began to suspect that my apparent shares in a number of our major assets might be almost worthless."

"So if you try to leave him, he can threaten to turn you over to the tax authorities? I'd have thought he'd be reluctant to do that. They're bound to go over his own affairs extremely thoroughly. On the other hand, if you do leave him, you will be . . . penniless?"

"Good as."

"Have you told Nancy any of this?"

"Most of it. Her line is that we should call his bluff. I actually know enough about his affairs to cause him serious trouble. Though it will be nothing to the trouble that I shall be in myself, it might still not be worth his while. What I would prefer, though, is to wait. Not to tackle Michael immediately, but to carry on as if I knew nothing, but meanwhile to play him at his own game, accumulating documentary evidence of his wrongdoing until I'm in a position to force him to play fair with me. I need, at the most, three months' grace."

He stopped and paced broodingly along the path, as if that was as far as his thoughts had taken him. I walked beside him, dry mouthed, appalled. The lake was a dismal grey sheet, blotched with blanket weed. The tired leaves hung motionless. The air was heavy with electricity and dim with the pestilent midges. There seemed to be no end to the path. Gerry's tone and demeanor were in keeping, those of one who is lost and knows it. For myself, I had listened sick-hearted. Did he really expect me to help him? Perhaps he had told me the truth about Michael's dealings with him, but surely not about his own naïveté and innocence. Michael might have led him step by step down the slope, each step seeming to follow logically from the one before, but surely there must have come a point, and far earlier than he had suggested, when he had looked around him and seen the pit he was in? If not the financial and legal trap into which Michael had coaxed him, then at least the moral repugnance of what he was doing?

How had he come to this? All those talents, that easy buoyancy, soured into this squirming mess? It didn't bear thinking of. Anyway, he was clearly about to ask for money, a loan of some kind, possibly a block of my shares which he could then use as collateral, either to convince Michael that he would not be in desperate financial straits if they parted, or else to persuade Nancy that they could afford to wait while he came to terms with Michael. Without thinking it through, I decided to forestall him.

"You want me to suggest some way of raising funds to see you over the gap?" I said.

"Well, something like that, but—"

"Before we discuss it, I want you to explain something to me. A few months ago you asked me to help you find a call girl. I told you to telephone Mrs. Mudge. You later told me she had not been able to help. Not long after that a young woman called Samantha Whitstable insinuated herself into a dinner party at the Seddons', dressed as a man. She was asked to leave, but before she did so she gave Seddon her card. Next you asked us to the opera, saying you had spare tickets. You suggested I should bring Lucy, which I did, but it turned out we were seated separately from you. Miss Whitstable was in a box with a man who tried to keep out of sight, but whom Lucy recognised as her husband. The girl pointed us out to him. After the opera Lucy and I followed them to Greek Street, and you followed us. Some thugs tried to abduct the girl, and you intervened. We then went off to supper as though nothing had happened. You had told me the tickets were available because friends of Nancy's had fallen through, but it became apparent that she was only reluctantly there, and she very much gave the impression that you had made her come. Wait. Next day I telephoned Mrs. Mudge, and she told me that the girl she'd suggested to you was this same Samantha Whitstable. She said that you'd persuaded the girl to leave her agency and implied that the fracas in Greek Street was an attempt on the part of her friends to take the girl back. Did you, by the way, know that something like that was going to happen? Was that why you followed us?"

"No."

I waited while he paced on in silence. But for the single syllable I might have begun to feel that he hadn't heard anything I had said. I pressed him again.

"I want to know what on earth you thought you were up to with this scheme. I want to know whether it was your idea, or one of Michael's you were carrying out on his behalf. And then I want to know why you should believe, after what you appear to have done, that I should either trust or help you in any way at all."

"Because you have to," he said. "Like me, you have no other course of action, unpleasant though it may seem. I will answer your earlier question. When I followed you after the opera, I had no idea that that woman was going to try and get the girl back. I just wanted to see that you didn't get into trouble."

"What kind of trouble?"

"The attack could equally well have been on you, if it had been noticed that you were following the girl. She is now under the protection of a much larger and more ruthless organisation than anything Mrs. Mudge can command. Now as to why you are forced to help me. You have to understand that Michael has two complementary drives. The first is to achieve total power over those he chooses to dominate. Second, to revenge himself in any way he can on those who defy or remove themselves from his control. He doesn't want to hurt them physically, but so to speak spiritually. He will go to almost any lengths to achieve this in certain cases. I tell you, unless you help me to reach a stage where he can himself be controlled by the threat of exposure of his affairs, he will in the end destroy Lucy."

"Lucy?" I said.

"I didn't at first realise it, but that is what the business with the Whitstable girl has been about," he said.

"But why Lucy?"

He stopped and looked at me. The midges haloed his large face. He was sweating lightly.

"You didn't know?" he said.

The next I remember was that I was sitting in the driving seat of an unfamiliar car and looking in vain at the dashboard for somewhere to insert the ignition key. In front of me was a blank stone wall. Somebody was tapping at the window. It was Lady Vereker. The dreamlike moment endured another few seconds, nonsensically ominous, and then the real world flooded back. I had had some kind of blackout. I could clearly remember Gerry and the swarming midges, but nothing after that. I was now, in my own mind, on my way to London, escaping, running desperately away, but had somehow wandered up to the Stables and climbed into Lady Vereker's car, which she garaged in the coach house when she was not using it for indoor riding. I seemed to have locked the door but had no trouble finding the catch and opening it. I climbed out.

Like many apparently scatty and irresponsible people Lady Vereker was rather good in a crisis. She didn't bother me with questions but led me into her living room, shooed several affronted dogs off the sofa and shut them out, made me lie down, and telephoned Nancy. She then made me a cup of weak, sweet tea, which I was drinking by the time Harriet and Bobo arrived to take me back to the house. By then I had physically pretty well recovered, and my main thought was still to find my own car and leave.

"What happened?" said Harriet. "Do you know?"

"No. I was talking with Gerry by the lake, and I don't remember anything after that till I was sitting in your mother's car. Don't worry. I'm all right now. I'll just pack up and go."

"You'll *what?*" said Bobo.

"I've got to go back to London."

"Bloody nonsense," said Bobo. "You're not fit to drive, for a start. What happens if you have another blackout on the road?"

"We'd much better put you to bed and get Dr. Jericho out to have a look at you," said Harriet.

"It's very—"

"Balls," said Bobo. "You can kill yourself and that's your lookout, but if you kill some other poor sod in the accident, then we'll be to blame for letting you go. You can give me your car key, and any more of this bullshit and I'm going to lock you in and sleep on a mattress outside your door, and you won't hear the last of that for a while."

They were perfectly right. I remembered the coronary-like sensation I had experienced on arrival. Though I might now feel I was up to the drive, it would be irresponsible of me to attempt it. I thought of asking for someone to drive me in to Bury to catch a train, but decided that I'd prefer not to face the inevitable refusal.

Just before the Stables drive turned onto the circuit round East Lawn, I paused. I'd have liked to ask Harriet alone, but there was no help.

"Look," I said, "I'm sorry, but I don't want to meet Gerry."

"He's probably still with Nan in the Yellow Room," said Harriet. "We'll take you up the back stairs."

So we went round by the servants' entrance and climbed the worn steep flights. I went obediently to bed. The doctor came, a rubicund, short, grinning man who told me he could find nothing wrong. He said I had been overworking and must rest, and forbade me to drive until I had been thoroughly examined by my own doctor. Supper was brought by a maid, but I ate very little. I didn't feel like reading, so I lay in the darkening room with the windows wide and the curtains open, trying not to think and watching the blinks of sheet lightning, eerily thunderless, flickering behind the cloud mass. At last, but without a sense of relief, it started to rain.

There was a tap at my door. I assumed it was the maid come for the tray, but when I called out, Lucy slid in and came to the bedside. She tried to take my hand but I drew it away. She seemed to understand the gesture almost at once.

"Gerry told you about me and Michael," she said.

"Yes."

She turned and sat on the edge of the bed, staring blankly at the window. The lightning glimmered across her face.

"I should have told you myself," she whispered. "Long ago. Long ago."

Lucy

NINE

August 1956

I haven't much to say here, because Paul's put most of it in. I think I really want to talk about Ben. The obvious question is why on earth did she agree to marry Michael, but it isn't obvious to me. Or rather, it isn't much of a question because it's the answer that's obvious. Michael could be extremely attractive, especially to risk-takers like Ben and me (he'd never have got anywhere with Harriet, for instance). He seemed dangerous, but worth it. Suppose he'd wanted to marry me, instead of just living with me for a bit. I'm sure he'd have gone about it differently, and I think very likely I'd have said yes. But of course that wouldn't have stopped him being perfectly foul afterwards. I don't think he'd started being foul to Ben yet, apart from the odd little tweak and pinch just to keep her guessing, but he was going to be one day. One day he was going to tell her about me, I'm sure, but he was still saving that up, savouring it.

So why did he marry her? Well, she was glamorous and interesting, for a start, the right sort of wife for someone like him to show around. And she was a challenge. The big thing in her life was dancing, and he could have the fun of showing her who was boss by not letting her. And then of course she was a way of getting at me.

Gerry seems to have told Paul a lot of lies by the lake—no, not lies, but half-lies, all twisted and with things left out—but I'm sure he was right about one thing. Michael never forgave anybody. He was never going to forgive me. He might wait twenty years, but in the end he was going to see to it that he hurt me really badly, and the best way to do that was to hurt my family, to split us up and make us enemies of each other. And I think, without us knowing it, that was already starting to happen, and we knew we had to stop it, and that was why we all wanted to come together that week-end and make ourselves whole again.

I know this doesn't make sense when you think that with another part of our minds we—Nan and Harriet and me, that is—were trying to get Gerry to split up with Michael, which looked like as good a way as any of making Ben into an enemy, but there it is. People are like that. You want two opposite things at the same time, with different parts of you, so you think about one of them at a time and blank the other one out, and hope. Of course it doesn't work, but you never learn.

Anyway, I'm sure Ben felt like that. She was in terrific form, alive and funny and friendly and full of Paris gossip but so obviously happy to be home and ready to make things up with Nan after letting her down by getting married in a rush, and not saying anything about it being really Nan's fault because of the letter she'd written. I can remember that Friday afternoon net as if it was yesterday, and Paul's right, it really did feel as if we'd gone back at least ten years to when things were far, far easier and anything was possible and we weren't trapped and hedged in by all the things we'd done and mistakes we'd made between. And that was a terrific shot. I can shut my eyes now and feel the swing of the bat, part of me, weightless as my own arms, and the sweetness of its smash into the ball at exactly the right moment to a millionth of a second, and the ball sailing away, and the glass breaking, and Mr. Chad saying exactly the same thing he always used to about us growing up. . . .

Oh dear, I'd like to stay talking about that for ever, but I'd better get on. I was back at Seddon Hall and dressing for dinner, nearly finished, when my house telephone rang and it was Rodrigo, the butler, saying there was an urgent message for me to call home. I did. Harriet answered and told me that Paul had had some kind of a stroke or heart attack while he was talking to Gerry by the lake, only according to Gerry it wasn't like that because he hadn't fallen down or anything, he'd just rushed away and for some reason Gerry hadn't followed to see he was alright and the next thing anyone knew he was in Mother's car trying to drive himself to London and the doctor was coming and they thought I'd better know at once. I said I'd ring back and went through to tell Tommy. (Even when we used to sleep together, we'd always had officially separate bedrooms and bathrooms and dressing rooms with a little breakfast room between them, though we practically never had breakfast there—by the way I can't remember if I said, when I was talking about the reasons for not breaking up completely with Tommy, that one of them was the sheer luxury of being married to a terrifically rich, kind man.)

Tommy was brushing his forelock into the exact shape that he thought suited his profile. He didn't stop while I told him.

"You'd better go over," he said at once.

"Oh, but . . ." I began, of course thinking about the dinner table where the numbers had worked out right for once without our having to do anything special about it.

"Even I have some sense of priorities," he said. "Take a bag in case you want to stay the night."

He really was a lovely man, in his weird way. I put my arms round him and pecked his cheek, taking care not to muss his hair.

"An illness in the family should cover it," he said.

So I drove over, feeling very odd and churned up, but

that may have been partly the weather because it was an extraordinary evening, tense as a drum, with a great black lid of cloud sitting straight overhead as if somebody was just getting ready to clamp it down. I could see almost all the way round the edges, a thin strip of clear sky above the horizon, silvery and still, except where the sun had gone down like a furnace in the west. And I thought something must be wrong with my eyes because of the way the light kept changing until I worked out that it was lightning, overhead, not bolts flashing down to earth, but sheeting to and fro out of sight above the car. By the time I reached Blatchards, the rain was sluicing down.

I let myself in. I could hear clatter and chatter from along the West Corridor so I knew they were still having supper, but I went up to Miss Bolton's room and tapped on the door. He says he called out, but I didn't hear him. I just crept in. He was lying on his back with his arms outside the blankets and his head propped up. It was pretty dark and I couldn't see his face properly till I got nearer. Then I saw how gruesome he looked. That afternoon when I'd met him on the lawn he'd just looked jolly tired, but I knew how hard he'd been working so I wasn't surprised, but now he looked like death, with his cheeks sunk in and his eyes large and strange. I tried to take his hand but he wouldn't let me. I didn't have to guess—I knew. Gerry had told Nan, so he'd tell Paul. I couldn't imagine why, but I was certain.

Of course Paul had always known he and Tommy weren't the only men I'd ever gone to bed with, but we'd never talked much about any of the others. Sometimes in ordinary conversation something might come up, like a place I'd visited because I'd spent a holiday there with one of them, or something, and I couldn't make sense of what I wanted to say without including that I'd been there with someone and it was pretty obviously a man, but I was always vague as possible about it because he really didn't want to know. He didn't want to make the picture in his mind, *his* Lucy, the girl who'd shown him how to collect the hen's eggs, lying on the brass-knobbed bed with the sunlight through the shutters making bars across her naked body, and a man—not just a vague shape but a particular man with a face you could recognise, fingers as solid as his own, leaning down over her. Still, I should have told him. It was at least half my fault.

I took his hand again and this time he let me hold it, but he closed his eyes and when I tried to say something he shook his head. I was still like that when Harriet came up for the tray. I went out into the passage with her.

"Is anyone sleeping in my room?" I said. "I've brought a bag."

"No, you'll be alright there," she said.

"What did the doctor say?" I asked.

"He's been overworking and he's got to rest," she said.

"Fat chance," I said.

"I think he and Gerry must have had some kind of a row by the lake," she said. "That's why Gerry didn't stay with him. In fact I think Gerry probably asked him for money, and that was what the row was about. Gerry tried to touch Bobo, you know, and not just for a fiver either, just before he married Nan. You can imagine what Bobo said about that. Supper's been dire. The reason it was me called you was that Nan and Gerry were having a set-to in the Yellow Room, so they've both been less than the life and soul, and I'd no idea what was going on and couldn't stop worrying about Paul, and Bobo never wanted to be here in the first place and neither did Teddy, I gather, and all the while Janet and Ben were carrying on as if all was sunshine and laughter and not noticing anything wrong, and in the middle of it all Michael came in soaked to the skin—his taxi had broken down and he'd walked the rest of the way—but still behaving as if he was Louis XIV making a grand entrance at a court ball."

"Where is he now?" I said. I couldn't bear the idea of meeting anyone, especially him.

"He piled himself a mountain of cold chicken, and Gerry took him up to the Yellow Room," she said.

"I don't want to come down," I said. "Tell Nan I'll keep an eye on Paul. Just give me that tray."

I went to my room and finished Paul's supper, which he'd hardly touched. Then I crept along to his room and asked if he wanted anything, but he just shook his head and when I kissed him good night he didn't stir, so I went away feeling utterly wretched. Nan was waiting for me, looking pretty washed out.

"He doesn't want anything," I said. "What's happening with Michael? I suppose you can't throw him out of the house for me?"

She managed to smile and shook her head.

"Not the moment," she said. "I think it may be alright. I was listening behind the secret door, but I only heard bits."

"Do you think they knew you were there?" I said.

She shrugged.

"I bet Michael did," I said. "He's nightmare like that."

"I don't think it matters," she said. "Gerry started, and he must have been saying what we'd agreed, because Michael broke in with his mouth full and said, 'You'll get twelve years, at least,' and Gerry said, 'Five, and about three for you, and Nan will stand by me, what's more.' We'd talked about that, you see. The whole point was to make Michael understand that Gerry wasn't afraid of going to prison if the worst came to the worst. After that Gerry did most of the talking, but I couldn't hear what he said. Michael yelled at him several times, telling him he was a total idiot, risking everything they'd worked for, but Gerry stuck to his guns. Then Michael said, 'Let's have a drink. I've got to think about this.' He always brings a bottle. He says our brandy's not fit for cooking. Gerry said no—I'd told him he must, till it was over. Then Michael said, 'Alright, let's look at some figures.' Then there was nothing for a bit, and then Michael said, 'This is a bloody stupid notion and it won't work and you'll finish up in the shit, and you've let me down badly, but you can go to hell your own way provided you don't take me with you. I'll sort the details out Monday morning. Now I'm going to bed, and I'm going to have a much better time rogering young Ben than you've ever had with that bitch of yours.' "

"I told you he knew you were there," I said.

"It doesn't matter," she said. "As a matter of fact, Gerry and I have pretty good times when we're on speaking terms."

"What did Gerry say?" I said.

"I don't know. He locked himself in," she said.

"Oh," I said.

"It's alright," she said. "He does that. He'll have a couple of brandies and pass out, but he'll wake up in the small hours and come to bed. He'll tell me what happened in the morning."

I still wasn't happy about it, and I don't think she was, either.

"Well, good luck," I said. "But watch out for Michael. He's totally ruthless."

"So am I," she said.

When she'd gone, I went to bed and read till getting on midnight and then went and looked in on Paul. His bed was empty and his clothes gone from the chair. I was rushing off to look for him but it was getting chilly with the rain after the heat wave, so I went to my room for a coat to put over my nightie and I was just coming out when I heard the fifth stair creak the way it always did, so I lurked behind my door and saw Paul come creeping past fully dressed, with his shoes in his hand. I tiptoed along to check, but I heard the key turn in his lock, so I went back to bed and tossed and turned and listened to the rain sheeting down, and prayed that Michael had got wet enough to catch pneumonia and die. Just as it was getting light, I fell asleep, deep, deep, like a drowned man, and what felt like an instant later I was woken by the fire alarm.

Paul

TEN

August 1956

It was impossible to sleep. I lay in the dark. The lightning flashes continued through the rain, by now a steady, drenching downpour. Lucy came back once, but I refused to acknowledge her presence—mean-minded of me, as I could sense her distress, but I was unable to cope. My sole thought was to leave, to get clear away, without having to talk again to any of the Verekers or anyone else connected with them. I listened for the movement of doors, and as soon as I was sure that everyone on my floor at least had gone to bed, I rose, dressed, and stole in stockinged feet along the corridor and down the stairs. There was a telephone in the old butler's pantry, well out of earshot of any of the bedrooms, but to my dismay it turned out that raising a taxi at almost midnight on a wet Saturday night in Bury was not a practical possibility, though I offered all the money I had on me. In the end I was forced to accept an offer to collect me from the drive gates at half-past seven next morning, for a fee of twenty pounds on top of the fare.

I went back to my room, locked the door, and lay down in my clothes, taking the precaution of setting my alarm for half-past six. I did in fact then sleep for a while but woke soon after first light and wrote a note for Nancy, apologising for leaving and saying I would arrange to collect my car and case later. Though still deeply miserable, I was feeling physically almost normal, but I wasn't prepared to risk carrying the case the length of the drive. I longed to write a note for Lucy, but I could think of nothing I could bear to say, so I left it at that and crept once more downstairs.

I now realised that I was hungry enough to raise the possibility of my collapsing again on the journey. The chances of finding anything to eat in Bury on a Sunday morning were nil, but I remembered from my telephone call last night that the remains of supper had been cleared onto the pantry table. I found an electric kettle, tea in a cupboard, milk in the fridge, bread rolls, butter, and cheese. It was half-past six by the time I finished. I now felt fully up to the journey—in fact if Bobo had not taken my key, I would have paid off the taxi and driven myself to London. The risk of harming some other road-user at that hour would have been negligible.

By now I was anxious to be gone. There was a risk of someone else coming down for an early snack, or of Lucy waking and going along to my room to check on me. But the rain was sheeting relentlessly down outside the window, and again, after what had happened the evening before, it would have been stupid for me to wait half an hour at the gate in weather like that without protection and then journey, soaked, to London. I needed an umbrella, a raincoat, boots. Luckily I knew just where to find them, in the Gun Room close to my way out. It was a hundred to one, knowing the habits of the house, that Lord Vereker's boots, which fitted me, would still be there. Almost cheered by the neatness with which matters were now arranging themselves for my escape, I stole back down the West Corridor, across the Central Hall and straight on towards the main door under the porte-cochère, turning left just before I reached it down the shorter corridor that led to the Gun Room and the East Stairs. The boots were exactly where Gerry had found them for me after Lord Vereker's funeral. Probably I was the last person to wear them. It took me a short while to choose an umbrella and raincoat that wouldn't be needed for a few days. Nervous now that I might meet someone and have to argue with them about my determination to leave, I paused at the Gun Room door and listened. Perhaps some primal instinct of the hunted caused me at the same time to sniff the air. I think so, because I immediately smelt something of which I had perhaps been vaguely aware before, a definite odour of gas.

I sniffed again and was sure. The house, it will be remembered, was heated by its own gas plant, a Victorian device whose intricacies only Mr. Chad understood. It was located in the cellars below the East Wing. Clearly there must be a leak. I felt I had to investigate. It might be extremely dangerous, and whatever my own urgencies, I couldn't leave a house full of sleeping people like that. The smell seemed to be coming from my right, and grew stronger as I turned in that direction and stronger still as I climbed the East Stairs. By the time I reached King William's Room, it was so powerful that I felt it would be dangerous to go on. (This was old-fashioned town gas, which contained a proportion of lethal carbon monoxide.) I retreated, hurried down the stairs, and ran, still in gumboots and raincoat and grasping the umbrella, back to the Central Hall, up the Main Stairs and on to where Nancy and Gerry slept. I hammered at their door with my fist and tried the handle. The door moved, but then was almost pulled from my grasp, and Nancy stood there, fully dressed. She stared at me, took in umbrella, raincoat, boots.

"There's a gas leak," I panted. "In the Yellow Room, I think. It was so bad I stopped at King William's Room."

She seemed to take it in absolutely at once. She pushed past me and ran down the corridor, which spanned almost the full width of the house on that floor. I followed but lagged behind. When I reached the cross-corridor at the far end, she had disappeared, but the false specimen case on the right wall was hinged out. The cavity opened onto the spiral stair down to the secret door in the Yellow Room. As I reached it, I heard thumps, and Nancy's voice crying, "Gerry! Gerry!" The gas smell here was strong, too.

I waited, getting my breath back. There was no point in two of us crowding down there and being overcome, and if she didn't return soon, I might have to try to haul her out, but the thumps and the calling stopped and she came climbing back, white faced.

"He didn't come to bed," she gasped. "We've got to wake everyone up. Then we'll try again. You do this floor. I'll do upstairs."

She rushed away. I had no idea which rooms were being slept in, so would have to try them all. From the Main Stairs I heard a tinkle of glass, followed by the clamour of several electric bells. Fire alarms. A door opened at the other end of the cross-corridor, and Harriet looked out, still in her nightdress.

"Yellow Room's full of gas!" I shouted. "Gerry's in there. Tell Bobo to come and help. Get everyone else out of the house."

She seemed to understand at once and vanished. Not for the first time I was thankful for her unimaginative practicality. Anyone else would have hesitated, checked that they'd heard right, or something. I ran back to the spiral stair and down, lifted the door handle, and flung my weight against the door. It seemed totally solid, and the twist of the stairs precluded a proper charge. There was nowhere for leverage. I climbed the stair and found Bobo in the cross-corridor wearing grey flannel trousers over his pyjamas and pulling a jersey on as he came towards me.

"That door's locked," I gasped. "We'll have to try King William's Room. It's full of gas."

I ran but he overtook me on the stairs and led the way. I followed with relief. I am not a man of action. Bobo was. Indeed he already seemed to have a plan. At the foot of the stair he picked up the short bench that had always stood there and hefted it onto his hip. The gas smell was now sinisterly strong.

"Right," he said. "First thing is air. I'll go and get a window open upstairs. You do that one there. When I call, take a good lungful and then hold your breath and come on up."

I saw his own lungs fill. Still carrying the bench, he climbed purposefully up the stairs. I followed him to the landing, loosed the catch of the landing window, slid the sash up and leaned out, breathing the rain-washed air. In a few seconds I heard his call and followed him on up. He was kneeling on the bench, which he had climbed on to reach the window catch, and had his head and shoulders out into the open. As I joined him, I could see the raindrops beginning to gather on his already sparse blonde hair. Mercifully the draught was inwards.

"Christ," said Bobo. "Did you smell it in here? Must be solid gas in the Yellow Room. I tried a squint through the keyhole, but the key's in the lock. Stupid bugger. He'll be a goner all right, if he's in there. Ready? We'll use this bench as a ram. You take that end. Five swings and back to the window. I'm not going to kill myself for bloody Gerry."

We swung the bench rhythmically against the lock with Bobo grunting the time. At the third strike something splintered. At the fifth the lock gave. Bobo booted the right-hand leaf and propped it open with the bench. He barely glanced inside before inspecting the other leaf. He found the bolts and slid them free. Over his shoulder I saw that the curtains were drawn in the Yellow Room but the lights were still on. A pair of legs, presumably Gerry's, were visible. The body itself, slumped in the armchair on the far side of the fireplace, was hidden by a draped table on which stood a decanter and siphon. Bobo followed me back to the window.

"Looks like a piece of cake," he said. "I'll go in and get him out. You stay by the door. Don't come in unless you can see

I'm having trouble. If anything goes wrong, get me out, not him. He'll be a goner. Grab a fresh lot of air before you try anything. If you don't think you can do it alone, go and get help. But it's not going to come to that. Soon as I'm out, get some air, then go in and turn the gas off. Keep counting while you're in there. Soon as you reach twenty-five, head for the door. More air, go back, get the windows open. Just don't try to do any more in one go than you can. And for God's sake don't touch any switches. I'll be back as soon as I've got him outside. Right? We're off."

Bobo had never looked a natural athlete, effective rather than deft, and was a large man now, but he was still keeping himself in trim. Holding my breath and counting the seconds, I watched from the door as he walked calmly into the room. By five he had reached the chair. He took Gerry by both wrists, heaved him into a sitting position, half knelt, and dragged the body over his shoulders. Gerry was in his shirtsleeves, with gaudy Eton Rambler braces. I glimpsed his face, a dark yellow-ish purple. Eleven. Bobo stayed kneeling, adjusting his hold. Fourteen, fifteen. He rose, shrugged his load into position, and strode out and straight to the window. Twenty-two. I joined him. Edward Voss-Thompson was out on East Lawn under a golf umbrella, wearing a dressing gown.

"Want any help?" he called.

"Not yet," I answered. "Stay where you are. Send for an ambulance."

"Right," said Bobo. "Your turn."

I held my breath and walked back into the Yellow Room. Five, and I'd reached the gas tap and turned it off. Plenty of time. I stood and looked around. Gerry's smoking jacket lay across the desk, beside a brandy bottle and a half-empty water jug. There was a balloon glass on the table beside the armchair where he had been slumped. An upright chair stood close in front of the fire itself, facing the room. Fifteen. As I picked it up to carry it over to the window, my fingers went straight through the cloth at the back. Ridiculously, I paused to see why, and found that the whole area was scorched. The padded front, on the other hand, was for some reason damp. I actually stood there, staring at the object as if it mattered, before carrying it on to the window and climbing onto the seat. The window catch, out of sight above my head, was of an unfamiliar pattern with some kind of locking device. Obstinate, I fiddled with it, realised I had lost count, came to my senses, and dashed for the door. My haste, verging on panic, caused me to catch my foot on the bench which Bobo had used to prop one leaf open, and I went sprawling, with the hoarded breath bursting from my lungs. Nothing could stop me gasping a breath of the poisonous mixture, but I forced it out again, crawled blindly for the window and hauled myself up. This time, though, I deliberately stood to one side, invisible from below, while I gulped the sweet inflowing draught. The bench had made my mind up.

I truly believe that since that first whiff of gas outside the Gun Room I had sensed, guessed, known, that something more complex and more potentially disastrous to us all than an accident, or even a suicide, was in process. Perhaps some such awareness had been in my mind ever since Nancy's ominous remark on the telephone: "It's going to happen. Or else. . . ." The sisters at their net on the lawn, Nancy at the window, Mr. Chad on his ladder; the locked doors; Nancy up and dressed and apparently waiting for my alarm, Harriet ready for it, too, Bobo knowing so clearly what was involved, bringing the bench; the water jug, the chair both scorched and wet . . . I also knew that such intricacies invariably come apart under the pressure of the real world. Every section of the machinery carries the possibility of betrayal. It was never going to work. It must be covered up. Buried.

I knew what I wanted to do, but not how. Bobo would be back any moment. All I could think of, no doubt from forgotten boyhood reading, was oily rags. Bonfires. The Gun Room. I left the window and dashed downstairs.

Matches and paraffin were there, but no cloth. I opened the can, wadded a handkerchief over it, and tilted. A missile. There was a wastepaper basket full of old cricket balls. I took one and ran back up the stairs, knotting the sodden handkerchief round the ball as I went. I remember hearing footsteps along the passage below, Lucy's voice calling my name. No more.

Lucy

TEN

August 1956

The first I knew was the fire alarm—I think I've said that. There were feet stamping about, and voices, and it was dreadfully early, and I wanted to put the pillow over my head and go back to sleep, but then Nan rushed in and hoicked the bedclothes off and yelled that the East Wing was full of gas and we'd all got to get out, so I pulled some clothes on and went down and out through the double saloon doors on the South Front, where luckily there was always a stand full of brollies, so I took one and stumped crossly round in the pouring rain to the East Lawn to see what was happening. Teddy Voss-Thompson was there, shooing everyone up to the Stables, but he told me Paul and Bobo were up in King William's Room trying to get Gerry out, and a moment later Bobo came staggering out of the East Door with a body over his shoulder. I ran to help.

"Don't look," he said, but I'd seen already. It was Gerry. I knew he was dead. That colour.

Bobo laid him down. I took off my coat and covered his face and then ran into the house. I was desperately worried about Paul. After last night, and then creeping round fully dressed when everyone else was in bed, I thought he might do anything. As I turned into the East Corridor, I just glimpsed him

running up the stairs. I called his name. Bobo was a bit behind me, so I don't think he'd seen Paul. He was telling me to come back. He caught me up and held me by the elbow, but I jerked it away and said, oh, I don't know what, and he gave in, so we started up the stairs together.

We hadn't quite reached the landing when there was a colossal explosion and a great whoosh of burning air and we were knocked flat. They told me afterwards that if we'd been anywhere except on the stairs, we'd have been killed. Paul, too. He must have been just below the top, because the explosion knocked him all the way back down to the landing. I didn't see or hear him fall, but we found him there, with his clothes on fire, when Bobo grabbed me by the shoulder and started to drag me up towards the window, which was open.

Bobo was absolutely terrific. I'll never hear a word against him since then. Quick as a flash, he let go of me and simply rolled Paul up in the landing carpet, banging the flames out with his bare hands as he did so, then he picked Paul up and carried him to the window, sat and swung his own legs over, and jumped.

I rushed to the window too and climbed out. I could see Paul and Bobo lying in the laurels beneath me. It wasn't far, really, not a whole storey anyway because of the landing, but I still couldn't make myself jump, though the house was like a furnace behind me. I climbed out and hung from the sill but I still couldn't let go, and then Mr. Chad arrived with his ladder and got me down.

I was perfectly alright, hardly a scratch, just my hair a bit singed, but Bobo had broken both ankles it turned out, in spite of the soft ground under the laurels. We got them out— I can't remember who else was there, but Mr. Chad kept shouting at everyone that we'd got to get well clear because the equaliser tank hadn't gone up yet. He and Teddy were carrying Paul, still rolled in the carpet, and I was trying to keep the rain off Paul with a brolly, when I remembered about

Gerry and looked back over my shoulder. So I actually saw the next explosion.

It was like films of the Blitz, though I don't think I've ever seen a film of a big bomb actually hitting a house, but I'm sure that's what it would be like. Before I heard the noise or anything, I saw the East Front sort of shrug, and then came the roar and the wall of hot air whumped over us and the house was breaking up, floating apart, huge blocks of brickwork and stone sailing through the air and the ball of boiling fire mushrooming up beneath them. Mr. Chad staggered against me but we didn't quite fall, and then we started to run as best we could carrying Paul, while the bits of house came crashing down through the trees around us.

We all got up to the Stables somehow. Somebody must have helped Bobo; I didn't see who. No one else was hurt, though a lot of Mother's windows had been blown in by the blast and I could hear the horses screaming in their stalls and thrashing around as they tried to escape. Mother's flat was all on the ground floor, so we carried Paul into her bedroom. One side of his face was ghastly to see and his right sleeve had really caught fire, so I told them to bring me scissors and a lot of cold water and towels, and I bathed and bathed the burnt bits, the way Nanny always said you had to, though the doctors then said grease was better, but now they say water after all. It was when I was cutting the burnt sleeve away that I smelt the paraffin. I've made too many bonfires not to know what it was. That's how I knew he'd started the fire.

It didn't make any difference. It was all over, done, and a lot of it was my fault. All I knew was that I wanted to do the best for him I could. When the ambulances came, I insisted on staying with him. They didn't want me to, but I told them who I was and people still used to pay attention to that sort of thing then.

The ambulance didn't have proper windows, just a couple of titchy little panes in the back doors, but as we swung round into the drive, I got a glimpse of what had happened to the house. The whole of the East Wing was gone, and a lot of the centre block. You could see right into the rooms beyond—the wallpaper and the fireplaces and a bath hanging in midair— like you used to on bombed sites during the war. The East Front had collapsed outwards onto the porte-cochère. There was just a pile of rubble there. Gerry was underneath it.

Paul

ELEVEN

Autumn 1956

I woke in considerable pain. The whole side of my face, as well
as my right arm, was burning and throbbing. My right eyelid
seemed to be glued shut, and when I opened my left, I could see
nothing. From the sense of touch in that cheek, just discernible
against the steady pain on the other side, I was aware of a
dressing of some kind over my face. I moved my left hand to
feel the place, but fingers caught my wrist and restrained me.
Lucy's voice said, "Try and lie still. I'll send for someone. Are
you terribly sore?"

My lips wouldn't articulate. I was forced to groan an affir-
mative.

"You're in hospital," said Lucy. "Try to lie still. You'll be
all right. Everyone's all right. We all got out."

Somebody came and gave me an injection, morphine presumably, and the pain died and I slept. The pattern was
repeated again and again. Sometimes Lucy wasn't there, but
more often she was. When my hurts became more bearable
and the painkillers could be reduced enough for me to feel no
more than drowsy, she read to me, and all through the six-
month process of healing and having my face rebuilt she was
with me most hours of most days. As soon as I was well enough
to pay any attention to my business, she made herself my

channel for all my dealings. I had known from her rare references to her wartime work that she must be competent enough at that sort of thing, but had no idea how quick, clear, and sensible she was, knowing exactly when to act on her own responsibility, and so on. My affairs, which I had left in a state of controlled tension, were by now in crisis. I just managed to restore them to decent order. There was luck involved, as always, but I know I could not have done it without Lucy's help. And I doubt if I would have healed as well as I did, or found the energy for my work, or regained my belief that there was any point in working or living, without her company. But at no point did I ask or say anything that might in any way open up a discussion of the events around Gerry's death. It was a subject far too dangerous to talk about, to think about, to remember in any way at all.

I had one relapse. It came while I was in another hospital, undergoing the drearily painful business of having my face rebuilt by skin grafts from my buttocks. Lucy was there as much as possible. She will say that she was using the need to visit me as a way of escaping from the reverberations of the so-called Seddon Affair, then in full swing, but all that mattered to me was that she came. In the course of one visit she happened to mention that Nancy was going to be "all right" financially, because on her marriage Gerry had taken out a large insurance policy on his own life. That night, for the only time, I rejected a graft. I never made the connection that this news had provided me with the one missing piece of machinery for the dream structure I had been building, starting from that first flash of intuition as I lay sprawled on the floor of King William's Room gasping the poisonous air, and continuing as I came and went through the morphine haze, but never acknowledged by my waking consciousness. I now "knew" the motive for Gerry's murder.

I was too ill to attend the inquest and so gave an affidavit in which I described my talk with Gerry, saying that he had seemed depressed but not overwhelmed about his finances, but omitting of course his apparent attempt to blackmail me with threats about what Michael might do to Lucy. I said that I had fallen ill during the conversation, gone back to the house, and gone to bed; that I had decided to leave early next morning for personal reasons and had telephoned for a taxi; that on reaching the Gun Room I had smelt gas, woken the household, returned with Bobo and helped him break into the Yellow Room, watched him retrieve Gerry's body, and then gone into the room myself and turned off the gas; that my intention had been to open a window, but that I could not remember doing so—indeed could remember nothing else at all until I woke in hospital. Apart from the omission referred to, I was not lying. That indeed was all I remembered. It was only the shock of Lucy's question in the garden last July that allowed me the glimpse of memory that prompted my reply to her.

Instantly the door tried to close, but I knew I must not let it. Lucy is dying. There is unfinished business between us. The urgency with which I have felt compelled to write this memoir tells me that the time has come. The memoir itself is a tool for prying out into the open this thing that I have refused to look at or think about for thirty-six years, and now that I have it in plain view, what have I got?

There is a story in, I think, Oliver Wendell Holmes about how in the dentist's chair, under the influence of laughing gas, he saw with great clarity the secret of the universe, but on coming round from the anaesthetic could no longer remember it. He insisted on being given the gas again, saw the secret again and this time, with great effort, clutched it to him as he swam back up into consciousness. It turned out to be this:

> Hoggamus Higgamus,
> Men are polygamous,
> Higgamus Hoggamus,
> Women monogamous.

What I have discovered after all my effort appears to be a secret of that order. The intuition on which I acted so disastrously came to me in two parts, like the piers of a bridge, with a vague-seen structure in between. First, that everybody in the house, to judge by their reactions when I panted the news of the gas leak to them, already knew what to do. Dressed as I was, and after my breakdown the previous night, Nancy would have had every excuse for taking me for crazy when I confronted her, but she did not. Scenes like those which then took place—Nancy trying the door on the spiral stair and then setting about evacuating the house, Bobo taking the bench on his way up to the Yellow Room, to use it as a ram—had already been mentally rehearsed. My intervention was if anything a convenience, providing an uninvolved witness to the events.

Second, the episode on the East Lawn the previous evening had indeed been a charade. Lucy had struck the ball towards the house on purpose. She could not hope to hit one of the Yellow Room windows at that distance, but that didn't matter because Mr. Chad, the intended witness, had his back to the scene, and Nancy, watching her moment, broke the pane from inside, threw up the window and tossed out a cricket ball she had ready. Even I, watching the flight of the ball as it started, had assumed that I'd been mistaken in its line, so obviously did the tinkle of glass attach itself to the missile. The sisters, of course, had not intended that I should be watching. Nancy had pointed me out, no doubt in some alarm, and Lucy had immediately come over to check whether I had noticed anything wrong.

The rest of the structure, which, as I say, I put together in no better than a half-waking state, and then dopey with morphine, can be summarised as follows: If Gerry failed to come to acceptable terms with Michael, Nancy decided that she would be better off getting rid of him and taking the insurance. She was the instigator, and the perpetrator. Her sisters, acting out of that intense family solidarity I had sensed when I saw them on the lawn, had been more or less active accessories. The intention was that Gerry's death should look like an accident. The fire must seem to have been on, and then the gas to have failed while Gerry was in his stupor, and then come on again but not relit, thus filling the room with gas. There must be a reason for the fire to have been on on a summer evening. The doors must be locked, so that nobody in the house could be suspected of being involved. Another way into the room must be arranged for.

All this Nancy achieved. The only element outside her control was Gerry's actually drinking himself into a stupor, but she saw to it in her interview with him before supper that he would have every incentive to do so if he failed to break with Michael. At the same time she prepared events by spilling water over one of the chairs and putting it in front of the fire to dry. Presumably she listened outside the door while the interview with Michael took place and failed. Perhaps Gerry then locked himself in, perhaps not—it didn't matter. If not, she could have gone in and upbraided him, perhaps even incited him to drink by doing so herself, and meanwhile checked on her other arrangements. If he did, then she would have left and waited until the household was asleep, fetched Mr. Chad's ladder, removed the soft putty from the pane she had broken that afternoon, turned off the gas (to judge by the charring of the chair and Gerry being in shirtsleeves, he had not done so), waited for the elements to cool and turned it on again, locked and bolted the doors if necessary, and then left, reputtying the pane into place. She was, I gather, skilled enough to do so. She would have brought a flashlight to work by. She then went back to her room and waited for the earliest moment at which it would seem proper to wake the household. She had been on her way to do so when I had knocked on her door. There were other apparently corroborating details— Bobo's participation, for instance, could be accounted for by my awareness that Gerry had asked him for money, as he had attempted to ask me, and perhaps also with the threat of some piece of knowledge Bobo would much rather not have made public—but it would be tedious to go on.

The structure does have a sort of coherence, but it is the coherence of the paranoid, in which everything that might support the delusion is twisted to fit and everything that contradicts it—in particular the sheer messiness and lack of structure in the everyday world—is ignored. Even if I allow myself a serious misjudgement of the character of one of the sisters, Nancy, and make her a monster rather than a moral tough, what about others I love or like or admire? What about Lucy and Harriet? And then, suppose those three were monsters, how could I imagine that they would take the risk of letting Janet play a part in their conspiracy? Or, for different reasons, Ben? And if those two were not in it, one of them at least would have spotted that the ball wasn't going to hit the window, even if the actual impact was out of sight. And then, how could anyone believe in a conspiracy which hinged on the certainty that the victim could be relied on to drink himself into insensibility at the appropriate time? And so on.

So a totally different question now arises: why did I feel impelled first to create this nonsensical structure, and then to bury it out of sight? By the same token, why did I choose to extend the amnesia surrounding the actual explosion—a normal enough response to extreme physical trauma—into the minute or two before, during which I took the steps that were to destroy the house? The shock and pain buried the first, and that is mercifully irrecoverable, but I then chose to bury the second, which I have now disinterred. The answer is that I needed the act of destruction, for my own purposes, and that I invented the structure to justify it, but because the structure was no more than invention and as such would not stand the daylight of honest reason, I was forced to bury it.

I had certainly been overworking and was possibly due some kind of a breakdown. What I took for a severe pang of nostalgia on my arrival may have been a premonitory symptom. My blackout during my interview with Gerry would then have been the true onset. My behavior that night, the secrecy, the creepings about, the reluctance to insist on a taxi being sent for to take me away, the wish to do everything for myself, and so on were mild manifestations, and then my so-called "intuition" and consequent burning of the Yellow Room were the full-blown products of delusion. I wanted, no doubt, to destroy the past, to destroy Gerry (though he was already dead), and thus at least symbolically wipe out the dreadful thing he had told me by the lake, but perhaps I wanted more than that. Did I in fact at some level know that the explosion in the Yellow Room was going to set off the far larger one, which effectively destroyed the whole house? I wanted, I had always wanted, in spite of my apparent tolerance, Lucy for myself alone. Other men were not really my rivals. Blatchards was. Now she could never go back there.

No wonder then, as the rest of that year went by and the next began and the outside world occupied itself according to its interests, with the ludicrous Suez operation and the Seddon Affair and the uprising in Hungary—all things to which I paid at least superficial attention—I used my energies in rescuing my business from the brink and my spare time in talking to Lucy about anything and everything except our own lives, or listening to her read (Walter Scott mainly—she had a talent for the dialects), or if all else failed, playing endless games of cribbage.

I was throwing earth into the grave, burying the things which I could not afford to face, what I believed her to have done, and with it, deeper still, what I myself had.

Lucy

ELEVEN

1992

He didn't mean to end there. He'd just got to a stopping place and went out to fossick around and think. When he'd finished a bit and got it the way he wanted, he used to print it out and give it to me to read, but he didn't this time. It was still in his word processor and I had to get Mrs. Wrasse—she's our cleaner—to press the keys while I told her what to do so we could get it out. That was next day, or the day after—I don't remember.

He'd told me he'd be clearing leaves from the rockery if I wanted him, but he didn't come in for tea—not like him— he'd got a stopwatch in his head, though I used to tease him by saying it was in his stomach—and I went out and found him lying facedown among the cyclamen. I wanted to leave him like that. I knew at once he was dead. It looked right. Just leave him lying until they were ready for the funeral— much nicer than any kind of mortuary place—but I knew I wouldn't be allowed, so I went and got help, and everybody was very kind and sorry for me, which was quite unnecessary really. It was the best thing that could have happened.

I'm in a home now. Timmy and Janice wanted me to go and live with them—I really think they meant it, and not just saying so because they felt they ought—but I said no. I want to get this boring business of dying over as tidily as possible (and as quickly as possible, I hope), and at least they're used to it here. I'm quite a lot worse already. In fact I can't always remember where I am. So before I lose touch completely, I want to get this all tidied up.

I thought of asking them to burn everything Paul had written and just wipe my tapes away by putting a lot of Mozart or someone on top of them, but then I thought no. I want it finished. I don't want it all wasted. Tombstones are boring— they don't tell you anything. No. This is all anyone is going to know about us, Paul especially. He never knew how to behave with children, so he kept in the background when they came to visit and I don't think they'll remember much about him, and I shall soon be gone, and there's no one else left. But he's here alright, in these pages. Sometimes when I've been reading, I've felt I could almost reach out and hold his hand.

That's what matters to me now. I suppose people will want to know what happened to the rest of us, and how Gerry got killed, and I'll do my best. Somebody said you've got to have a story, and he was right. I always feel miffed if I'm left in the air. So here goes.

The first thing was the inquest. I didn't give evidence, but Bobo did, and Nan, and Michael, and Mr. Chad about the gas plant. (Paul's wrong about that, by the way. The gas plant was in the Brew House, because it would have been dangerous to have it in the main house, but the trouble was it was too far away and the gas didn't flow evenly, so Mr. Chad's father, before the First War, put something called an equaliser tank into the cellars under the Billiard Room. It still didn't get enough gas to the West Wing, but it was OK for the East Wing, which was why the Yellow Room fire was pretty good. It was the equaliser tank which exploded in the fire.)

The family line was that Gerry's death was an accident. We all thought so anyway, except me, and I wasn't going to say anything. So without actually conspiring, we agreed to play down Gerry's worries about money, and the row he'd had with Nan before supper, and so on. Only bloody Michael went and spoilt it, and he was vital because he'd been the last person to see Gerry alive. He'd arrived soaked to the skin because his taxi had broken down, and supper was almost over by then, so they'd taken a tray up to the Yellow Room, and Gerry had lent him a dressing gown, and they'd put his clothes over a chair in front of the fire to dry. He said that Gerry was very depressed about money because of the cost of running Blatchards now that Dick Felder's alimony wasn't coming in anymore, and he'd wanted to borrow a lot of money from Michael. He said he'd tried Paul and Bobo and they'd said no (I expect Gerry really did tell Michael this). Michael said he'd promised to do what he could, but it obviously wasn't going to be nearly enough. So in the end he'd taken his clothes and turned off the fire and said good night. Of course the lawyers—Nan had one, and so did both the insurance companies—asked about this again and again. It was vital. If the fire was off when Michael left, somebody must have turned it on again, and if the doors were locked, it could only have been Gerry. The life insurance lawyer was an absolute terrier about it, because if Gerry had killed himself on purpose, they wouldn't have to pay up. (The house insurance man was more interested in all the things Mr. Chad had done, electrics as well as gas, without being properly qualified and without telling the company.)

Luckily all this happened at Bury—where everybody knew us, and Mother and Father had opened all the village fetes around for years and years—and the terrier-lawyer put the coroner's back up, and the jury's, too, and they brought in a verdict of accidental death (after all Gerry could have turned the fire back on to keep warm, and it gone out after that), but the coroner did say a lot of fatherly things about getting properly qualified workmen to mess around with gas and electrics, and Mr. Chad was desperately hurt, but worse still, the house insurance people tried to get out of paying up. In the end Nan got her own lawyers and went after them and they had a sort of compromise, but it wasn't enough to rebuild.

Not that any of us would have wanted that. Even if they'd put up an exact replica, down to the gouged panelling in the Morning Room where Mother let old Flossie scratch, it would never have been our Blatchards. That was gone. And a good thing, too—Paul's right. It took me about three years to realise it, but actually what I mainly felt about the house being burnt down was an enormous sense of release. All my life it had been summoning me back and back and back, and now it couldn't do it anymore.

I'll come back to that in a minute, but first I've got to deal with the famous Affair. (It was really bloody at the time, absolutely horrible, so I find the only way I can talk about it is treating it like everyone else does, as a bit of a joke. Just remember, it wasn't.) The first I knew about it was when I got a message from Tommy saying he wanted to talk to me urgently, and could I be in Eaton Square for breakfast on such-and-such a morning. I'd hardly seen anything of him at all. I was officially spending the holidays with the children at Seddon Hall while he was desperately trying to get the French and everyone else to be sensible about Colonel Nasser and longing to spend any spare time he had with Sammy Whitstable, and I didn't mind leaving him a free hand for that, as it meant I could spend more time with Paul. I felt I had to. You see, I'd smelt the paraffin and seen the way his sleeve had burnt, so I was practically certain he'd started the fire. And I'd seen him sneaking around the night before, in all his clothes, so I was as sure as I could be that he'd been up to something he didn't want us to know about, and when Gerry was killed, I put two and two together.

What I thought was this. He'd gone to see Gerry late that night, because he was a bit off his rocker, and he'd found him passed out in the Yellow Room. I had no idea how he'd got in and out, leaving it locked behind him. That's what I've always longed to know about—that's what I asked him in the garden, wasn't it, that Saturday morning last summer? All I knew was that he must have, somehow. I don't know. Anyway, what I decided was that finding Gerry like that, he'd decided to get rid of him by turning the gas on and not lighting it. And then in the morning he'd got up early and woken us all up by saying he'd smelt gas. And then perhaps he'd thought perhaps he'd made some mistake and left fingerprints or something—I don't know what—and decided it would be safer to start a fire, only he got it wrong. He's quite right about not being a man of action. Absolutely not. I've never understood why plants grew so well for him. They were the only things he could ever make work. Perhaps it was because they were so slow.

Sorry, I've got lost. Oh yes, the thing I was most sure about of all was that he'd done it because of me. I've never been one of those people who go round looking for things to feel guilty about—quite the opposite, in fact I probably haven't felt guilty nearly enough—but I did about that, so I wanted to be there when he remembered and tell him it was all alright, it wasn't his fault—only he never did. I knew something was worrying him in a puzzled sort of way, like a dog which is being punished because it's done wrong, and it really does know it's been wicked about something and it's anxious and ashamed and sorry, only it can't remember what it was.

Well, then, Tommy sent me this message, so I went up to London and spent a night at Eaton Square, and there he was at breakfast next morning opening his post, so I pecked his cheek and settled down to my grapefruit and the crossword the way I'd always used to when things were better, but when I looked up, I saw him watching me. I raised my eyebrows.

"Do you want a divorce?" he said.

"Oh. Why?" I said.

"I cannot divorce you, because of my faith, but you can divorce me if you wish, and I will provide you with the evidence," he said.

"I don't understand," he said.

"I greatly appreciate your willingness to keep up appearances over the past few months," he said.

"It wasn't only for that," I said.

He just nodded and went on.

"It's not going to be necessary much longer," he said. "I am proposing to resign."

"You can't!" I said. "I mean . . . Why on earth . . . ?"

He watched me, smiling, while I burbled on aghast. Then he shook his head. The only thing I could think of was that they were trying to make him dish Colonel Nasser in a way which would be even worse for his career than refusing to do it.

"I must resign before I'm forced to resign," he said. "My friendship with Miss Whitstable is about to become public knowledge."

"I thought you'd been so careful," I said.

"We had," he said. "Or so I thought. However, I was approached last week by a man who said he had information to give me. What he in fact had was photographs. He wanted a substantial sum for the negatives. I told him to go to hell. The probability is that he will now attempt to sell them to some Fleet Street rag."

"That's extraordinary," I said.

"Not very," he said. "If one lays oneself open to black-mail . . ."

"That's not what I meant," I said. "I mean, what sort of a man?"

"Like a seedy solicitor's clerk, I suppose," he said.

"With a great big ring on his hand which he kept tapping to show he meant what he was saying?" I asked.

I don't think I'd ever seen Tommy startled before. He sat

bolt upright and gawped like a schoolboy. For a moment he actually let me see what he was like inside. Then he pulled himself together.

"Has he been after you, too?" he said.

"No," I said. "It was someone else. I'm afraid I can't tell you. He asked for advice. It was because I'd been in security."

He thought about it.

"Perhaps I should know his name," he said. "Assuming he is to be trusted, we may be able to act together."

"I'll ask him," I said. "But what did you say? Where did this all happen? How did he get hold of you?"

"He was waiting for me on the steps of the Athenaeum. It was a mistake on my part even to speak to him, but I was taken by surprise and allowed him an opening. As soon as I came to my senses, I tore the pictures up and told him to clear off. Of course I have always been aware that something like this was going to happen in the end."

"What did he want?" I said.

"Money, naturally," he said. "Was that not the case with your friend?"

"It was more complicated than that," I said. "It was help in doing something very tricky about exchange controls, and if it had worked, it would have been worth, I don't know, millions."

"That does not sound like my man," said Tommy. "Altogether too sophisticated and grandiose. What did your friend decide?"

"I don't know," I said. "The man was coming back, but I'll ring him up and ask, if you like. Anyway, what about us? Do you really want me to divorce you? Do you want to marry Miss Whitstable?"

"I should not be able to regard myself as divorced, though you could," he said. "As for Miss Whitstable, no, far from it. I recognise perfectly well what is happening to me—in fact I am fascinated by the irrationality of my own behaviour. I was no more strictly reared and schooled than others of my class, but there was never any need to discipline me, because I disciplined myself. I believe I never knowingly broke a school rule. As an adult I not only observed the rules of my class and culture but invented further rules for myself. To my colleagues, to my staff behind my back, to the public at large, I am a figure of fun."

"And now you've found out what you've been missing?" I said.

"You don't understand," he said. "The excitement and satisfaction of what I have been doing over the last few months depend on there being rigid rules for me to break. The whole point of my relationship with Miss Whitstable is that it is illicit. My own self-disgust provides a kind of pleasure. So does the knowledge that in the end I shall have to pay the price of public humiliation. That time seems now to have come. I shall not ask you to share it with me."

I expect this all sounds desperately pi, too high-minded to be true, but all I know is that I felt terribly moved. He'd never talked to me like that before. I could see he was forcing himself to say these things because he felt he owed it to me. His face was like a wooden doll, with his lips just moving up and down. I reached out and took his hand, half expecting him to pull it away, but he didn't.

"I'll do whatever you want," I said. "But if I get a vote, I'd like to sit tight and tell them all to go to hell. I don't want everyone thinking I ran away just because you were in trouble."

"And I don't want them thinking I was content to let them pull you down with me," he said. "What I suggest is that we bring the whole thing to public notice by your suing for divorce, citing Miss Whitstable. I will not defend the action. We will behave as if we had nothing of interest to conceal, and if all goes well, the press will assume that that is indeed the case. They are certain to paw our affairs over to some extent, but we may be able to arrange for the process, though unpleasant, not to be unspeakable."

"I'll have to think about it," I said. "It feels like running away."

"There are the children's interests, as much as yours and mine," he said.

I'm afraid I'd forgotten about them. Tommy was always a much better father than I was a mother, though I got fonder of them as soon as they started to grow up. Anyway, we left it at that for the moment, though I rather gloomily decided he was probably right.

I rang David later that day, and he told me the man had come back only a few days before, and this time David had been ready with a lot of technical difficulties, only the man just wanted money now, and not an awful lot of it, either, and he hadn't any idea what David was talking about. In fact David said he got the impression that the time before the man had been sent by somebody and told what to say, and this time he was acting on his own for what he could get, so as soon as David realised he couldn't do him any harm with anyone who mattered, he started to ring up the police, and the man saw that he meant it and ran off. He said he thought the whole thing was now over.

He was in for a shock. We all were. It began with the TV programme about racketeering landlords, the one Teddy Voss-Thompson had started off with and then left because of Michael being his brother-in-law. I never saw it, but I heard about it over and over and over. It was almost the first time TV had really shown what it could do about something like that. They talked to the tenants, ordinary, harmless old people, who'd been frightened and harassed out of their homes. Most of them wouldn't talk, but they managed to trap one of the frighteners on the job and question him, and he got rough, but they had pictures of him and connected him with a lot of criminals in the East End—remember that party Michael took me to? I think that was them—and they didn't just do frightening, they drug-trafficked and did protection and ran call girls, and so on, and all that was exciting enough.

But on top of that they'd got a lot more stuff about Michael, and how he did things. Remember Nan telling me that she'd got a stick for Gerry as well as a carrot? What it was was that before she'd agreed to marry him and start the family he so longed for, she'd made him tell her a lot of stuff, names and dates and money and so on, about what he and Michael had really been doing, so that she could force him to break with Michael and force Michael to let him go by threatening to publish it all herself. With Gerry dead, that was too late, of course, but she still didn't want Michael to get away with it, so she asked me how I'd found out what I'd told her, and I explained about Teddy Voss-Thompson's talk with Paul, so she passed everything on to him. That was enough for the TV people to take the risk of giving Michael's name and asking a lot of suggestive questions about him.

So next day there were reporters trying to get hold of Michael, and he was threatening everyone with libel writs, and other reporters swarming all over the East End, and I think somebody must have run into the man with the big ring, because next thing wasn't a newspaper story but a question in Parliament about the Lord Seneschal (that was Tommy) and his connection with people who were in turn connected to the Yugoslav security services. Not all in one go like that, of course—a harmless-seeming question first and then a snide supplementary and points of order and a terrific burst of excitement like you get when you're hunting and the hounds all get a scent together and give tongue.

It was all absolutely typical of the whole business. Most of what anyone said was just hints and guesses and nosing around, and a few lies, but just enough truth oozing out all the time to keep the excitement going. Apart from Tommy (and me) it was poor David who took the worst hiding. The man with the ring must have passed on those photographs, too, and said where they were taken, and somebody else (I bet it was Biddy Trollope, who never means any harm but just blurts things out and causes havoc—it keeps happening to her, like being accident prone), somebody let on that David and I had been lovers. Heavens, it had been six or seven years before, and it had lasted about a couple of weeks, but now David had gone to Yugoslavia and some idiot in the secret police had tried to blackmail him, and *then* it came out that our friend Mikovicz, who everybody thought was rather a jolly Yugoslav playboy enjoying the fleshpots of London and pretending to run UF-TFA, hadn't just been a pretty bloodthirsty resistance leader against the Germans but had moved on to becoming a high-up in Tito's secret police. And what's more, Sammy Whitstable was spending just as much time with him as she was with Tommy. And while they were still frothing at the mouth about that, one of the reporters who were nosing round the East End met somebody who remembered me going to that party with Michael. And to cap it all, there was Michael's crony dead in an explosion in a country house. Luckily the inquest was over before any of this came out, but even without that, just imagine! Two titles, a government minister, a kinky tart, the minister's wife who'd been a society beauty but slept around with mysterious businessmen (that's Michael, David, and poor Paul), East End criminals, racketeering landlords, a dead body, and cricket! (They'd got on to Blatchards *v.* The World and kept making frightful cricketing puns in the headlines.) It all simply reeked of the Establishment leaping in and out of bed with each other and having kinky sex on the side, between driving poor, honest pensioners out of their homes and betraying their country to the Reds.

Some of it was a hoot, such as the notion of David being part of the Establishment, let alone a mysterious businessman. But most of it was hell.

I never met Sammy Whitstable again, after that one party where she'd come dressed as a man, but there we were in the newspapers day after day, me looking cold and upper-crust and her looking earthy and sexy. Actually she behaved rather well. One of the papers paid her a lot of money for her life story, and according to Teddy Voss-Thompson, the hack tried to make her say all sorts of things that weren't true and she dug her heels in and wouldn't name names of other men or say what they'd done together. So perhaps Mrs. Mudge was wrong about her. I hope so. I'd rather liked the look of her. Then she just disappeared. I don't think I saw her name again till she died (much too young), and the obituaries raked the whole thing over again. Apparently she'd got religion and become a Buddhist. That's all I remember.

I had a pretty bad time, of course. I was used to being photographed, but not like that, stalked, lain in wait for, peeped at, ambushed. They actually found out I was visiting Paul in hospital, and some of them dressed up as orderlies and sneaked in and tried to interview him. Fiends. Then, mercifully, Suez happened, and then Hungary, and they had other things to think about.

People still remember the Affair, of course. Every few years there's another book or a TV programme. When Michael died, there was a flurry, because you can't libel dead people and at last they were allowed to say things about him which he'd have sued them for. But because people are so obsessed with sex and spies, there's always more in them about poor Tommy and Sammy Whitstable, and the fancy orgies our friend Mikovicz was laying on. Usually there are bits about me. You can't imagine what a cold-hearted man-eating bitch some of them make me out. And then there'll be a chapter about Gerry. I remember one year there were two books which came out almost together and one of them said he'd been killed by the CIA and the other said it was the KGB. A few times people have said it was Michael, or Michael's East End cronies, but they couldn't say how anyone had got into the room. And most of the sensible writers decided in spite of the inquest that Gerry had been Michael's stooge and he realised what he'd let himself in for and he'd killed himself for the insurance for Nan and the baby. That's what anyone who remembers the Affair comes up with. "Gerry Grantworth, that crook who killed himself."

Now I've got to tidy up. I hate stories which don't explain bits and leave all the characters dangling in midair. I want to know how they all got on after. So I've made a list—explanations first, then loose ends.

Let's start with all the sexy bits—David and his girl in Yugoslavia, Tommy and Sammy Whitstable, Mrs. Mudge, the man with the ring on his finger who had the photographs, all that. Despite what Nan said, I don't think this had anything to do with Michael. Michael would have known there wasn't a hope of blackmailing Tommy, but he easily might have chatted to Gerry about Tommy's hangups and told him what sort of a girl he'd go for. I think it was something Gerry and Mikovicz cooked up between themselves, because they needed the money, Gerry to take over paying for Blatchards, and Mikovicz for the orgies and his general life-style. Mikovicz was one of Gerry's group in the war, Tommy told me. They knew that something like Suez was going to happen, and they knew it was bound to mean trouble for sterling. (Paul says Michael talked in the Yellow Room about the Americans not letting us get away with it, and Gerry believed Michael was pretty good at that sort of thing.) So they needed three things, an exact date (which they thought they could use Sammy Whitstable to get out of Tommy), someone like David to put the deal through, and enough money—about two hundred thousand pounds, David told me—to set the deal up. If Mikovicz had been acting for his bosses, he could have got it from them, so

I don't think he can have been, because that must be what Gerry was trying to borrow money for, first from Bobo, then from Paul, and last of all (I'll come to this later) from Michael.

Have I left anything out? Oh, yes. David said he'd been moaning to everyone about not being able to get to Yugoslavia the way he wanted. He's bound to have told Biddy Trollope, who was always trying to help people about that sort of thing and getting it wrong, and she could easily have asked Gerry because he was in Yugoslavia during the war.

By the way, I don't think Gerry ever spied for anybody. I think he was supposed to be what they call a "sleeper," which is why somebody had got silly Annie Dunwoody to snitch his file from the F Block, but I don't think they'd have had much luck if they'd ever tried to wake him up. Oh, yes, and I think Gerry really meant it when he told Paul he didn't want to involve Michael in getting hold of Sammy Whitstable. He might even have talked to Michael about the idea, and Michael had told him to leave it alone because it was far too risky. Michael was doing quite well enough out of his horrid property deals. And—I know this sounds extraordinary after all the things I've said about him, but even the foulest people have little good patches—Tommy was his friend. There can't have been a lot of people who actually liked Michael. Tommy did.

So Gerry and Mikovicz set things up to blackmail Tommy and David so that they could make a pot of money buying sterling futures on margin, but then Gerry got killed and the plot came to bits and the man with the ring, who was acting for Gerry, tried to make some money for himself by ordinary blackmail, but both Tommy and David told him to buzz off so he sold the pictures to newspapers instead.

I think that's all about David except, just tidying up, to say that Teddy left Janet for a TV newsreader, and Janet married David instead, and they had three more children and were rather happy together—in fact they became more and more like Father and Mother apart from David making pots of money until he died—it was a coronary—and then Janet cut loose and went New Age and lived in Devon where she became a witch and joined a coven and had a generally terrific time, channelling and things, until she had a stroke at one of the meetings and went into a coma but the others thought it was all some sort of spiritual transfer and left her alone so it was too late by the time they realised and got her to hospital.

Well, then, what really happened in the Yellow Room? The first thing is, I don't believe any of it was planned. I agree with Paul about that. Of course I know Paul's other theory, the one about us all being in it, is nonsense because I wasn't. I did hit that ball, for fun, not on purpose. It was beautiful, everything just right, the bat feeling part of me, weightless as my own arms, and the timing spot on, and the ball sailing away. Of course it would have been even better if I'd done it to Ben's bowling, but you can't have everything.

Sorry, I must stick to the point. Nobody planned it, nobody made Gerry get drunk and lock himself in. He did. And it wasn't an accident. There was nothing wrong with the Yellow Room fire. Mr. Chad was terribly conscientious about the gas system, and he always checked everything over. But Gerry didn't turn the gas on again to kill himself after Michael had turned it off, because Michael had never turned it off. He must have lied at the inquest. That is, if Paul's right about picking up the chair from in front of the fire and finding the back of it was burnt and the front was still wet. Michael said he took his clothes off the chair, where they'd put them to dry, and then turned the fire out. That's why the chair was wet, because the clothes had been sopping. But if the clothes had been hanging over it, how did the back get burnt? It couldn't have. They must have left the chair standing there to dry out after Michael had taken the clothes away, with the fire still burning, long enough for it to char. Gerry would have passed out by then, or he'd have noticed the smell of burning. So he didn't kill himself. So somebody made the fire go out, after Michael had left the room and Gerry had locked himself in. I'm certain as I possibly can be that it was Michael.

I don't know what Nan had said in her letter to Ben, but I guess Ben showed it to Michael, or asked him about it. All Michael would think was that Gerry must have told Nan some of what was going on. That's why he rushed ahead and married Ben, to have some kind of a hold over Nan. I don't know whether Michael had had it out at all with Gerry in London. They may not have had a chance, because first Michael was on his honeymoon with Ben and then Nan and Gerry had theirs at Blatchards, mainly because Nan wanted to keep him out of Michael's way. So that meeting in the Yellow Room may have been the first chance the pair of them had to try and sort things out.

So Michael showed up with his clothes all sopping, and they turned the fire on and put his coat on the chair to dry. Gerry knew that Nan would be listening, so he started to say what they'd agreed, loud enough for her to hear, but after that they mostly kept their voices down. Why? Because Gerry as well as Michael was talking about things they didn't want her to hear. You remember Gerry locked himself in and deliberately passed out when it was over? I thought it was funny at the time, though Nan seemed to think it was alright, that he didn't at least let her in to tell her how things had gone, and I'm pretty sure the reason was that he'd got Michael to agree to something he—Gerry—wanted, but it wasn't what Nan had wanted.

He wanted to borrow money.

Alright, I don't suppose it was as simple as that. Michael probably hadn't got the money—not enough of it—to lend him. What Gerry was probably asking for was to use some of their joint property as security for a loan, or something like that. Yes, that makes sense, because in that case he actually couldn't ask for a split-up. The point was, a split-up wasn't going to get him the money for the loan soon enough, and even when it came, it wasn't going to provide enough for him to run Blatchards. He absolutely had to get his scheme using David Fish through first, and then he'd be in a much stronger position to deal with Michael.

And just as he had with Paul, he tried to blackmail Michael into letting him do what he wanted. He said what Nan had told him, about how much he'd found out about the way Michael had been setting him up to be a stooge in case what they'd been doing ever came out. The funny thing is, I think Michael gave in, at least for the moment. It sounds like that. Perhaps he was hoping to find a way out by Monday. Or perhaps he was prepared after all to let Gerry take the risk, and hope he got away with it. I don't know.

But then he heard Gerry lock himself in. He waited outside the doors into King William's Room to see if Gerry let Nan in, and try to hear what they said, I expect, but Gerry didn't, so he went upstairs to Ben.

I don't know when he had his idea. After they'd made love, I should think. He used to lie on his back and think then, and he shut you up if you tried to talk. Then he went quietly down and along to King William's Room to see if the Yellow Room lights were still on. They were, so he went on down to the cellars and found the equaliser tank and traced the separate pipe that led up to the Yellow Room—Mr. Chad had showed him all this, Paul says, remember? It would have its own tap. Turned it off, using his handkerchief because of fingerprints. Waited for the elements to cool so that the fire wouldn't relight, and turned it on again. Then back to bed with Ben. He'd wake her up and make love again, I bet, because he was feeling pleased with himself.

So why was he so keen at the inquest to make sure it was suicide, not just accident? What did it matter to him? Because, when the Affair broke and everyone was after his blood, *then* he said that he hadn't quite told the truth at the inquest. It was to spare the family, he said. What he and Gerry really talked about, he said, was that Gerry had admitted he'd got their partnership into a mess in various ways, a lot of them crooked, without telling Michael. He'd done it because he was desperate for funds with which to run Blatchards, and could Michael help him out of the jam? And Michael had told him no, it was too serious for that, and they'd have to split up because he wasn't going to have any part of it. He'd been Gerry's last hope, he said, and that was why Gerry had killed himself. He announced that he was doing everything he could to make up for Gerry's crimes, and he made a great public fuss about it, but he didn't really do much, just enough to get by. Nobody who knew him believed him, but nobody could prove anything, either.

What else? I bet I've left lots out. Oh, yes. Nan was up and dressed because Gerry hadn't come to bed and she was going to look for him. Bobo knew what to do about breaking into the Yellow Room because he was like that.

Well, that's that, and I've almost finished. Just a bit more tidying up. Paul's said what happened to Harriet and Bobo, and I've done Janet. Tommy and I stayed officially married, but after a bit we stopped living together, though we were good friends always. He gave up politics and wrote books about it. He had a secret life I didn't ask about. He died in his sleep a few years ago. I miss him.

Ben. You know, I think she'd have stuck with Michael if he hadn't started beating her up, but she left him in the end and married Gino, who was a sweetie apart from having phases when he felt he'd got a duty to Italian manhood, or something, to lay every moderately pretty woman he came across. She left him too and didn't marry again. She went to live in New York where she switched to modern dancing because her height wasn't a problem for that, and became a complete New York intellectual. (They never seem all that intellectual to me, but my goodness, they talk better intellectual gossip than anyone else, anywhere.) Then, poor woman, a shortsighted jogger ran into her in Central Park and knocked her over and broke her hip and it didn't mend right, so she had to stop dancing, and without that she became more and more reclusive and wouldn't go out, and in the end they found her dead in her apartment because she hadn't had anything to eat for days. She was still quite young. Only fifty-something.

Nan. She held herself together and had the baby—it was a girl, and she called it Gina—but then she fell apart for a bit, drank too much, wore thick makeup, like armour, rushed up and down to London, slept around and didn't enjoy it—she told me all this one afternoon in Eaton Square, where she'd come to pick up the baby who she'd dumped on Nanny—I'd only expected her for five minutes but she stayed four hours and cried in my arms—Nan!—about how she missed Gerry, dreadfully, much more than she missed the house. (She'd pulled it down and converted the old Brew House into a pretty little cottage.) I'd no idea. They were like a couple of trees that have grown into each other in a hedgerow and got themselves all out of shape, but when one dies, you can still see from the other one exactly where it used to be.

Then she did one of her deliberate self-changes and joined what they hadn't quite started calling the Jet Set and met a wildly rich Lebanese grain merchant and lived very plushly with him for several years, trailing Gina around with her. They were on a Caribbean cruise when they ran into Dick Felder, and Nan dropped her Lebanese—left him flat, between lunch and supper, she told me—and remarried Dick. I used to visit them most years, and they seemed as happy with each other as if they'd been married all along. Dick was an ordinary millionaire now, but they did pretty well. He adopted Gina, who turned out to be something like Gerry, only small and neat, but full of sparkle and amazingly good at everything at school. Dick was determined she was going to be an Olympic horsewoman and lavished wonderful horses on her and she started to win all sorts of prizes, but then she said no. She was studying law and married a boy she met at law school, and they did well in an ordinary kind of way, and now they live in a rambling timber house by a lake in Connecticut with woods all around and they've got six children, and in a funny way, I suppose, it's a bit like an American version of Blatchards. It's a place where you are happy to visit, even though you feel you are somehow still being left out of the inner circle of happiness, which the family keep for themselves. So now at least I know what people mean about visiting us in the old days.

When Dick died, Nan stayed on—went native, in fact, golf and diets and charities and facelifts. She got very involved with a guru who said you could be immortal if you only tuned yourself in to the right cosmic resonances, but she kept her sense of humour and died of cancer like anyone else, about twelve years ago. I miss her, too.

Who does that leave? Teddy got famous, so you'll know about him. And Michael. I know if I was just hearing this as a story, I'd want Michael to be punished, really hurt and humiliated, but it didn't happen like that. Like I've said, he managed to wriggle out of everything during the Affair—I don't know how many libel writs and injunctions he issued, but it worked—so he just became a respectable property developer and pulled down nice old chunks of London and put up enormous office blocks nobody wanted, but that didn't seem to stop him becoming enormously rich. You didn't hear about him much, because he did his best to stay out of the papers. I saw him a few times, in restaurants and places like that. The last time must have been somewhere in the late seventies, I suppose. It was in the Gay Hussar. We'd just come in from the opera, and his party were finishing, coffee and liqueurs, but Michael was wolfing another steak, the way he used to. He had a blonde dolly-bird on one side and a smart mean-looking beauty on the other, and everyone was watching for what he was going to say next so that they could be the first to agree. He looked gross, repulsive, slimy, evil. The thought that I'd once let him touch and stroke me made me feel ill. When he got up to leave, he needed two sticks to walk with. I told myself that I could see from the way he moved and talked that he knew exactly what sort of thing he had become. I don't know if that's true, but I hope so.

Somebody told me he'd had a stroke not long after. It was the sort which leaves you so you can't move or speak, only sit there with your head on one side and your mouth hanging open, waiting for the next person to come and feed and clean you. You know all about it, but there isn't anything you can do except make little grunting noises nobody understands. Then he died.

Well, that's it. Only there's one more thing I want to say. I realise that all this sounds terribly narrow and obsessive, as if we'd all of us spent all our lives worrying about Gerry and longing to be back at Blatchards when we were girls and everything seemed easy and golden. It wasn't like that, really it wasn't. We've all had proper lives, full of interesting other things, and other people and places.

I've always been a tidy person. I try not to leave clothes on chairs and shoes all over the house, but especially before I go off on holiday, I sort everything out and fold them up and get them into their drawers. It just seems decent, I suppose. Well, this is like that, a last bit of folding up and tidying away, so that I can go off with a clear conscience. That's all.

SOMERVILLE PUBLIC LIBRARY
35 West End Avenue
Somerville, N.J. 08876-1899
(908) 725-1336